Glowing endorsements for "The God Virus"

Skip Coryell has written ... now things can go terribly w ... aration, keeping a cool hea ... an get you through it. The ... pared still rings true. And a good gun helps too.

– George Hill
author of *Uprising USA* and *Uprising UK*–

Skip Coryell just keeps getting better with each book. I didn't want to put it down. *The God Virus* makes you ask the question of what would you do if all the lights went out and not just briefly, but for real. This chilling description from the book sums it up: "...*as if the hand of God had reached down and flicked a switch*." What do you do when society is no longer polite and you don't know who to trust?

– J. Keith Jones,
author of *In Due Time* –

The God Virus is a compelling and well-crafted story of a world gone dark. However, Skip Coryell, still finds some brightness in this outstanding drama. It did what few books do for me, grabbing me from Page One and holding me to the end!

– RG Yoho,
author of *Death Comes to Redhawk* –

Skip Coryell is at the top of his game with his latest page-turner, The God Virus. With realistic characters and action that makes you want to apply 3-D glasses in order to capture its full magnitude, Skip has written his best book to date. Readers will have a hard time putting this one down--I know I did.

– Josh Clark,
author of *The McGurney Chronicles* series
and *Dakota Divided* –

Skip

Coryell

The
God Virus

The 1,000-year night begins...

Published by White Feather Press. (www.whitefeatherpress.com)

ISBN 978-1-6180802-0-2

Printed in the United States of America

Cover design created by Ron Bell of AdVision Design Group
(www.advisiondesigngroup.com)

White Feather Press

Reaffirming Faith in God, Family, and Country!

For Sara Sunbreak.

The light of my life.

CHAPTER 1

The Treachery - September 7

STEVEN Maxwell was a Cyber Terrorism Specialist for the United States Department of Homeland Security. To put it plainly, he was a government geek. To be even more specific, he was assigned to the National Cyber Security Division. His job was to simulate attacks on the private sector power grid and then develop procedures for defending against any cyber weaknesses he discovered.

And Steven Maxwell was very good at his job.

Despite that, he had grown unhappy with his position and with his meager pay. If that had been his only complaint, he would have simply gone to the private sector and gotten a raise. But the roots of his discontent ran deeper, much, much deeper. And that's why he was sitting in a coffee shop, waiting for a man he'd never met, contemplating a terrorist act, the same kind he worked so patriotically to guard against every single day. He looked around him now. It was an open room, with tables all around him, and he felt hemmed in by people. It's not that he hated people. He liked them as everyone else did, on a case-by-case basis. The woman to his left was typing on a laptop. It was cheap hardware and Steven turned his nose up. She was cute though.

He looked back down at the walnut-veneered table top beneath his folded hands, sitting calmly beside his Blackberry. The question nagging him right now was this: Was he a traitor? Was he capable of selling out his country?

Steven pushed the self-indictment aside. No, he could never betray his nation. But still…he was here wasn't he? The man had left a message and Steven had responded. He hadn't said no. On the other hand, he hadn't said yes either. Besides, it wasn't all black and white. The country was already lost. The government deficit was closing in on thirty trillion dollars, and hyperinflation was beginning to set in. If the Chinese ever called in their loans, the game would be over. He mused about it for a second. And then there was the proposed government take-over of the internet. Not just regulation, but an actual iron-fisted, jack-booted cyber-shackled software tyranny. From what he'd been seeing around the office, the higher ups had been preparing for it for years, and now they were ready to erase the final vestige of American freedom. Maybe he was doing the country a favor by bringing down the house of cards now before the commies took the first shot. Yes, maybe he wasn't a traitor? Perhaps he was America's first cyber savior? Interesting thought. He had to admit that the hacker part of him would revel in laying low the powerful.

The blonde waitress walked over and placed a napkin down in front of him and then his glass of Mountain Dew on top. She was shapely, with a face that merited a second glance. He smiled weakly without looking up.

"Thank you."

The waitress walked away silently. Steven stared at her butt as it moved out across the room. He had always been polite. He looked down at the green liquid, watching the fizzy bubbles break free one at a time from the side of the glass and float quickly up to the surface beside the crushed ice. He smiled nervously. Yes, he'd always been polite ... not very confident though, especially with the ladies. He wondered why they never asked him out?

He ran his fingers through his greasy, long hair and took a sip of his Dew before glancing down nervously at the time on his Blackberry. The man was late. He put his drink back down on the table, and that's when he saw the writing on the already-dampening napkin in front of him. He picked it up. It was written in black ink, a barely-readable scribble of characters. He squinted his eyes to read it.

"Go out the back door.
Turn left down the alley
Wait by the dumpster."

Steven looked up nervously, placing his palm over the napkin so no one could read it. He glanced around the café, wondering if they could see him right now. He was scared, but it was a thrilling fear, one that gave him chills and made him feel more alive than usual. He got up and pretended to walk to the restroom, but then he kept going down the dark hallway and out into the shadowed alley. The wooden door slammed shut behind him like a vault, and he cursed himself at his lack of stealth. The warm, muggy air hit his face and he breathed in the late summer humidity. His asthma didn't like it. He looked to his left and then to his right. No one was there, so he walked over to the dumpster, barely discernible ten yards away. He got the feeling someone was watching him, and he caught himself wondering if anyone was hiding inside the trash. He laughed nervously at his paranoia. That was silly. He was just going to talk to a gentleman about a business deal. It's not like they were spies or anything.

That's when he felt the barrel of the gun press against the back of his left ear. He froze, and all he could think was, *I knew it! He was hiding in the trash!*

"Don't move, Mr. Maxwell. I'd hate to blow your head off before we have a chance to hire you."

The man had a chilling voice, like Anthony Hopkins in *Silence of the Lambs*. The adrenalin surge hit him hard and unexpectedly, and that's when Steven felt the wetness run down his legs and soak into his socks. Right now he felt like more geek than spy. Finally he found his voice. It wavered when he spoke.

3

"Why the gun?"

The man laughed, but ignored his question.

"In ten seconds a van will pull up at the end of the alley. You and I will walk slowly over and get in the back. You will cooperate. You will not cry out. Do you understand?"

When Steven nodded, the gun barrel rubbed softly against the hair on his scalp. It almost tickled. He heard the van's engine before he saw it. The gun pushed him forward and Steven walked. A few seconds later he was pushed inside and the door slid shut. He didn't resist as a pillow case pulled down over his head. It seemed odd to him, but as the van sped away, all he could think was *I hope I don't get in trouble for not paying for my drink.*

❧ ⸱ ❧

"We've been watching you closely, Mr. Maxwell."

The man paused but Steven didn't answer. He wasn't sure it was a question. Besides, on the ride over they'd already hit him twice for speaking, and he wasn't about to risk it again. In the past twenty minutes he'd been kidnapped at gunpoint, bagged, beaten, and now he was duct-taped to a chair. His first thought was *I've decided not to be the cyber savior of the world. I like my boring, government-geek job with low pay. In fact, I can't wait to get back to my small, cramped cubicle and churn out work that will be unappreciated by my boss and my peers.*

"I spoke to you, Mr. Maxwell and you didn't respond. That is very rude."

"Uh..." Steven hesitated, unsure what he could say to avoid another beating.

"Take the bag off his head so I can understand him, please."

The voice of this man was different than the Hannibal Lecter who'd abducted him. It was soft and measured, almost seductive in nature. He felt the bag being ripped off his face and the bright light hit him full in the eyes. He blinked several times until his pupils adjusted. The man across from him was sitting in the dark, just a shadowed form. Steven glanced up and the light overhead seemed to shine down on only him, blinding him, laying him bare, illuminating every shadow of his wrinkled soul.

"Now, Mr. Maxwell. Let's try this again, shall we? You would like to have a civil discussion with me, wouldn't you?"

Steven nodded his head up and down.

"I asked you a question, Mr. Maxwell, and if you don't answer me, then I'll take it as a rude gesture on your part."

Then Steven heard the Hannibal Lecter voice speak for the first time since the alley, this time in a hushed whisper.

"He nodded *yes*."

His inquisitor smiled.

"I can't hear your head rattle when you nod, Mr. Maxwell. I'm blind."

This time Steven found his voice.

"Oh, I'm sorry. I didn't know."

The man in the chair leaned forward as he spoke.

"Good, human compassion. I like that. No need to pity me though. I hate pity. It's only deserving of the weak, and I am anything but that."

He leaned back in his chair again before continuing.

"As I said before, Mr. Maxwell. We've been watching you closely, and we know that you are less than thrilled with your job, your boss, your pay, and, most importantly, the U.S. government."

The man paused.

"Mr. Maxwell, please be kind enough to wait for my pause, and then respond. Things will go much smoother if we have a conversational protocol. Do you agree?"

Steven started to nod his head, but caught himself.

"Yes, sir."

"Oh my! You are so polite! I like that."

5

"Thank you, sir."

"Now we're getting somewhere. You should respond now to my previous statement, Mr. Maxwell."

Steven thought for a moment, then spoke.

"Yes, all that's true. But how do you know all that?"

The man just smiled but ignored the question.

"We are here to help you, Mr. Maxwell. You've spent your whole life working hard and excelling at what you do, but no one has rewarded you. You graduated valedictorian of your high school then on to MIT where you graduated early, Magna Cum Laude. You spent ten years at Microsoft before being recruited by Homeland Security, and you've been there for six years without a single promotion."

The man paused.

"Steven?"

"Uh, yes sir. That is all correct."

"Good. You never married. You don't even date, although you do surf pornographic websites when your urges get too much to bear."

He paused. Steven lowered his head slightly.

"Yes sir."

"Nothing to be ashamed of, Mr. Maxwell, everyone looks at porn." He laughed out loud. "Well, not everyone. I'm blind, and braille just leaves way too much for the imagination, if you know what I mean."

He paused again.

"Yes sir."

"Now what I want to do, Mr. Maxwell, is to compensate you for the wrongs perpetrated against you by society. I'd like to place the sum of ten million dollars in a numbered Swiss account in your name. In return, all I need from you is a favor. A simple favor, really, only five minutes of your time. Are you interested, Mr. Maxwell? Shall I continue?"

Steven looked back up and thought for a moment. He remembered his boss at work, how he watched his every move, how he timed his breaks and lunch hours, how his peers laughed at him behind his back, and how the women never looked at him the way he looked at them. He weighed the morality of what he was certain they were going to ask him to do, because, in truth, he'd thought of it on his own many times. Getting back. Getting revenge. Getting rich. Bringing them all down to size. Then he spoke.

"Yes. Please go on."

The blind man smiled like a cat with a mouse between his paws.

"You have to understand that once I share this with you, that you must go through with it. If you don't, if you back out, if you turn on us, then my associates will visit you again, and they will do so with less subtlety than today. Understood?"

Steven nodded out of habit but quickly followed up with words.

"I understand."

"Good!" The blind man nodded to the person with Hannibal Lecter's voice, who then stepped forward into the light. Steven looked up and saw the black balaclava over his face, but cringed when he met the man's gaze. His eyes were cold, distant and hard. He never wanted to see this man again. Steven was reminded of the cold, wet urine on his pant legs which contrasted with the hot sweat on his brow and chest.

The man reached into his jacket pocket. He remembered the gun and Steven stiffened in fear. He pulled out a small memory stick and placed it in Steven's front, shirt pocket. The man's eyes smiled like ice, then he backed away and resumed his place beside the blind man who started talking again.

"On that memory device is a piece of software we'd like you to load into the proper computer system. We have chosen you because you have intimate knowledge of all power grid vulnerabilities. You know when, where and how to overcome all failsafes and defenses. Do you understand, Mr.

Maxwell?"

Steven looked around nervously. "You want me to take down the grid."

For the first time, the man nodded before he spoke.

"Yes, Mr. Maxwell. Will you do that for us, please?"

Steven didn't need to think about it for too long. He hated the government. He hated his job. He hated his life. And here was a chance to change it. This was his shot at happiness. He could be important. On the flipside, he comprehended that if he refused, they would kill him right there in the dark room. His body would be dumped somewhere cold and lonely and perhaps it would be eaten by fish or crabs. He considered both options and chose piña coladas on the beach in a warm, sunny island over sleeping with the fishes. Not only was he polite, but he'd also graduated Magna Cum Laude. He was no dummy.

"Of course, sir. I wouldn't want to be rude."

The blind man laughed out loud.

"I like you, Mr. Maxwell. I like you a lot. My associates will see you get home safely now."

The man stood.

"Oh, this must be done tomorrow at 4PM Eastern Standard Time. Is that good for you?"

This time Steven smiled.

"Yes sir. Nice meeting you, sir."

The blind man laughed as Hannibal Lecter led him away into the darkness.

"He's a polite man, such a polite man."

CHAPTER 2

DAN Branch raised the binoculars to his eyes and what he saw broke his heart. Oddly enough, it also made his blood boil. He loved his wife, and he was going to kill her with his bare hands.

He watched as she leaned across the table at the local Applebee's and kissed the other man full on the mouth. Dan ground his teeth but couldn't bring himself to pry the binoculars away from his eyes. In a fit of anger, the only question on his mind was "Which one of them do I torture first?"

Dan took a deep breath and lowered the binoculars. In his heart of hearts, he knew it would be foolish and wrong to do anything right now. He needed to calm down. He needed to get some distance. After all, this wasn't her first affair. Dan thought about that for a moment. *Affair*, it was such a harmless, such a benign word to affix to an act that almost always resulted in the destruction of a family, in the pain and loss of divorce, and in the heart-wrenching confusion that kids would feel for a lifetime. Instead of *affair*, maybe they should call it *treachery*. But somehow he just couldn't imagine his wife saying, "Hi honey. I'm having a *treachery* and I'm going to divorce you, break your heart and warp our children for life. You don't' mind do you?"

He reached down into the cup holder and picked up the mocha Frappuccino. He liked the glass bottle. It just seemed cool to him. He took a sip of his all-time-favorite drink, but the liquid had somehow lost its flavor.

Dan took the binoculars off from around his neck and laid them beside him on the seat of his old Ford, F-150 pickup truck. The body was rusted out, the frame was a bit bent, the windows sometimes rolled down but wouldn't go back up unless you pulled with one hand and rolled with another. But the radio worked very well.

A mighty sigh left Dan's tortured lips, and a tear rolled down his right cheek. He wiped it away, but another quickly took its place. He had to divorce her. He knew that. He had forgiven the first fling, but how could he let it go this time, assuming she even wanted to stay married to him, which he doubted. The woman had always confused him. She was so nice when she wasn't drinking too much and sleeping with other men.

It was 8 o'clock at night in early September with a heat wave hanging on like Velcro, so he had both windows open to keep the heat from killing him. The truck had an air conditioner, but it didn't work. He had married Debbie 6 years ago in a park just outside of town. It had been a beautiful wedding, but Debbie had gotten drunk at the reception and passed out on their way to the motel. The marriage had gone downhill from there.

He raised the binoculars up again and saw them holding hands atop the table. Suddenly, he felt very stupid and ashamed. She was making a fool of him for the whole town to see. Other people had to know. He could tell by the sympathetic looks they gave him at church and at work. He hated the pity. He put the binoculars down again and turned the ignition key. The truck turned over a few times and then clicked like the staccato of a machine gun.

"Darn it, you lousy piece of crap!"

He popped the hood latch, hopped out of his truck and slammed the door behind him in anger. The battery was old, and this would keep happening until he could afford to buy a new one. He opened the hood and looked down at the battery cables again. They were a little loose. Dan got a Crescent wrench from the toolbox in the truck bed and tightened them down. Just as he was finishing, he heard a voice behind him.

"Hey Dan. You need a hand?"

He turned around and saw Chris Flanders, his friend from work. He forced a smile onto his face. He didn't want Chris to know what he was doing here or that his wife was cheating on him.

"Hi Chris. Just have a loose cable. It should start up once I tighten it down. Just finished up."

Chris put his truck in park and shut off the engine. Dan's heart sank. *Great.*

"Well, I'll just stick around until I know everything's okay. What are friends for, right?"

Dan nodded. "Yeah, right. Thanks." He quickly hopped back into the cab and turned the ignition, but nothing happened. He slapped the steering wheel with his hand and then bounced his forehead off it for good measure.

"Ouch! Man that hurts!"

Outside he saw his friend shaking his head. Chris walked up to the open window. He was a big man, 28 years old, and always seemed too happy. Chris had that sympathetic look in his eyes, and Dan felt his stomach sink.

"Dan, I just came from inside the restaurant, and I saw Debbie in there sucking face with that no-good McKinley fella from Eau Claire." He reached through the window and placed his big, meaty hand on Dan's left shoulder and squeezed firmly. "You don't gotta take that crap from her. You need to do something, man!"

Dan looked up, and the tears were welling in his eyes again. But he shrugged his shoulders helplessly.

"What can I do, Chris? I'm at the end of my rope here."

Chris smiled. "That's his truck over there. The fancy, new, midnight blue four-wheel-drive with the custom flaming eagle paint job on the hood."

Dan turned his face to look at it. "Yeah, okay. So he's got

a nice truck. So what."

Chris shook his head impatiently. "Give me a break, Dan. Don't you have any self respect at all?" He turned away as if controlling his frustration. Then a moment later he turned back again. "Okay, here's the deal. I'll show you what to do the first time, but after this you're on your own. Agreed?"

Dan cocked his head to one side but finally nodded his head. "Okay, I guess."

Chris smiled. "Just watch and learn, my friend." He reached in through Dan's window and picked up the 12-inch Crescent wrench off the dash and walked over to the truck of Debbie's lover.

Dan sat inside his beat-up truck and watched in awe as his friend began to abuse the man's shiny, brand, new truck. First, Chris worked over the front end, breaking the head-lights and the turn signals. With his free hand he pulled out a jackknife and slit all four tires. Dan watched as the truck suddenly became about 8 inches shorter. Crack! The wind-shield was gone. Then as a final coup de grace, he scraped his knife several times across the flaming eagle on the hood. It sounded like fingernails on a chalkboard. The 3,000-dollar custom paint job was ruined.

Chris backed away and then nodded in satisfaction before walking back over to Dan. He reached in and set the wrench back on the dash.

"Ya see, Dan, none of what I just did will keep your wife from cheating on you, because she's a worthless, conniving bitch. But when people treat you like that and you do noth-ing, it leaves you damaged on the inside. You can't bury the anger. It's toxic man. Like a cancer it'll eat you alive." He paused as if forming his thoughts. "You have to dump her. It's the only way she'll respect you. And respect is a lot more important than love."

Chris turned to walk away, but then stopped and canted his head back toward him. "Stop by the house if you need to get drunk at a safe place. I'll buy the beer."

And then he got into his truck and drove away. Dan looked back over at the demolished truck and shuddered. All he could say was "Wow!".

≈ ≈ ≈

DHS National Cyber Security Division - September 8

The next day Steven Maxwell glanced down into the lower-right-hand corner of his computer screen. The time was 3:52PM EST. He reached down into his jacket pocket and his fingers closed over the thumb drive. Thumb drives were restricted here at DHS, so he'd been forced to smuggle it in. In truth, he liked the fear, even though the risk was great. Late last night he'd looked at the contents of the drive. There was the promised piece of software, which he immediately tried to open. It was locked. Then he saw a README FILE which he opened. It came up in MS Wordpad. In big, black characters it said:

```
4PM EST
You know what to do.
We are watching you!
```

Steven looked up and scanned the other cubicles around him. Where are they? Can they really get inside here?

"Steven! Did you finish debugging that tracer module yet!"

Steven jumped forward in his seat, almost falling off onto the floor. He pulled his hand out of his pocket to catch himself from falling. As he did so, the thumb drive fell to the carpet. He quickly placed his foot over it, hoping his boss hadn't seen it.

"I asked you a question, Steven! Did you finish the module or not!"

Steven knew it wasn't really a question, but a command. He lowered his head into his best bottom-of-the-pecking-order fashion and nodded his head slowly. He was very careful not to make eye contact.

"Yes, sir. I was just getting ready to send it on to you for review."

His boss smiled triumphantly.

"Good! I need it by 4:30 so I can run a test on the full tracer tool. Make sure I get it by then."

Steven nodded meekly.

"Yes sir. I will."

His boss walked away. Steven watched him go and glanced back down at his computer clock. It read 3:57 PM. He looked around to make sure no one was watching. Then he picked up a pen and clumsily dropped it to the floor. He slowly reached down to retrieve it and scooped up the thumb drive as well. The clock changed to 3:58PM.

He took the cap off the drive and inserted it into the USB port on his computer. He looked around again, trying not to look nervous. Of course, to anyone watching, he simply looked like a man who was nervous, but trying not to look nervous. The MS Explorer window came up and he looked at the two files. One said README. The other said THEGODVIRUS.EXE. The clock clicked over to 3:59PM.

What did the God Virus mean? What would it do? Would it bring down the whole power grid? If so, for how long? He'd been thinking about it half the night. He wanted so much to be able to explore the code. Apparently, the only way to find out was to double click.

A stubborn, cold sweat formed on his brow and he quickly wiped it away with his polyester shirt sleeve. He placed his right hand on his mouse and moved the pointer over the file. He hesitated, the small, black arrow poised like an electronic dagger, ready to stab. The digits on his computer clock rolled over to 4:00PM with a deafening crash. Time was up.

His right forefinger moved down and rested on the mouse button. He waited. He thought. He contemplated. He mused. But there was no answer. It was what it was, and the only way to find out was to...

Steven thought of his boss and double clicked.

ॐ ॐ ॐ

Menomonie, Wisconsin

The next night Dan walked into his house and heard loud music coming from his 14-year-old step son's bedroom. He walked to the door and knocked politely, but there was no answer. He knocked again.

"Jeremy! Can you turn that down please?" There was still no answer, so he opened the door. On the bed, in a tangle of naked arms and legs was his step son with the 12-year-old neighbor girl in the height of adolescent ecstasy.

"Jeremy!"

The boy looked up and immediately became angry.

"Get out of my room! Now!"

Dan's jaw dropped open, and he backed out and closed the door. Inside the room, he could hear the squeaking of springs over the chorus of some really angry music. Normally he would walk away, but this time the image of Chris Flanders came to mind. He saw the Crescent wrench come down on first one headlight and then the other. He heard the knife scraping over the paint job, and a newfound resolution steeled itself inside him. He hesitated, took a deep breath and opened the door.

"Get outta my room, old man!"

Slowly and ever so calmly, Dan walked over to the corner of the messy room and picked up the ball bat. He smiled and looked Jeremy full in the eyes. The boy's face took on a confused look. Dan took a full swing at the stereo and the music suddenly stopped. Dan swung again and again and again.

"What are you doing to my stuff! Are you crazy?"

Dan looked up.

"Tonya, it's time for you to go home now."

The young girl clutched the blanket over herself as she

picked up her clothes and hurriedly put them back on. The look of terror was ever so present, and Dan had a feeling she would never come back.

Jeremy stood up, totally naked. He was a big kid for fourteen, muscular, and broad-shouldered. He took a step toward Dan and raised his fists. Dan dropped the bat and punched his step-son in the face three times before the boy went down in a heap, clutching his hands over the blood.

Tonya skirted past him out the door.

"Have a nice day, Tonya. Tell your parents hello."

Then he looked down at Jeremy, naked and writhing on the floor. "I'm sorry, son, but you've had that one coming for a long time. Sorry to make you wait so long."

Jeremy pulled his hands away from his face and screamed as blood poured out his nose and mouth.

"I'm going to tell my mom, and she'll call the police! She'll take pictures of this and you're going to jail!"

Dan nodded resolutely.

Yes, I suppose so. But the thing is, Jeremy. I really don't care what she does. I don't care if I go to prison for a few years, so long as I respect myself. But I do care if my step son is screwing the neighbor girl in my house, which is against the law by the way, so you'll be joining me in prison. I also care if my wife stays out all night with other men. I care if she yells at me. I care if a young boy disrespects me in my own home. I care about all those things. However, I no longer care what the police might do to me if you call them."

Dan crossed his arms over his massive chest and smiled.

"So, I suggest you get dressed and clean up your room. It's a pig sty in here."

Dan turned and closed the door behind him. He went to the kitchen, opened the refrigerator door and pulled out an ice-cold mocha Frappuccino. He tore away the cellophane, twisted off the cap and took a long swallow.

"Smooth!"

And the drink never tasted so sweet.

ࡍ ࡍ ࡍ

Arlington, Virginia

Steven was home now, lying in bed, waiting for some-thing to happen. The blue, cotton sheet was pulled up tightly over his face, exposing only the red-streaked orbs he called eyes. His head pressed anxiously into the down-filled pillow until his neck muscles ached. The night was muggy and hot, and he had the air conditioner on full blast, but it still only brought the temperature down to 75 degrees. He needed to buy a new one. He just wanted this to be over.

Steven sat up in bed, swung his legs over the side and walked over to his computer desk. The only light in the room came from his computer screen. He pressed the "refresh" button, hoping to see new email. Nothing. He reached over and picked up his Blackberry. No text messages. No phone messages. Nothing! He was in the dark.

As he stood there, hovering nervously over the desk, his computer suddenly switched to battery power. Steven seemed confused by it. He knelt down and checked the power cord only to find everything in place. Then he picked up his Blackberry and tried to call his office phone. The phone was dead. A rush of adrenaline coursed through his bloodstream as he walked hurriedly over to the window. He looked out into the city and saw...only blackness.

Along with the adrenaline came uncontrollable anxi-ety. He got up. He sat down. He got up again, only to seat himself once more. Steven tried his computer, then his Blackberry. Nothing. Oddly, he felt a growing sense of ac-complishment. He didn't know what he had done, nor the extent of it. Steven only knew that he'd done something. He'd affected the world and the people around him for the first time in his life. For a moment, he thought he felt some-thing akin to pride. It was a new experience for him. But the feeling was short-lived. As Steven stood there in the dark, he heard a click at his door, then the slow creak as it opened.

In a final moment of enlightenment, he knew they had come for him. The sense of pride faded, and was replaced with terror as he watched the blacker-than-night shadow walk slowly toward him. Steven felt like a kid in his room at night who was having a nightmare. He knew the only way to end the terror was to move, but he was paralyzed into stasis.

Steven felt the black balaclava move toward him. He sensed the presence of the gun. His eyes saw the flash of light. Then another. And another. He stood there for a full 10 seconds, then, slowly, ever so slowly, his head filled with dizziness and he collapsed to the floor.

His last sensory experience was the feeling of the gun barrel pressed against his left eye. There was a final blast, a shock, and then total, ethereal darkness.

The man with Hannibal Lecter's voice smiled beneath the mask and then turned and walked away into the thousand-year night.

The White House

"Mr. President, sir."

President Bob Taylor looked up from the chair and grunted at his aide without speaking, all the while thinking *Why are you bothering me?*

"We have a situation, sir."

The President looked at him impatiently. Yes, and..."

The aide spoke with a nervous edge to his voice, afraid that delivering bad news of this magnitude might not be conducive to a long and happy career in politics.

"The country is under attack, sir."

"Excuse me?"

"Yes, sir, under cyber attack."

Bob Taylor was about to demand more details when the lights in the oval office flickered, died, and then came back on again as emergency power kicked in. A worried look came over his face.

"It's the power grid, sir. The Joint Chiefs and some of the cabinet are meeting you in the situation room in 15 minutes. It doesn't look good, sir."

The President thought for a moment, then braced his hands on the desk as he stood. The President was a tall man, handsome, and many thought, too young to be President, especially during a crisis. He walked around the desk and hurried out of the room with the aide following him. The two Secret Service men were waiting outside the door and escorted him down to the Situation Room.

Back in Menomonie, Wisconsin, Dan Branch waited on the sofa in his underwear for the police to come and arrest him for a crime he hadn't committed. While it was true he hadn't destroyed his wife's boyfriend's truck, he had beaten up her son. He was pretty sure that was still a crime.

The remote control was in one hand and a mocha Frappuccino in the other. Dan was utterly convinced this would be his last Frappuccino for the next few years, as he was certain they didn't serve Frappuccino in prison. Despite that, there was a smile on his face, and he felt pretty darn good. He wondered to himself *Can I go to hell for thinking like this?* He stopped channel surfing at the local Fox News station and listened to the talking head.

"The blackout appeared to begin on the eastern seaboard and has slowly spread inland. Experts say it's still too soon to tell how far the power outage will spread and how long the power will be out on the East Coast."

The announcer was a beautiful blonde, the one that Dan had always enjoyed watching. He instantly forgot about his own troubles and was absorbed in the news of a major power outage.

"We go now to our Fox News affiliate WPGH in

Pittsburgh to Professor Roy Percy. The professor is the foremost expert on power grid modeling and simulation."

Professor Percy showed up on the split screen. He wore a grey cardigan sweater and sported a bald head and black-rimmed glasses. Professor Percy was extremely overweight and had a very serious look on his face.

"Professor Percy, thanks for joining us today."

The professor nodded but said nothing.

"What can you tell us about the nature of this power outage that seems to be hitting the entire eastern seaboard?"

The professor shifted in his seat uncomfortably and pursed his lips tightly before speaking.

"This is widespread. It's serious. I would say that it's a matter of extreme national security."

The blonde reporter seemed confused by his statement.

"National security? This is a power grid problem. Isn't it?"

Professor Percy turned away from the camera for a second in order to form his thoughts.

"Yes, Eileen, it is a power grid problem. But the Capitol of our nation is without power, so the continuity of government is of major concern right now. We have no idea when the power will be restored, what caused the power loss, or even if it can be contained."

"So are you saying that this outage could actually spread to other parts of the United States?"

"Absolutely! For all we know this could be a cyber terrorist attack by another nation. The East Coast could be just the beginning of a very long, dark night for America."

The reporter hesitated and looked skeptical.

"Professor, assuming this was a terrorist attack, what country is capable of doing something like this?"

"The most likely candidate is China as we've long known they've been developing a cyber-attack scenario for several years now. Many times in the past two years the Department of Homeland Security has linked smaller cyber-forays into our power grid as originating from inside China. Kind of like a testing of their software and capabilities. They've been feeling us out, getting to know our weaknesses and vulnerabilities. I'm not the least bit surprised by this outage. Whether it's attributable to cyber terrorism or not, there are just way too many vulnerabilities in our power grid, and ..."

Suddenly, the professor's voice stopped in mid sentence and the split window turned blank. The blonde reporter seemed surprised and looked around the room for confirmation of what had happened. None came.

"I'm sorry folks, but we seem to have lost our connection with WPGH in Pittsburgh. We'll try to re-establish our connection. Stay tuned for more news when we come back."

The blonde reporter was replaced by a commercial featuring a singing, animated greensaver light bulb. Dan put the remote down on the coffee table and leaned forward. He thought to himself, *What in the world is going on?*

Just then his cell phone vibrated on the glass table top in front of him, making it move almost an inch with each pulsing vibration. His heart skipped a beat. Only one person sent him text messages, and that was Debbie, usually when she was going to be out all night, but didn't want to tell him with a phone call where he could ask questions. He picked up the cell phone and read the terse, unexpected message.

Alas Babylon!
Uncle Rodney

Dan's heart leaped into his throat. He hadn't spoken to his uncle in six months. More importantly, he knew the meaning of the message. It was a code that his uncle had set up with him long ago.

And it was not good.

CHAPTER 3

Menomonie, Wisconsin - September 9

_IT_ was 2AM as Dan pushed his overflowing cart towards the checkout lane at the local Wal*Mart. The store was usually empty at this late hour, but tonight things were different. The store had become packed within the last 10 minutes, with people frantically moving from aisle to aisle, loading up carts with food, flashlights, batteries and other supplies. Dan could see the fear in their eyes and feel the tension in the air. People had been watching the news about the power outages. They knew it was moving westward like an unstoppable wave and were stocking up just in case. Dan was suddenly happy that he'd come here so quickly. By morning the merchandise in this place was likely to be cleaned out.

As he moved to the checkout lane, he took one last look inside his cart. Among other things he had a case of Spam, two cases of pork and beans, ten 4-pound bags of rice, a camp stove, fuel, one hundred rounds of 12 gauge shotgun ammo (a mixture of buckshot, slugs, and field loads) fifty rounds of number 3 buckshot in four-ten gauge as well as fifty rounds of four-ten slugs, and one hundred rounds of nine millimeter pistol ammo. He also had an axe, a large Buck hunting knife, two sleeping bags, a machete, and last, but not least, one heavy duty truck battery.

The cashier's eyes looked tired as he rolled up to the checkout counter and began loading the supplies onto the conveyor belt. Right about now Dan was appreciative of his Uncle Rodney for keeping him fifteen minutes ahead of the shopping horde. He glanced discreetly over at the cashier, and she was staring at him out of the corner of her eyes as she worked quickly to scan each item. Dan shook his head from side to side as he unloaded the cart. His checking account was already overdrawn, and now he was about to compound the problem by maxing out his Visa card.

He thought to himself *Alas Babylon*.

The cryptic message still echoed in his head. Dan knew his old uncle was different than most people, but still … Uncle Rodney had never been one to panic. Dan groaned as he picked up the multi-fuel campstove. In a pinch it could also burn unleaded gasoline as well as the traditional Coleman fuel.

"Aren't you Debbie Branch's husband?"

The beeping scanner had suddenly stopped and the middle-aged cashier was looking over, trying to make eye contact with him. Dan avoided her gaze by continuing to load a large, blue poly tarp onto the belt.

"Ah, yeah, Debbie's my wife."

The lady nodded and started scanning again.

"Yep. I thought so. I cut her hair yesterday. I got a second job over at the "Clip Joint", but it's only part-time ya know. At least for now. As soon as business picks up there I can quit this midnight shift job and do hair full time."

Dan didn't say anything. He looked behind him at the crowds of people filling up their carts. They would be lining up behind him soon. He didn't want to encourage her, but despite his silence she just kept on talking.

"So what did you think of her new hair-do?"

Dan nearly dropped the bag of rice he was lifting. He hesitated a moment. The truth was she hadn't been home in three days, so he hadn't seen her hair close up, but he certainly didn't want to explain that to a total stranger.

"She was real excited about it, almost like a silly school

girl going on a first date or something."

Dan shuddered at the cashier's words and blood raced to his cheeks. He thought to himself, *Yes, it was a date, but certainly not the first or the last.* He smiled before speaking.

"You did a great job. Best ever I think."

The cashier smiled. "Yeah! That's what she told me too! She said she wanted something sexy, something that would light up the bedroom when she pulled up the covers, if ya know what I mean." She winked at Dan, and he was hating the woman more than ever now. He picked up the twenty-four inch long machete and gazed at it before finally placing it on the belt.

"So what you gonna do with all this stuff? Goin' campin' er something?"

Dan's frustration mounted as he lifted a case of Spam and then a one-hundred round box of shotgun shells onto the belt. The cart was empty now, and he was about to say something rude when someone spoke behind him.

"Excuse me, sir."

Dan turned and looked at the Menomonie Police Officer who was standing in line behind him with a bottle of Mountain Dew. Dan redoubled his patience and forced a disarming smile.

"Yes, officer. Did you want to go ahead of me?"

The man looked into Dan's eyes as if trying to read his mind. The officer shook his head. "No, I was just wondering why someone would need all that ammunition. Hunting season's a ways off yet."

Dan continued to smile and didn't miss a beat with his reply. "Oh, yeah I suppose it does look unusual. But you see I'm leaving for Montana in a few weeks for a big hunting, fishing and camping trip. It's a once in a lifetime deal."

The officer almost smiled. "Yes, I go there every year with my two oldest sons. It's a good time."

Dan nodded and started to turn away.

"But that shotgun ammo you've got isn't the best choice.

You might be better off with a high-powered rifle out there." He looked at Dan skeptically, but Dan didn't return his gaze.

"That'll be eight hundred sixty two dollars and seventy-three cents."

Dan turned around and pulled out his wallet. When he swiped the Visa card he prayed to himself, *Please, God, let the card clear just this once*. He had no idea what his wife had already charged with it. For all he knew she'd already sucked the credit cupboard bare. Dan waited a few seconds, but the cashier just stood there. The card reader screen in front of him seemed to be stuck on "Please Slide Card". Sweat beaded up on his forehead. The cashier reached over and held out her hand. "Let me see that card for a second."

Dan hesitated, looked over at the cop, then let her have the card. "What's wrong?"

The woman looked at the card, turned it over in her hand a few times, then smiled. "Yeah, just what I thought. The magnetic strip is all dirty and it's not reading it."

Dan relaxed a bit. "Can you punch the numbers in by hand?"

The woman laughed. "Men! You're all alike! I could punch in the numbers by hand, but then you'd still have this problem the next time you bought something! I got a better idea." She raised the card up to her mouth and slobbered out a gob of spit onto the magnetic strip. Dan grimaced and turned away. Then she used her shirt tail to scrub off the dirt. "There! Try it now!"

Dan reached out and reluctantly grabbed the card, being careful not to touch the magnetic strip as he swiped it through the reader.

"Waiting for Approval..."

"Waiting for Approval..."

"Waiting for Approval..."

Dan began sweating again as the police officer moved closer. Finally, the screen gave him mercy.

"APPROVED!"

The cashier laughed out loud.

"Man you were really sweating on that one weren't you."

Dan faked a smile, but inside his head he picked up the machete and hacked off her head, then laughed as it rolled around on the tile floor.

"Yes, you really had me going on that one."

Dan took his receipt, placed all the bags into the cart and nodded back to the police officer before walking away.

When he got to the parking lot he picked up his pace, hoping to get out of there before the cop made it out. After everything was loaded into the back of the pickup, he got in and drove away, leaving the obnoxious hairdresser and the nosy cop behind him.

Three blocks from the Wal*Mart Dan saw the police strobe light up the night behind him. He slammed his fist on the dash and cursed out loud before pulling over. He kept his hands on the steering wheel as the policeman walked up to the driver's side window.

"License, registration, proof of insurance please."

Dan looked over and recognized the cop from Wal*Mart. He was smiling. Dan reached back with his right hand to get his wallet, all the while noticing that the officer had his own right hand on the butt of his pistol. Dan moved slowly, but didn't say a word.

The officer looked down at the documents briefly.

"Please stay inside your vehicle. I'll run these and be right back."

Inside, Dan was fuming. *How could it get any worse?* His wife was screwing another man; his son was screwing the neighbor girl; but the only one screwing Dan was the Wal*Mart cop. To top it all off, his Uncle Rodney, the man who'd raised him after his father's death, had just told him to come on home, because the world was about to end. Immediately he winced. He knew better than to ask what more could go wrong. In Dan's world, it could always get worse.

Dan looked up and the police officer was standing outside the window again. It startled him and he jumped, all the while wondering, *How do they sneak up like that. It's like they take a class in sneakiness.*

"Mr. Branch, you don't mind if I take a look inside your truck, do you. I'm sure you have nothing to hide."

Immediately a red flag came up inside Dan's head. His Uncle Rodney had home schooled him, and he knew his rights.

"Actually, sir, I'm very tired, and I'd like to get home to bed."

The officer's jaw tightened, and Dan could tell he wasn't used to being refused.

"If you have nothing to hide, sir, then I see no reason why you wouldn't allow me to search your vehicle."

Dan sighed deeply. He knew this wasn't going to end well.

"Officer, with all due respect to your position and to you as an individual, you do not have permission to search my vehicle."

A determined look spread over the officer's face, and then he frowned.

"Keep your hands where I can see them and step out of the vehicle, sir."

Dan thought about asking him why, but he knew better. The best way to handle this was to comply with all his commands, even though his civil rights were being violated. Then he could file a complaint later on with the man's superiors.

"Of course, officer. I'll step out now."

Just then the entire city went dark. The only light came from the spotlight of the police cruiser behind him.

"What was that?"

Dan didn't answer the policeman. The officer glanced down at Dan and ordered him not to move. Dan kept his hands on the steering wheel in plain sight. The officer hesitated, then he reached up to his right shoulder and keyed his mike.

"Dispatch, this is Unit 17. "

There was nothing but static in response. He keyed the mike again.

"Dispatch, this is Unit 17. Is anyone there?"

Inside, Dan smiled. His Uncle Rodney had been right. There was a moment of indecision on the officer's part, then police sirens broke the silence further back inside the city limits.

Just then his microphone came back to life.

"Attention all units! Attention all units! We are now on auxiliary power. Return to base. I say again. Return to base immediately!"

The police officer threw Dan's driver's license and documents through the window and ran back to his cruiser. Dan listened as the tires squealed on the pavement and the siren started up.

A few seconds later, Dan was all alone on the side of the road. He let his hands drop off the steering wheel, and then he leaned his head out the window into the warm, humid, early September air. Looking up into the sky, he was awed at the sight of thousands of stars. He thought of his wife lying beside another man, and he knew he should be sad about it, maybe even crushed, but … right now, all he could think about were the stars. They were beautiful.

He reached down and turned the ignition, but all he heard in response was the staccato clicking of a dead battery. He let his head drop down onto the top of the steering wheel and laughed out loud. Dan reached down onto the floor on the passenger side and grabbed the Crescent wrench. Thank God he'd just bought a new battery with money he didn't have.

He stepped out of the car, looked up into the night sky and smiled. Yes, it could always get worse.

The White House - September 9

The situation room was buried deep beneath the White House. It was soundproof, bugproof, and electronically secure in every facet. The President sat at the head and each chair around the big table was already occupied. The meeting had been going on for fifteen minutes.

"So, Terrence, does the NSA agree with the FBI's assessment of the situation?"

The President leaned back in his big, leather chair to listen to the response. Irene Sebastion was a lean woman with ever-whitening hair. Five years ago, before taking this job, it had been jet black.

"Yes, Mr. President. We agree that this is an act of cyber terrorism. But we just don't know who is responsible. It could take weeks to figure that out."

President Taylor looked over to his Department of Energy. "Frank, how far is this likely to spread?"

The head of the Department of Energy was a bald man with a large, bulbous nose. He took out a handkerchief and blew before answering his Commander-In-Chief.

"I don't know, sir. I don't have a clue. This has never happened before."

The President looked displeased. He glanced over to his CIA Director, Anthony Hooker. "Tony?"

"Sir?"

"Who did this to us?"

He squirmed a bit in his chair but maintained eye contact with the president, which was no mean task at the moment.

"We're not sure, sir. But we do have a list of candidates. We're checking them out right now."

The President tried to maintain his patience, but it was failing.

"And the candidates are?"

"China is the most obvious choice, sir, with Russia close behind. We have a lot of other enemies, but none as sophisticated as the Chinese. It's possible that some of the richer oil-producing countries in the Mid-East could have purchased the technology, but not likely. My best bet is China."

The President moved his gaze over to his immediate right at the Director of Homeland Security.

"Eleanor, is there any chance this was domestic terror?"

Eleanor Freeland was in her mid-sixties with gray hair and a slender frame for her age. Her face was creviced with wrinkles and stress marks, and her piercing blue eyes lit up when the President talked to her.

"No, Mr. President."

"And how can you say that which such surety. You didn't even think about it."

She smiled dangerously.

"Because, Mr. President, in order for it to be domestic, it would had to have originated from inside my Cyber Security Division, and those people have been vetted with extreme prejudice. We run a very tight ship over there. I would say there's hardly any chance of this being an inside job. I agree with the FBI and the CIA. I think it's China."

The President threw up his hands in exasperation.

"What proof do we have? I can't attack China without proof? And if they are responsible and I don't do something, then they could follow up with a nuclear strike to finish us off while we're crippled."

The Commander of the Joint Chiefs thought this the right time to pipe in.

"Mr. President, if I may."

The President nodded curtly.

"Mr. President, we have time to think about this. The blackout is contained to the East Coast, and most of our nuclear assets are located either deep inside the heartland or out to sea in submarines. We can wait a while and still order a counterattack if need be. There's only one problem."

"Continue."

"What if it is the Chinese? What if the blackout spreads to our missile silos, to NORAD, to command and control all across the country. If it was the Chinese, I'd bet my money they're getting ready to follow up with a first strike as soon as the blackout reaches the plains states. And the first place they're going to hit, Mr. President, is right where we're sitting. Washington DC will be toast, and from a military standpoint, there's not a thing we can do to stop it."

For the first time in his presidency, Bob Taylor showed his fear. He didn't answer the Joint Chiefs. He didn't know what to say, and he certainly couldn't say what he was thinking at the moment. Namely, *I'm scared and I don't know what to do.*

Off to his left he heard whispering. He turned and saw Eleanor Freeland speaking with a short, unassuming man who sat behind her. The President waited a few seconds before interrupting.

"Okay, Eleanor, what's so secret you have to keep it from the President of the United States?"

Eleanor nodded to the man behind her then waved her hand to shut him up. He immediately silenced, and she turned back to face the table before speaking.

"It's nothing, Mr. President, just a suggestion that I believe is untenable and premature."

The President didn't like that answer.

"Hmm, well the problem I have, Eleanor, is that I seem to have zero options right now, so I'd really like to hear anything that might give me a handle on this thing."

He pointed to the man behind her.

"So who's your little friend who likes to whisper while I'm talking?"

Director Freeland tried to regain her composure before speaking.

"This is Sam Hollister, he's the Assistant Director of our Cyber Security Division."

The President interrupted her.

"Why isn't the Director here? Shouldn't he be?"

She nodded.

"Yes sir, but he's in Los Angeles on an inspection tour. Sam has been with the division since it began and is fully briefed on all the division's activity."

The President narrowed his eyes.

"Okay Sam, what do I need to know?"

Director Freeland started to speak, but the President cut her off with a wave of his hand.

"Let the man speak, Eleanor. I want the benefit of his opinion. Lord knows, no one else in here can give me anything else to work with."

Sam Hollister glanced at his boss and she answered him by lowering her head. He turned to face the President. His voice wavering as he spoke.

"Mr. President. I was just reminding Director Freeland about a counter-cyber-terrorism tool we've been developing over the past 3 years."

He hesitated, but the President prodded him on with a look.

"It's not a defensive tool, sir. It was developed to operate in a first-strike scenario."

Bob Taylor leaned back in his chair again,

"You're talking about the Ludlow Virus?"

Sam raised his eyebrows in surprise. The President smiled.

"Don't be shocked, Mr. Hollister, I am the President of the United States, and contrary to the mainstream press, I'm not a complete idiot. I read every report that crosses my desk, including ones written by you. So, tell me. How can this "tool" help us with our potential dilemma with the Chinese?"

Sam looked over at his boss again, but she looked away as if washing her hands of the whole affair. He sighed and plunged forward.

"Since the Ludlow Virus was designed as a first-strike option that is virtually untraceable, it allows us to attack without the recipient nation knowing exactly who is responsible."

The President interrupted him.

"How is that possible?"

Sam threw up his hands.

"Just look around you, Mr. President. We have been attacked and no one in this room, not the greatest minds in America, knows for sure where it came from. When delivered discreetly, no one need ever know it came from us. And it would shut down whatever country we send it to, just like this foreign virus is shutting us down."

Eleanor Freeland noticed the look in her President's eyes and she didn't like it. She'd seen it before and she knew that he was seriously contemplating use of the Ludlow Virus. She quickly spoke, trying to head him off from a hasty conclusion.

"Mr. President, I need to remind you that so far we've contained the power failure to the East Coast. If it stops there, we'd be sending a nation with 1.3 billion people back into the stone age. Many of them would die from disease and famine."

Just then, as if on cue, a Secret Service agent walked in and handed a note to the Secretary of the Department of Energy. All eyes moved to him as he unfolded the paper and read it silently. His face grew ashen. The President was the first to break the silence.

"Frank? Talk to me."

Frank looked up and spoke in a solemn voice.

"I'm sorry, Mr. President, but we've just lost all power east of the Mississippi River and south on down to the gulf. And it's still spreading."

President Taylor leaned forward with his elbows on the table. No one spoke. They just watched as he gazed ahead at nothing in something akin to a thousand-yard stare. Finally, Eleanor prodded him.

"Mr. President? Are you okay?"

He jumped as if startled. Then he looked over at Sam Hollister.

"Mr. Hollister. Tell me more about this Ludlow Virus. How does it work? How fast is it? How would we get it loaded? In layman's terms please."

Sam Hollister began to talk, but Eleanor Freeland couldn't hear him. She was too busy thinking about the severity of what they were contemplating. And then from somewhere deep in the recesses of her mind, she heard the voice of long-dead Jim Morrison. The DOORS song *The End* kept playing to her over and over and over.

> *This is the end Beautiful friend*
> *This is the end My only friend,*
> *the end of our elaborate plans,*
> *The end of everything that stands,*
> *the end*

CHAPTER 4

DAN Branch sat alone in the dark eating a large bag of Buffalo Ranch style Doritos and drinking Mountain Dew. He never mixed Frappuccino and Doritos. It just wasn't right. It had been two hours since his incident with the Wal*Mart cop. After changing the truck battery, it had started right up, and he'd driven straight home. Thankfully he'd already filled up his gas tank along with four other five-gallon cans. He knew that no one would be buying gas anytime soon now that there was no electricity to work the pumps. He'd listened to the news on a Minnesota station on the truck radio which confirmed that all power was out east of the Mississippi river, and no one knew the cause or when it would come back on.

In the back room he could hear his stepson snoring. Jeremy had left hours ago after their skirmish, but then returned while Dan had been at Wal*Mart. Dan assumed he was drunk and would be sleeping until morning. Just thinking about his stepson and their altercation made him sad. Over six years ago when they'd first met, Dan and Jeremy had gotten along well, very well, and Dan had found himself excited at the prospect of raising Jeremy as his own son. That had lasted until about two years ago when the boy had fallen into the wrong crowd and started up on drinking and drugs. Dan had never really thought of Jeremy as a stepson, and he felt pretty guilty right about now for punching him, even though he'd had it coming in a major way. In truth, Dan still loved the boy ... and his mother.

His thoughts returned now to his Uncle Rodney and the ciphered message. He knew his uncle was sincere, and that he wouldn't joke about a thing like this. And the fact that half the country was sitting in the dark right now supported the idea that this was indeed a true crisis. But ... *Alas Babylon*... Could it really be that bad?

From age twelve Dan had been raised by his uncle in northern Michigan after his father had died of cancer. Dan had never known his mother or any of her relatives. As a child he'd accepted that without question, but since then, he'd realized how odd that was. His mother had just up and left him. To this day, that very thought was a mood-altering experience for him.

As he sat alone in the dark, he thought to himself, *Am I being left again by the woman I love?* The answer rang back painful and obvious. *It's 4AM. Do you know where your wife is?*

On one occasion he'd asked his father about his mom, but only once. That was the only time he'd ever seen his father cry. He suspected that Uncle Rodney knew the inside story, but he'd never had the guts to bring it up after that. Besides, the past was the past, and he'd best leave it there. Nothing but pain in the wake of that ship.

He heard the creak of Jeremy's door as it opened. Dan waited a moment, then turned on the big flashlight sitting on his lap. The room lit up and Jeremy covered his eyes and turned his head away.

"What the hell are you doing? My head is killing me! Turn off the light!"

Dan left the light on, but did lower it away from Jeremy's face.

"You okay, son?"

Jeremy stopped and turned back toward him. Dan could see the black eye and the swollen face even in the dimness.

"Of course I'm not okay! My dad just beat the crap out of me, and my head is killing me!"

Dan sighed.

"Yeah, well, sorry about that, son. But you should know better than to come at me while I'm holding a ball bat. That was really stupid. I could have killed you with that bat."

Jeremy didn't say anything. He just stood there. Dan got up and moved over to the wall where he stood. He was surprised to hear whimpering.

"What's the matter?"

"Just leave me alone!"

He reached out and touched Jeremy's shoulder, but the boy pulled away and pressed himself up against the wall.

"Don't touch me!"

Dan nodded. "Yeah, okay, fine. I can understand that." He paused and then continued. "But I think we need to talk about something."

"I got nothing to say to you, old man!"

Dan smiled sympathetically and he shook his head, more in pity than anything else.

"So you're admitting that you just got your butt kicked by an old man?"

Jeremy said nothing, so Dan continued.

"Listen, Jeremy, we've got some real problems here. This blackout isn't only here in Menomonie. I was listening on the news until the outage, and it's happening all over the country."

Dan waited a few seconds. Finally, Jeremy lowered his hands from his face and glanced over at his stepfather.

"You serious?"

"Yes, I'm afraid so."

"How could that even happen? I mean, it's never happened before, right?"

Dan nodded and placed his hand on Jeremy's shoulder again. This time the boy shrugged, but didn't move away. Dan's hand remained on the boy's shirt.

"Jeremy, this could be really bad."

His son looked back toward his room.

"I got some candles."

Dan sat on the couch again, and a few minutes later Jeremy returned with two lit candles. He set them on the coffee table and they cast eerie shadows all across the room. It reminded Dan of times when he was a kid when the power would go out in Michigan during a thunder storm. Back then it had been exciting. But not today. This was different.

"Do you think it was an EMP burst?"

Dan had been trained in the basics of NBC warfare years ago in the Marine Corps, so he knew a little about EMP, but he was surprised by Jeremy's question.

"How do you know about EMP? Do they teach that in school?"

Jeremy shook his head. "No, I saw a TV show about it called *Jericho*. It was about a nuclear missile going off over the United States, and it fried every circuit board in the country. Nothing worked anymore. Not Facebook, not Twitter, YouTube. Nothin'!"

Dan nodded his head. "That's the Compton effect."

Jeremy looked over at Dan.

"Yeah, how'd you know that?"

"I learned all about nuclear, biological and chemical warfare when I was in the Marine Corps."

Even in the dim light Dan could see Jeremy's facial expression change.

"Oh...yeah. I forgot you were a Marine." He paused. "No wonder I can't whip you."

Dan smiled involuntarily. Then he chuckled.

"Don't worry. Time is on your side. Soon you'll be kicking my butt every day and twice on Sundays."

Jeremy smiled as well.

"Don't try to be nice to me. I'm still mad at you. You beat me up pretty bad."

Dan shifted his butt on the couch so he was facing the

boy straight away. He let out a long sigh.

"I was wrong to hit you. But I was mad, and you were way out of line. You've got no business taking advantage of that girl. It was immature selfishness on your part. What if you've gotten her pregnant?"

This time it was Jeremy's turn to laugh.

"She's not pregnant. I was wearing a rubber."

Dan narrowed his eyes. "Where did you get them?"

A stupid grin spread across Jeremy's face, causing him to wince out loud when it reached his battered cheek.

"I took them out of your sock drawer."

Dan shook his head from side to side.

"I hate to break this to you, sport, but those rubbers are five years old and full of holes."

Jeremy's smile began to fade.

"I don't believe you."

"You don't have to believe me. We'll just wait a few months and find out for ourselves. Are you ready to be a father, get a job, settle down?"

Jeremy didn't answer for almost a minute, and Dan decided to let him squirm for a while. He still loved the boy, but he needed a good scare for his own good.

"I guess I screwed up." He shook his head as he spoke. "I just really like sex. I didn't know it was going to be so nice."

Dan nodded. "Yeah, I know. But sex at the wrong time can really screw up your life, not to mention the girl you're with."

The boy moved his right hand up to his chin and held it there in thought.

"We can talk about that later, Jeremy, but right now we need to figure out what to do about the power."

Jeremy still didn't answer, so Dan kept talking.

"Can we call a truce right now until this crisis is over?"

Dan extended his right hand outward and held it there, waiting for the boy to take it. Jeremy hesitated, looked at it, then he thought about the darkness. He would never admit it, but he was deathly afraid of the dark. He reached out his hand and squeezed as hard as he could. Dan squeezed back, matching him pound for pound. In the end, Jeremy relaxed his grip and let his hand drop. It was all crimped together from the pissing match he'd just lost.

"Okay, but just until Mom gets back. Then all bets are off."

Dan smiled and offered him some Doritos.

The next day Dan woke up at 1PM to the sound of gunfire in the distance. He propped himself up in bed on one elbow and was immediately awake. He'd expected this to happen, but not so soon. If it had been only him, Dan would have loaded up and left town last night, but Jeremy had refused to leave without his mother. The sun was high in the sky and shining in on his face through the window. He looked over and saw the empty space beside him.

She hadn't come home last night ... again.

Dan thought about what that meant. *She slept with the man from Eau Claire and is probably nursing a hangover this morning.* His mind drifted back eight years to when they'd first met. Dan had been visiting the local Baptist Church and he'd seen the most gorgeous, slender blonde woman at the end of the pew where he was sitting. She'd looked back at him and smiled.

Three hours later Debbie had showed up at his door wearing a mini skirt, stiletto heels and black, fishnet stockings. Apparently she'd copied his name and address off the hospitality book they'd passed down the row. Everyone signed it, but Dan had never imagined signing the church book would result in the wildest time of his life. It had given him a whole, new outlook on church hospitality.

He had been twenty-six years old at the time, and was taking night classes from the local University. He was accepted into the Engineering Technology program, but never really got around to taking any actual engineering classes. Oddly enough, he was more interested in the humanities, and kept taking history and literature electives, making him wiser, but bringing him little closer to graduation. Prior to his college days he'd spent four years in the Marine Corps as a grunt. Now, at age thirty-four, he was at a dead-end factory job, with a shattered marriage, and the world was about to end, not with a bang, but a whimper.

One day, after 3 months of incredible bedroom passion, Debbie had announced she was pregnant. The next week he'd married her. Dan was old-fashioned at heart and known it was the right thing to do. He looked back on that now and shook his head in disgust. He'd also known the right thing to do was to wait for marriage to have sex, but that idea had gone out the window when she'd kicked off her stiletto heels and wrapped her long, slim legs around him.

In retrospect, any person who viewed church as a pick-up bar probably wasn't marrying material. Debbie had been twenty-one at the time and her son, Jeremy, had been six years old. Dan punched his pillow several times in frustration. *I was such an idiot!*

Just then he heard police sirens downtown, and looked up as Jeremy walked in his bedroom through the open door.

"Can you hear that? I just went over to Jason Mather's place and he said the college kids were looting downtown. The police are running out of places to put them."

Dan nodded his head. They were renting a small house on the Red Cedar River about a mile out of town. He knew that would buy them a little time, but he also knew that within a few days downtown Menomonie would be gutted, and the police would no longer be able to control all the hungry and terrified people. Once the population realized the lights weren't coming back on anytime soon, law of the jungle would take over, and the Golden Horde would spread out across the countryside. Thank God they were in northern Wisconsin and not closer to Chicago. His Uncle Rodney had taught him that The Golden Horde referred to the Mongolian conqueror, Batu, who had spread out across Russia during the thirteenth century. His Uncle had said that after the collapse, it would be an American horde that spread out across the land like locusts, consuming and destroying everything in their path. Dan knew their only hope of making it to Michigan was to stay ahead of the horde.

"We have to get out of here, Jeremy. In a few days Menomonie is going to be a war zone and we don't want to get caught up in it."

Jeremy glanced over at the empty half of Dan's bed. Dan lowered his head.

"She didn't come home last night did she."

Jeremy looked out the window.

"I guess I didn't expect her to, but...I was just hoping, ya know."

Dan nodded. "Yeah, I know. I've been hoping for a long time."

Jeremy's eyes misted over, and it was hard for Dan to believe this was the same kid he'd punched out just yesterday. He sat up in bed and swung his feet out onto the floor before finding his pants and pulling them on.

"We'll spend the rest of the afternoon packing up the truck and getting things we need, then slip out of town after dark. We'll take back roads all the way. They should be less dangerous than the interstate."

Jeremy plopped himself down on the chair beside the bed. He had a faraway look in his eyes.

"I'm staying here."

"Excuse me?"

Jeremy looked over at him.

"You know I can't leave mom here by herself."

Dan stood to his feet and zipped up his trousers. Then he slipped on his boots and began lacing them up.

"It's a mistake, Jeremy. She may never come home, and

even if she does, she won't be here long. She's a wanderlust, son, and she's just not the settling-down kind."

"Then why did you marry her?"

Dan flinched as if stung by a bee.

"Because I was stupid. I thought with my Johnson instead of my brain."

"That must be old people talk, because I don't even know what that means."

Dan finished lacing his boots and walked over to the dresser. He pulled out a grey t-shirt and pulled it over his head.

"It means that the weakest part of a man is just below the waist."

Jeremy cocked his head to one side.

"You mean you were screwing my mom?"

Dan turned his head away in shame and embarrassment.

"Don't rub it in! I feel stupid enough as it is right now."

Jeremy looked down at the floor.

"So, let me guess, my mom faked a pregnancy, and you felt obligated to marry her. Am I right?"

Dan tucked his shirt in and put on a belt.

"Something like that."

Jeremy laughed softly.

" That's the oldest trick in the book. And you had the nerve to lecture me about Tonya."

"I'm running into town to check things out. When I get back I'll start packing up the truck. It would be nice to have your help if you're still here."

Dan walked out the door, and Jeremy called after him.

"Can you pick up some more milk? Everything in the frig is all warm."

Dan shook his head from side to side and muttered to himself. "Warm milk. That's the least of our worries."

CHAPTER 5

The City - September 9

MENOMONIE, Wisconsin was first settled in 1830 when James H. Lockwood and Joseph Rolette built a lumber mill near the confluence of Wilson Creek and the Red Cedar River. Over the years, Menomonie had been claimed by Spain, France, England, and the United States. The latter finally won out, and the city had now grown to a population of over 14,000 people. Up until twelve hours ago, for the most part, those 14,000 residents got along pretty well, but once the lights went out, about 6,000 of them went nuts!

When Dan turned right off river road on the outskirts of town, he knew he was going to have trouble. Black, billowing smoke rose up from the heart of town. There was a conspicuous absence of sirens that bothered him. He could hear plenty of screaming though, and then a few more gun shots. He wondered to himself, *How could it break down so quickly?*

Then off to his right he saw a police car with its strobe lights still blinking. There was an officer lying face down on the side of the road, and he wasn't moving. Dan's first instinct was to stop, and he did so. Before getting out of the car he looked around carefully. His nerves were tighter than a gnat's butt stretched over a barrel. When he walked up closer, he saw the dark liquid drying in the hot sun beside the cop's head. On closer inspection, Dan could see half the man's face had been blown away, probably by a shotgun.

Flies buzzed around the officer's head, landing, then taking off, then landing once again, only to repeat the deadly dance over and over as heat radiated up off the black pavement. It was then he recognized the corpse of the Police Officer who'd pulled him over last night after shopping at Wal*Mart.

At that moment, Dan took back all the skepticism he'd ever given his Uncle Rodney. All the while Dan was growing up, he'd seen the way people had responded to his uncle's eccentricities. Some had even laughed behind his back, saying it was some kind of neurosis he'd picked up in Vietnam. He doubted they were laughing at him now. Before, he'd never taken the man seriously, but now, only twelve hours into a world without electricity, he suddenly believed. With the conviction of Noah, building an ark in the desert, he believed with all his heart.

Dan looked over at the police car. It was filled with bullet holes and steam rose up from the hood. Things were scattered out onto the pavement, and he knew it had been ransacked of anything valuable or dangerous. The cop's jacket was crumpled in a heap a few feet away, and Dan walked over to it. He picked it up and brought it back to the body, where he laid it over his mangled head. Dan read the man's name tag: Sergeant Jim Miller.

Yesterday Sergeant Miller would have called for back up and a SWAT team and 50 officers would have saved him. Today, it was a different world, and any person with a gun and enough savvy to stage an ambush could kill a cop with impunity. Dan realized that if the police weren't safe here, then neither was he. He'd seen enough. Dan jumped back into his truck and came to a decision. He fired up the truck and did an illegal U-turn … because everything was legal now. Without the rule of law, all things were legal to those who had the power.

"Somebody killed a cop?"

Dan nodded his head without speaking. He was sitting in the living room on the couch with his head down almost between his knees, trying to get over what he'd just seen. Jeremy sat across from him in the recliner, leaning forward, trying to get his father to talk about it. He would never admit it, but his young heart was excited by all that had happened, even though he knew it was wrong to think so.

"How did it happen?"

Dan shook his head back and forth. "I don't know. It just did, okay, and I don't want to talk about it anymore." He got up slowly. "We should be packing our stuff and loading up the truck right now, because we're leaving by day's end."

Jeremy popped up beside him. "But my mom! What about her? We can't leave my mom here by herself!"

Dan turned on him with more vehemence than he knew was in him. "She's not alone, Jeremy, remember? She's with another man, and she may or may not be back." Dan took his head in both hands and squeezed his temples in an attempt to make the throbbing go away. Jeremy grabbed his wrist.

"Please, Dad. Please. She's my mom. I know she's been bad to you, but ... I still love her."

Dan stared out over Jeremy's head into the blue painted wall behind him. His body was in the room, but his mind was somewhere else. "I can't, Jeremy. Even if I wanted to get her, I have no idea where this guy lives in Eau Claire. We'd never find her."

Jeremy let Dan's wrist drop. "I know where she is, Dad. I can take you there."

Adrenaline surged into Dan's blood, and his muscles tightened up like knotted rope. "How? How could you know where he lives?"

Jeremy looked down at the floor and spoke to the dirty, yellow, shag carpet in a hushed voice. "I've been there before, several times."

Dan tightened his jaw. "So you knew all along about her

affair?"

"The whole town knew, Dad! Mom's been cheating on you for years. How could you not know that?"

In his heart, Dan had known all along, but it's one thing to know, and quite another to accept what you know. "It's too dangerous in Eau Claire. If people are berserk in Menomonie, can you imagine how crazy things are in a bigger city? We have to assume the worst."

Dan started to walk away, but Jeremy's next words stopped him cold. "He lives four miles outside of town in the country. We can take back roads all the way, and we should be safe."

Dan turned around and stared back at his son, but Jeremy wouldn't make eye contact.

"Please, Dad, just try and if she won't come or we can't find her, then I'll go to Michigan with you."

Dan heaved out a sigh and rubbed his eyes with his left hand. Suddenly he felt very alone ... and very betrayed. He looked back up and choked back his emotions.

"All right, son. Let's load up the truck first. Then we'll get going, but if we can't find her, then we head north to the upper peninsula."

His son nodded, and without saying another word they both went off to pack.

It took them six hours to get everything loaded up. Dan drained the hot water heater in order to fill up all the plastic bottles he could find, then he drained the gas out of the old Buick that had been sitting in the front yard for over a year. Before loading everything into the truck bed, they lifted the cap onto the back and bolted it securely in place.

As the sun was getting low in the sky, Dan made his final check around the house. He walked back to the bedroom and looked at the bed where he'd slept with Debbie. The covers were all messed up, and he didn't bother to fix them. Dan knew if he drug this out he would cry in front of his son, so he slowly backed his way out of the room. He closed and locked all the windows, and turned off the main breaker switch just in case power came back on while they were gone.

As he walked out of the kitchen, the Bible on the counter caught his eye. He stopped and reached down to stroke its leather. He thought, *Why not?* and picked it up on the way out. It couldn't hurt to take God along on the trip.

Once inside the truck, he fired up the engine and didn't look back. Jeremy glanced down at the large pistol on Dan's waist. "You're not going to shoot anyone are you?"

Dan didn't answer. He just gripped the steering wheel as hard as he could and took the back way out of town. He was painfully aware this was a new world with new rules. The old law said "No Guns Allowed", but the new law said, "No Guns - No Survival!" And Dan chose to survive.

☙ ⸰ ⸰ ❧

As Dan drove through the back roads of Dunn County, he did so with reservations. On the one hand, he knew that if he left his wife here in Wisconsin, he would always feel guilty about it, would always wonder what happened to her and if one more try might have made the difference. Despite the fact she was with another man, and had, in effect, already broken their marriage vows many times before, he still felt conflicted. On the other hand, he had no desire to see her with this man again. It had killed him in the Applebee's parking lot to see them kissing. A big part of him wanted to drive north and forget he'd ever seen her, to leave her cheating heart and all the chaos that followed her behind him forever. Nonetheless, he did still love her. Love was a funny thing. He loved her and wanted to kill her simultaneously. He wondered if that was normal.

"So why did you grab that Bible?"

Dan was snapped out of his thoughts. He didn't want to talk right now.

"I don't know. I saw it on the counter and something just came over me all of a sudden and I wanted it with us on this trip. Like maybe if we had it that God might help us out a little bit."

His son shook his head back and forth and laughed out loud. His response annoyed Dan.

"What's wrong? Why is that so funny?"

Jeremy looked down at the Bible on the seat between them. "I don't know. It just seems funny that you packed up six guns and a thousand rounds of ammo, but decided at the last minute to bring a Bible."

Dan grunted out loud. "Nothing odd about that. Christians need guns to protect themselves from bad people just like the atheists do I suppose."

Jeremy turned his head and hung his right arm out the window as they passed a field of corn that was over seven feet high and beginning to yellow. There was a distinct smell of cow manure in the air.

"Are you going to shoot Pete when you see him?"

"The man's name is Pete? I didn't know that?"

"Yeah, his name's Pete. He's a tool and die maker."

Dan glanced over for a second, then quickly back to the road. "Is he a nice guy?"

His son turned his head, and the shiner on his eye showed up pretty good in the fading sunlight. "Well, he's pretty nice. At least he hasn't beat me up yet."

Dan forced a playful smile on his lips. "Well, he doesn't know you yet. Give it some time."

"That's not funny, Dad!"

He laughed nonetheless. "Yeah, I know. Sometimes I make light of things to keep from crying."

Jeremy brought his arm back inside the window. "You cry sometimes? I didn't think old people did that."

"Stop calling me old! I'm only 34. And yes, I've been crying a lot lately. Seeing the woman you love with another man will do that to you."

Jeremy shrugged. "I suppose. I don't really know much about love. It seems over-rated from what I've seen between you and mom."

Dan was quiet for the rest of the drive. Ten minutes later Jeremy pointed at a gravel driveway. "Turn left here." Dan pulled in, drove about 50 yards before coming to a stop on the grass. A run-down, double-wide trailer was off to their right. "There's mom's car. I don't see Pete's truck."

Dan answered with a grimace. "It's probably in the auto-body shop."

"Why would it be in the shop?"

But Dan ignored him.

"Maybe you should stay out here, Dad. They might not like seeing you, and I think mom might act better if it's just me."

Dan nodded but said nothing. He was completely happy staying out in the truck. The last thing he needed was to see the two of them together again. Jeremy got out and slammed the truck door. He walked a few steps then turned back.

"Don't come in with that gun, okay. I don't want you shooting anyone."

Dan nodded. "Be careful, son. If she doesn't want to come, just back on out and we'll get out of here."

Jeremy walked away without looking back. When he reached the porch, he opened the door and walked in as if he'd been living there for years. Dan thought to himself, *Yeah, Pete must be a real nice guy. All adulterers are like that. Real sweethearts!* Dan sighed out loud, as if every cubic inch of air was leaving him in one mighty gasp. He looked down at the Bible on the seat. He touched it with the fingers of his right hand. Then his hand brushed against the holstered pistol on his right hip. It was a Taurus Judge, a five-shot revolver chambered in four-ten shotgun shells or 45 long Colt. It was large and bulky, but packed quite a punch at close range. The first three chambers he had loaded with number three buckshot. The last two were slugs. Jeremy was right; it did look odd to him, the huge gun on his hip only inches away from the word of God. Bibles and bullets. He wondered, *Was he a hypocrite?* Then he laughed to himself. Of course he was a hypocrite. Wasn't everyone?

"BOOM!"

The gunshot rang out, breaking the silence of the sunset behind him. Then he heard screams. Without thinking he jumped out of the truck and ran toward the house. When he reached the trailer door, he was surprised to see the big pistol already in his right hand. He hesitated, more screams, then he threw open the door and jumped inside not knowing what to expect. The living room was empty; it was a pig sty with pizza boxes and beer cans all over the floor. "BOOM!" Part of the wall to his left exploded, showering his face with powdered dry wall. It came from the next room over.

"Mom! No! Please!"

Dan moved to the doorway. He had the gun tight in both hands out in front of him and peeked carefully around the corner. He saw Debbie swing the gun over in his direction. "BOOM!" He jumped back just in time, but dry wall and wood splinters smashed against the left side of his face, blinding him for several seconds. He worked quickly to wipe the blood and dust from his eyes. He could hear Jeremy pleading with her.

"Mom, please. We're going to Michigan where it's safe. We want to take you with us. We still love you mom!"

"Shut up you little puke! I don't want to hear it from you! Now get out of here before I shoot you both."

Dan crawled slowly back over to the door. He had seen her up on the bed. Pete was lying next to her with his eyes closed. By the color of his skin, Dan was sure he'd been dead for quite a while. His son and his wife were both crying inside the room.

"Why did you bring him here! I didn't want him to see me like this! Now he won't love me anymore!"

Dan wasn't sure she was talking to him or to Jeremy. She

always talked crazy like this when she was drunk, but she'd never used guns before. She didn't even like them.

"Don't shoot me momma!"

"I want you outta here, boy! You just go back home and wait for me there."

Dan peeked around the corner and saw Jeremy nodding his head. Tears were running down his cheeks and his black hair was covered in dry wall dust. A huge, gaping hole was above him, letting in light from the outside. Dan thought quickly. If he rushed her, she'd shoot him for sure. If he did nothing, she might shoot Jeremy. She was crazy when she was drunk. A thought came to him quickly, *Had she killed Pete?*

"I'll leave momma. Okay? Just don't shoot me. I'll go home and wait for you."

Debbie lowered the shotgun.

"Yeah, and don't forget to feed the cat."

"We don't have a cat, Momma."

The gun came back up.

"Don't argue with me, son! Now get home and feed the cat! And cook me up one of those TV dinners with macaroni and cheese and fried chicken. The dark meat, not the white!"

He watched as Jeremy got up slowly and walked toward the door. The gun followed him as he went.

"Okay. Bye Momma. See you when you get home. Don't be late."

Jeremy reached the door and walked past Dan, who was already crawling backwards. Once outside, they walked back to the truck. He held his son as he heaved sob after sob upon his father's shoulder.

"She was gonna kill me, daddy!"

Dan stroked the back of his head. "Shhh, hush now. It's going to be okay." Jeremy hadn't called him daddy in years. "We're just going to wait out here until she passes out, then we'll sneak back in and carry her out. Okay?"

Jeremy nodded with his face pressed tightly against his

father's muscular shoulder. For the longest time neither man moved. They just stood there hugging each other in the fading sunlight, waiting for the drunkard to sleep it off.

Two hours later, Dan walked back into the house alone. Five minutes later he came out carrying his wife's body. She was already dead.

CHAPTER 6

The Exodus - September 9

DAN drove north through Colfax, hopped on County Road M to Sandy Creek, then cut over to New Auburn. From there he took 40 up to Island Lake and then Ladysmith. He figured so long as he stayed off the big highways, they would be okay. Actually, Dan was quite versed at getting out of Dodge in time of crisis. After all, he'd been raised by a Vietnam vet and a hard-core prepper. To be truthful, he hadn't heard the term "prepper" until a few years back. A prepper was someone who prepared religiously for a break-down in society where food would be in short supply, police and emergency services would be nonexistent, and the law of the jungle reigned supreme. For the past ten years, hardly a month had gone by when he hadn't received something in the mail from his Uncle Rodney. Once it was a book called *How to Survive the End of the World as we Know it*"; another time it was a DVD on home canning and food dehydrating; once he'd even received a small bag of junk silver coins. At the time, he hadn't known what junk silver was. Apparently the U.S. government used to make coins out of ninety per-cent silver, but ceased doing that in 1965.

Dan glanced down at Jeremy who had finally cried him-self to sleep, and then down to the Taurus four-ten gauge revolver on his right hip. He remembered the day Uncle Rodney had mailed him the gun. Debbie had opened the box and freaked out upon seeing it. She hated guns and had given him a ton of grief for it. It wasn't just that the gun was unregistered or that it was illegal to send it through the mail, but his Uncle Rodney had shipped it fully loaded. The next day Dan had called to scold him for his foolishness, but his Uncle, the king of overkill, had laughed at his concerns and simply said, "Now why in the world, son, would I mail you an unloaded gun? It's no good without the bullets! And the last thing I'm gonna do is register it, because then the government will know I have it! Think, boy, think! I don't need any ATF thugs sniffing around my door!"

That was his Uncle Rodney in a nutshell, no pun intended.

Everytime Dan went through a small town, he kept a very watchful eye and didn't stop or slow down. Most of the people in rural northern Wisconsin were different than in Menomonie. They probably knew what was going on in a general way, but were less effected by it. Northern country folk were more independent and less prone to over-reacting. But Dan knew that in a few days, these small towns would be visited by refugees from St. Paul and from Milwaukee, maybe even Chicago, and unless the people got organized, they would be picked clean like vultures on roadkill. The thought just occurred to him that his Uncle Rodney would be having the same problem with refugees fleeing Grand Rapids and Detroit. He needed to get there quickly.

His wife's body was in the back, rolled up in sheets and blankets, and he knew she would start to bloat, smell and draw flies in a few more hours. Jeremy had pleaded with him to take her along, so despite the impracticality, he'd carefully laid her in back under the watchful eye of his son. It was about a nine-hour drive to his uncle's house, then they could give her a decent burial and a ceremony. Dan figured they could bury her on the hill overlooking the house. She would like it there under the oaks. For a moment he pondered the absurdity of his last thought. *How could she like it there? She was dead.*

The reality sunk in like lead in the pit of his stomach. A few days ago he'd been willing to fight to get her back, but now ... if the truth be known ... deep down inside, a part of him felt relieved to be rid of her. Sure, he was sad, and he still loved her, but ... she was an incredible burden and a heartache he'd been suffering through for years. Despite that, the feeling of relief carried along with it a flipside of guilt. In fact, he was feeling so many conflicting emotions right now, that he couldn't sort it all out. Guilt, pain, sadness, relief, and even a bit of anger. It was all lumped in there like a recipe for peach jam that just wouldn't gel.

He glanced down at Jeremy again. He saw the tear tracks running down the boy's cheeks; they were still drying. Maybe he would sleep through the whole trip. It would be good for him. Had it really only been a little over 24 hours since he'd caught him in bed with the neighbor girl? It seemed like a lifetime ago.

He was headed east now on highway 8. His plan was to take it all the way into the Michigan Upper Peninsula and then hook up on U.S. 2.

A pick-up truck passed him coming the other way. It was loaded down with supplies and had a man and a boy perched on top with shotguns pointed over the cab. Dan was surprised at the lack of police officers out here in the sticks. True, there weren't that many to begin with, but he expected the rule of law to still be in force out here in the country, at least in the form of the County Sheriffs. But he hadn't seen a single law enforcement officer since leaving the edge of Menomonie. The last policeman he'd seen was missing half his head.

Dan looked down at his gas gauge. It read three-quarters full. Along with the gas he had in back, he would have no problem making it home to northern Michigan. His plan was to drive straight through until morning.

It was after midnight now and pitch dark outside. His eyelids were starting to droop a bit so he reached into the console and pulled out one of the Mocha Frappuccinos. He'd purchased a twelve pack last night at Wal*Mart, and he had a strong suspicion that once these were gone, it would be a very long time before he drank another one. He peeled away the cellophane, twisted the top and took a sip of the warm fluid. It was like magical, life-giving nectar.

Dan tilted his head back to take a deeper drink, and when he lowered his head back down the White-tailed deer was already full in his headlights. He slammed on the brakes, throwing Jeremy into the dashboard. The big doe bounced off his grill, got back up again and bounded off into the alfalfa field to his left.

"What are you doing?"

Dan saw steam already rising up from the hood of his truck. He let out an exasperated sigh and his forehead came down hard on the steering wheel. All he could think was *At least the radio still works*.

"Calm down, Jeremy, I told you to stop swearing!"

Jeremy was holding his head in his hands. Blood poured out from between his fingers from the new gash in his forehead. Dan slammed the shifter into park and reached over to his son. "Let me take a look at that cut." Jeremy pulled his hand away, but all Dan could see was blood in the dimness of the truck cab. He turned on the dome light and then wiped away the blood with an old, fast-food napkin. "This cut's pretty deep. You're going to need stitches, son. Here, hold this napkin over it. Press down hard until it stops bleeding."

Jeremy complied with a painful moan.

"What happened to the truck?"

Dan opened the door and stepped out to take a look at it. "I hit a deer." He moved to the front and looked down at the steam rising from beneath the hood. It was either a broken hose or the grill was shoved through the radiator. In the present situation, neither prospect was a good one. Up ahead he saw a driveway surrounded by pine trees. He didn't see any buildings, so he hopped back in and slowly nursed the truck forward. As the truck turned left onto the gravel drive, the headlights revealed a hundred plus marble and granite headstones. He thought to himself, *How apropo.*

"Dad, this is a graveyard! We can't stop here."

Dan looked over at his son impatiently. "We don't have a choice. We've lost our water, and if we keep going we'll over heat and burn up the engine."

"Is Mom okay?"

Dan parked the truck behind a row of bushy spruce trees. No sense in bringing undo attention to their presence. He then looked in the rear-view mirror and saw his wife's body had been slammed forward by the sudden stop and was now scrunched up against the truck cap window.

"Yeah, your mom's fine."

The bleeding had stopped now, so Jeremy took the bloody napkin away from his head. "What are we going to do?"

Dan thought about it for a second. He glanced down and saw the remains of his Frappuccino soaking into the floor carpet. "I don't know, son. Let me take another look under the hood."

Fifteen minutes later he determined that a plastic grill shard had sliced through the radiator hose. He repaired it temporarily with a liberal amount of heavy duty duct tape.

"What now? Will it still run?"

Dan shrugged. "I don't know. Probably."

He looked up into the darkness and saw a million stars. It was peaceful here among the graves. "We'll get a few hours sleep, then at first light we'll drive a bit and see what happens."

Dan moved to the back of the truck and spent fifteen minutes laying the air mattresses and sleeping bags on the soft grass underneath the pine trees. He then got out two MREs and an electric lantern. Dan opened his plastic bag of food and started to squeeze a thick stream of "Spaghetti with Meat Sauce" onto his tongue.

"What the hell is this stuff?"

"I thought I told you to stop swearing. Why do you do that?"

"I just want to know what I'm eating, that's all."

Dan lowered the tin foil pouch of tomato, pasta and meat mush before answering.

"Well, I think you can ask questions without swearing. If you don't learn to talk respectable then you'll never get a decent job in life and succeed."

Jeremy looked at him in disbelief. "You've got to be kidding me! First you tell me it's the end of the world, then you tell me I have to stop swearing or I won't succeed. Make up your mind! Which one is it?"

Dan thought for a moment. "Oh. Right. I guess you can go ahead and swear now." Then he added. "But you don't have to be so grumpy, and you could be a little more grateful for what you have. It could be worse. These could be those old C-rations my Uncle used to feed me when I was growing up."

"So, what's a C-ration?"

Dan finished swallowing his food before answering. "It's food that came in olive drab tin cans left over from the Vietnam War. Instead of spaghetti and meat sauce it had names like *Turkey and Turkey Parts*."

Jeremy looked at him blankly in the dim light.

"Turkey parts?"

Dan smiled and nodded. "Exactly what I used to think. It could have been beaks, talons and gums all ground up in a can for all I knew."

"Damn! That's some nasty stuff!"

"Will you stop swearing!"

Jeremy cocked his head to one side in disbelief. "Dad, you're kidding, right? In the last 24 hours my hometown has become a war zone; my Dad beat me up; my mom killed her boyfriend, then overdosed on drugs; I'm sitting in a cemetery eating liquid food surrounded by dead people, and the truck is broke down."

Dan thought again and conceded his point. "Okay, so you've had a bad day. No one denies you that. But you have to look on the bright side. I gave you the cheese tortellini. You should eat it up and get some sleep. Tomorrow's a big day."

Jeremy threw the MRE down onto the grass and screamed as loud as he could. "I HATE YOU! You are so stupid! You don't care about me! You are the worst dad in the whole world, and I hate you!"

With that, his son turned his back and crawled deep into his sleeping bag and pulled it up over his head. Dan sat there dumbfounded, holding the half-eaten spaghetti pouch in his limp hand. He looked up at the stars, then at the pine boughs. He could smell them in the humid night air. Dan thought to himself, *Yes, it can always get worse.*

He put away all the food except the spaghetti he was eating to keep it away from wild animals, then climbed into his sleeping bag. There was an owl hooting a ways off, and tree frogs singing close by. A few weeks ago he'd heard Cicadas buzzing in the tree tops, but they were gone now. A part of him wanted back the past, but another part, a deeper part, felt more contented than he'd ever felt in his entire life. He didn't understand that. Dan finished sucking down the spaghetti, all the while wondering, *Why do I feel so at peace in this graveyard?*

Dan crawled down into his sleeping bag. He rolled onto his right side like he usually would, but the bulk of his pistol revolted against him. He thought about taking it off, but then rolled over onto his other side. The gun gave him comfort.

He listened to his son whimper for a half hour, then it was replaced by his deep, steady breathing. Only then could Dan's mind drift off into the night.

CHAPTER 7

The Men - September 10, 2AM

DAN woke up in the middle of the night to the sound of screams. At first he thought they were his own, but when he sat up in the sleeping bag and touched his mouth, he knew it wasn't so. He looked over to his left and saw Jeremy still sleeping in his bag. The scream came to him again. It was blood curdling and it was close by. With the hairs standing up on his arms and neck, he jerked out of his sleeping back, and put on his shoes. He hesitated a bit, then walked over to his truck cab and quietly opened the door. The scream sounded again. This time he could tell it was from the far side of the cemetery. He looked over and saw a dim light. From behind the seat he pulled out the scoped, Winchester Model 1800 shotgun and quickly slipped off into the night in search of the unknown terror.

☙ ⁕ ⁕ ☙

The woman's back was pressed down on the bed of the pick-up truck by four men. Two kneeled up by her head, pinning her wrists down on the plastic bed liner while two others were stationed at her legs trying desperately to pry them apart. A fifth man, the one in charge, threw the woman's skirt up onto her writhing belly and began to unbuckle his belt.

"Hold the witch still!"

The woman screamed again as she thrashed on the truck

bed. The man unzipped his pants and let them drop to his ankles. He laughed out loud. "Man I love it when they scream and fight like this. It just turns me on!"

He moved closer to the truck bed. "Slide her in closer, boys." The man smiled as he leaned down near the woman's face. She was tear-stained and bloody. "Don't worry, little lady, this will only take a few seconds. I'll try to be gentle." The other four men laughed with him and the lady screamed again.

Dan's first shot took off the leader's head at the base of the skull. It seemed to explode in the dimness of the night, and then his silly, bare legs collapsed, followed quickly by his torso. Two seconds later the man holding her right leg was hit in the back. The 12-gauge slug passed cleanly through his heart, then slammed into the shoulder of the man still holding her right wrist. Both men fell, one squirming on the truck bed, the other on the grass beside his leader. The man on her left wrist jumped up and out of the truck bed. The one who remained standing was hit high in the leg and went down to the grass. The truck engine revved to life and sped off into the graveyard, knocking down headstones and bouncing radically up and down. Dan fired his two remaining shots into the driver's side of the cab, but it was difficult hitting a moving target with a scope in the darkness. The truck reached the paved road and accelerated into the night. A few seconds later, the truck engine began to wind down, and the truck coasted to a stop.

"Dad! What's going on?"

When Jeremy ran up behind him, Dan reached out to grab his son and pulled him down behind the large, granite headstone beside him. "Stay down, son. Two of them are still alive."

Dan gazed out into the darkness. Only the truck's headlights almost 100 yards away lit up the night.

"I'll get a flashlight!" Jeremy jumped up and ran off before Dan could stop him. As his son's footsteps faded, Dan started to hear other sounds. One of the men was in his death rattle; he was gasping for air, as the muscles around his airway began to relax. It was a pitiful sound that Dan had heard several times before on deer he'd shot. But this time it was different. These were men, and he had killed them.

Off in the distance the truck's engine purred lightly. Then it stopped altogether. Dan knew that inside the cab, the man was either dead or dying. The adrenaline surge that had hit Dan's body just one, short minute ago began to make his hands shake as the realization of what he'd done began to set in.

The death rattle stopped, and quiet recaptured the night. Dan lay on the ground dumbfounded that it had all happened in just a few seconds. Suddenly, fear for his own life took over and he fell apart and sobbed on an unknown grave. Off in the distance, he heard Jeremy rummaging through the truck cab for the flashlight. About two minutes later, Dan heard his son's footsteps coming up behind him. He reached up to wipe away his tears, then he gathered his wits and grit his teeth so his son wouldn't see him crying.

"I got two of them, Dad."

Dan said nothing, but reached over and accepted the big Maglight from his son. Leaving the shotgun on the ground, Dan got up and moved to the cover of a tree three feet away.

"Stay down, son. I need to make sure."

Safely behind the thickness of the Maple tree, Dan turned on the flashlight and lit up the darkness around him. He wasn't prepared for what he saw. Three bodies were stacked twenty yards away, almost on top of one another. Dan searched for movement, but saw nothing. He looked over at his son. "Jeremy, I need you to watch for movement, if you see anything, yell to me and tell me where it's coming from, relative to my position." He saw his son nod and his flashlight turn on. Jeremy's eyes were as big as saucers.

Dan stepped out from the tree and ran twenty feet to the next Maple. They were all about 10 inches in diameter, and had been planted in a line. They were perfect for his purpose. After three more movements, Dan was within 10 feet of the bodies. He shined the light all around, but couldn't find the fourth man. By now his hands had stopped shaking, and an eerie calm overtook him. He shined the light on the three bodies. A cold front had moved in, and a billow of steam was now rising above the death. He could smell the blood in the cool, night air, and it threatened to close up his nostrils. Dan moved the flashlight to his left hand, loosened the thumb break on his holster and eased out the big, Taurus Judge revolver. He walked over to the pile, and saw two shotguns and a rifle lying on the ground beside them. Two of the men also wore sidearms. The whole thing had happened so quickly, they hadn't been able to draw their guns and return fire. Dan thought about what he'd learned in the Marines. *The element of surprise can overcome superior numbers and superior firepower.* Until now, all his learning had just been book knowledge and hear-say.

That's when he saw movement 20 yards away. The man was on the ground, crawling slowly. Dan looked at the grass and saw the thick trail of blood. He was surprised that human blood shown in the light just the same as deer blood. Dan slowly closed the distance to only six feet, keeping straight behind the man as he moved. That's when he saw the gun in the man's right hand slowly raise up and point in his direction. On reflex alone, Dan moved to his left while shooting. The four-ten buckshot tore into the man's upper body. Five shots later, Dan heard the hammer clicking on empty cylinders. He forced himself to stop pulling the trigger and lowered the gun. The man was no longer moving, and the Glock pistol lay on the grass beside him. Dan holstered his Taurus and picked up the Glock. He felt the sticky blood on the grips. As he knelt beside the dead man, Jeremy walked up and stood beside him.

"Dad, you killed four guys, man!"

Dan nodded. "Yes, but there were five of them. I need

you to stay here behind that headstone while I go up and check out the truck."

Jeremy looked down at the dead man, and obeyed his father without question. Dan walked away, then he stopped and turned back around. "If you see a woman, don't hurt her. They were raping her, and I think she's still here hiding somewhere. We need to find her and help her."

It took Dan about two minutes to reach the stalled truck. The headlights were still on, so he approached from the rear. There was no sign of the woman. Suddenly, he was reminded of the Menomonie police officer who had snuck up behind his car the night of the blackout. Things had changed so much in so short a time - as if the hand of God had reached down and flicked a switch.

Dan shined the light into the back of the cab window and saw the man slouched over the wheel. He moved carefully up to the driver's side door and pulled on the handle. It opened easily. When he shined the light on the driver, he could see the gaping wound on the left side of his neck. The shotgun slug had done its job.

Dan looked around the truck and off into the darkness on the side of the road. He called out, but found no trace of the woman. He reached in and turned off the truck's headlights. That's when he heard his son yell to him. Dan sprinted back to the cemetery. When he shined the light down on his son, he saw Jeremy holding the shoulders of a woman close to him. She was sobbing, and Jeremy hushed her gently.

"It's okay, lady. My dad's the good guy. He saved you."

Dan shoved the Glock into his belt at the small of his back and dropped down beside the two. He felt like a clumsy cowboy when he spoke to her for the first time.

"It's okay, Ma'am. They're all gone now."

CHAPTER 8

The Woman - September 10

AFTER taking the woman back to his truck, Dan returned to the road and drove the other pick-up back to the cemetery and parked it behind the trees beside his own. The truck was new and shiny, still boasting dealer plates from Milwaukee. Without a doubt, it was stolen.

It was a grisly job in the eerie darkness of the graveyard, but he then piled all the corpses together. With that task done, he washed his hands and face using a hand pump by one of the graves. Then he brought the lady a rag and a pan of water. She had stopped crying now.

Dan and Jeremy waited a few yards away on top of their sleeping bags for her to finish. Jeremy tried to ask questions, but Dan shushed him into silence. The moon was high in the sky by now, and lit up the grave stones all around them. Dan quietly reassessed the events of the past hour. He thought it odd, that he was replaying the shoot-out in his mind, analyzing it, and picking out things he should have done differently. He felt a strange numbness, akin to the feeling he'd experienced the first time he saw his wife kiss another man. Inside him, a door had opened with a rusty scrape and then a thud, unleashing something, a part of him that he'd kept penned up inside his whole life. But now it was out. Just for a moment, he wondered if life was still worth living.

The woman finished washing and walked back to the sleeping bags where she sat down on the grass. Dan moved off his sleeping bag and offered it to her, but she just stared straight ahead as if she'd seen or heard nothing. Jeremy looked over at his dad, wondering what to do next. Dan nodded to him.

"Just go ahead and get some sleep, son. We've got a long drive tomorrow." By now the last vestige of adrenaline had worn off and Dan felt exhausted. Despite that, he took the time to reload first the shotgun and then the Taurus pistol. After reholstering, Dan brought the woman an MRE and a mocha Frappuccino. He laid them at her feet like a gift, and then backed away. "Go ahead. We have plenty." She looked down at the food. Her hand ran silently over the glass Frappuccino bottle, but still she said nothing.

"I'm Dan, and this is my son, Jeremy."

She looked out over the graveyard and directly up into the moon, staring at it like a coyote.

"Are you okay, ma'am?"

Dan noticed in the dim light how frail the woman looked. She was slender with a light complexion, and he couldn't help but notice how attractive she was, even after the ordeal she'd been through. Dan thought to himself, *I've just killed five men, and my dead wife is bloating up in the back of my truck, but for some reason I still notice attractive women. I'm going to hell for sure* He looked away, ashamed of himself.

"Well, okay. I can see you don't want to talk right now and I don't blame you." He pulled up a blade of healthy, green grass and began to tear it up with his fingers. "I've had a rough day myself." He threw the grass bits onto the ground. "Listen, I'll just sleep inside the cab tonight, and you can use my sleeping bag when you're feeling up to it." Dan glanced up at the moon. "We can talk in the morning when we all have some sleep under our belts." He hesitated. "Sound like a plan?" She didn't answer, so Dan got up and walked over to the truck. He piled in the front seat and stretched himself out as best he could. It was then he noticed the smell of decay, and realized his wife would never make it back to Michigan. In the morning he'd tell Jeremy they had to bury her here in the cemetery. Dan wondered why he didn't feel sad about that. Truthfully, he wasn't feeling much of anything right now. His feelings felt all blurry, like he knew they were there, but couldn't quite make out the details.

He thought to himself again, *Am I going to hell for all this? Did I do wrong?* Dan had never been as religious as he should, but still, he was no moral vacuum. Yes, he'd made mistakes, like anyone else, but he usually tried to do the right thing. After a few minutes contemplation, he concluded that killing the five men was less wrong than watching the poor woman get raped. He'd acted almost solely in accordance with his instinct and his personality. It worried Dan that his response had been instant, without thought, and totally merciless in its execution. He thought again about books he'd read over the years: *Lord of the Flies* by William Golding and *Heart of Darkness* by Joseph Conrad, and even the *Bible* for that matter. All of them proclaimed that man was inherently evil, and when left to his own devices, without accountability and the rule of law, that society would break down and the human heart would become evil and desperately wicked. Lying in the cramped cab, with the stench of his rotting wife behind him, and the five bodies piled up outside … Dan wondered.

When Dan finally woke up, the sun was already high in the sky. He jerked himself up and a savage pain shot through his neck where he'd been laying it against the door. His left leg was asleep, forcing him to wait a few minutes for the frozen numbness to thaw out and then for the tingling to go away. He heard a car drive by on the road, then voices.

"So what happened after your car broke down?"

Jeremy's voice was clear and easy to understand, but the woman's reply seemed muted and sad.

"Scott left me alone in the car to walk to the next town for help, but he hadn't gone two hundred yards when those people stopped and got out of their truck. Scott started running back to me, not knowing what they wanted, whether they were friends or not." She hesitated. "At first they were smiling, so I rolled the window down an inch to talk. I told them we'd run out of gas and that was my husband running back toward us."

From inside the cab, Dan thought her voice sounded tired and stressed simultaneously, like a balloon blown to the point of bursting.

"But once Scott got back to the car, their smiles went away. They stepped in front of Scott when he tried to open the car door and get inside with me. That's when I noticed the guns on their hips, and I knew for sure we were in trouble. That man with the black hair, the leader, he nodded to the others and Scott was immediately attacked and thrown to the pavement. I started honking the horn, hoping someone would hear and come help or that it would scare them away. But it was useless. While I watched, they ... well ..." She started to cry again, regained control and finished the sentence. "Well, Scott is dead. They beat him to death on the pavement."

The woman broke down entirely and cried on the grass beside Jeremy. Dan felt guilty for listening and sat up in the cab. He cleared his throat to let them know he was awake and stepped out onto the grass and walked over to them. Jeremy looked up at his father. "Her name is Kate." And then he added without tact; "They killed her husband, beat him to death about ten miles up the road. She wants us to bring him back here and help her bury him."

Dan thought for a moment. *He had a shovel in the truck, and they had to bury Debbie anyways, and this was the perfect spot.* Dan took a few steps and then kneeled down beside the crying woman. He thrust out his right hand awkwardly. "I'm Dan Branch, from Menomonie. This is my son, Jeremy." But Kate didn't accept his hand. She didn't even look up from her crying. Dan sighed and stood back up.

"We'll take the new truck there and back. That way we save twenty miles worth of gas."

Jeremy looked surprised. "Dad, why don't we just take that brand, new truck all the way to Michigan?"

Dan shook his head. "No. It doesn't belong to us." Then he walked back over to the dead men's truck and hopped inside. "What kind of car was it?" Dan heard Kate softly say, "A blue Ford Taurus."

Dan slammed the door and yelled to Jeremy as he started up the engine. "Come on, son. You can help me, and we need to talk anyways." Jeremy got up slowly and then hesitated. "But what about Kate? Maybe I should stay and make sure she's okay." Dan replied by shaking his head resolutely. Jeremy got in the truck. Dan called out before driving off. "We'll be about thirty minutes, Kate. If anyone bothers you, there's a loaded shotgun behind the seat in the cab." Dan saw Kate's head nodding in reply. He revved the engine once and pulled out onto the road.

"Dad, I don't think we should leave her alone. She's not doing very good."

Dan gripped the steering wheel firmly. There was blood all over the upholstery. Dan wondered how the shotgun slug had missed the windshield. "She just needs some time alone, son. Besides, I wanted to talk to you about something."

Jeremy went silent and turned to his right to gaze out the window. Dan let out another huge sigh. "Come on, Jeremy, don't make this any harder than it has to be!" He fixed his eyes on the road straight ahead. Jeremy snapped his head around as if on fire. The shiner on his eye was in full bloom now, not to mention the swollen gash on his forehead.

"I'm not going to let you bury my mom out here where I can't visit her! I want her coming with us to Michigan!"

Dan gritted his teeth and squeezed the steering wheel until his knuckles turned white. "Son, I'm telling you we don't have a choice anymore. Didn't you notice the smell back there? It's been two days and her stomach's all bloated up to near bursting! We need to get her in the cool ground. It's the only dignified thing to do."

Jeremy didn't answer at first. Dan looked over and saw the tears streaming down his face. "Why is this happening to us, Dad?" Dan reached over with his right hand and placed it around his neck. When the truck slowed to a stop, Dan threw the shifter lever in park and slid over next to him.

"It's not just us, son. It's everyone. I think the whole world is like this now, and it's going to get worse, much. much worse. We need to get on the road and back to Michigan where we can survive. Getting caught on the road like this is sure death. You saw what happened to Kate. The longer we wait, the more dangerous it's going to get. People from the city will be out here soon, looking for food and a place to live. We have to bury your mom and get over to my Uncle Rodney's house. He's prepared. Trust me when I say he's probably the most prepared man on this planet."

Jeremy kept crying, and Dan just held him for a minute or two. A car passed by. It slowed as it did and the two men inside craned their necks as they rolled by. Dan's eyes met their hard gaze until they were gone. "We gotta go, son. It's too dangerous here." He released his son and slid back over on the seat, put the truck in drive and sped off.

A few minutes later Dan saw a blue, mid-sized car parked on the side of the road up ahead. Jeremy stopped crying and looked up as Dan brought the truck to a halt behind it.

"You better stay here, son. Let me see what the deal is. This might not be very pretty." Dan jumped out of the truck and walked slowly up to the car. His right hand rested heavily on the grip of his big revolver. There was no one in the car. No broken windows. No blood. No body. No sign of a struggle. Dan was confused. Then he saw the paper shoved under the driver's side windshield wiper. He took it off and opened it up. The note read:

Hank, I ran out of gas. Don't worry though. The Thompsons picked up me and the kids and we're at their house waiting for you. All is fine.

Love, Christie

Dan got that hollow feeling in the pit of his stomach again. He felt a sudden need to get back to the cemetery. He dropped the note, got back in the truck, and drove ten miles back as fast as he could. But he was too late. The woman and his truck were already gone.

CHAPTER 9

The Betrayal - September 10, 10AM

"*WELL,* Dad, you were right. Things are getting worse. Now we've lost our truck, all our supplies, and she's stolen my mom. We have to get her back."

Jeremy shook his head from side to side as he spoke. "Boy, she just didn't seem the type to me. I'm surprised."

Dan looked out the truck window, his eyes scanning every inch of the cemetery, but for what, he didn't know. "Listen, son, just because someone is in trouble, doesn't mean they have character. She was a stranger and we helped her. But, as it turns out, she was one of the bad guys too."

Jeremy looked over at his father. "I don't want to believe that, Dad. I talked to her for a long time while you were sleeping. She was a really nice lady."

Dan didn't answer. He just kept scanning the graveyard while he tried to think of what to do. She had all their equipment, food, gas, and an arsenal of guns and ammunition.

"I'm serious, Dad. Did you know she was a nurse at a hospital in Milwaukee. She was heading to her cabin in the Upper Peninsula to wait until the power comes back on."

Dan looked back over at his son with a frown on his face. "Jeremy, do you remember that time you had a girlfriend on Facebook? You said she was sixteen years old and beautiful, and you wanted to meet her so bad. Do you remember that?"

Jeremy winced but didn't answer.

"So, how did that date work out for you, son?"

"That's different, Dad. That was online. I met Kate in person, and I know she wouldn't lie to me."

Dan rolled his eyes in disbelief. "Son, she already lied to us! We went to her car, but it wasn't hers. There was no dead husband! She's a liar! She's a thief! She stole everything we own along with your mother's dead body! Wake up! That woman, whoever she is, has yet to tell us a thread of truth!"

The boy looked out the window again. A light breeze blew on his face, gently moving a few locks of his blonde hair. Dan started up the truck and drove out of the cemetery driveway.

"Dad, you're going the wrong way. Michigan's east of here."

Dan growled out loud. "You don't think I'd leave Wisconsin without giving your mother a proper burial do you?"

His son's eyes smiled ever so slightly. Then Dan gunned the engine and squealed the tires on the pavement, throwing Jeremy's head back into the seat.

"Besides, all our gas was in that old truck, and this one only has a quarter of a tank. Without that truck, we're screwed."

Rodney Branch sat up on the side of the hill overlooking his compound through the scope of his .308 caliber hunting rifle. He called it a compound just to make himself feel better, but, in reality, it was just a house, built into the side of a hill with a chicken coop, goat yard, and a pig pen. But, regardless of whether you called it a compound, a dump, or a rolling estate, it still belonged to Rodney Branch, and he was willing to die defending it. That's just the way he was, with no apologies or hesitation. Some people called him dedicated; some called him eccentric; but most people called him just plain, crazy.

But Rodney didn't mind at all. In fact, he found it rather liberating, because society expected so little from insanity. For years, the normal people had been laughing at him as he prepared for the end of the world as we know it. Rodney smiled, his yellow teeth almost visible beneath his beard and moustache in the sunlight. Then he said out loud, just barely audible to himself and to no one else.

"I don't hear anybody laughing anymore. The goose is cooked. The deal is done. The lights are out. We're having fun."

Rodney's old mind drifted off to the only person on the planet he cared for. He'd raised his brother's son from a pup, but now he was in Wisconsin, hopefully, making his way back home. The old man prayed for his safety, not just for Dan, but also for himself. Because Rodney knew that a lone wolf would not survive this hunt. It would be too long, too hard, and too fierce. The lights were out for good, and this was just the beginning of a very long and brutal thousand-year night. He whispered to God almighty, wanting a reply, but not really expecting it. "Hey God. I know you're up there. I can hear ya breathing." Then he laughed softly to himself. "Just get the kid home safe, okay? We got a deal. old man?"

There was sudden movement down below, about fifty yards from the house, and Rodney swung the scope around slowly to check it out. He saw the man carefully making his way through the trees. He carried a light backpack with a shotgun in his hands. Rodney laughed out loud. "He's dressed like a peacock! How's he supposed to sneak up on me like that?" The man was dressed in bright green dress pants with a red, short-sleeved shirt and tie. Rodney shook his head back and forth in disgust. These morons had been flooding out of the city for a day now, driving until they ran out of gas, then walking, trying to take advantage of the first people they came upon. The old man felt sorry for them. He knew they wouldn't survive, realizing that most of them would die on the road, or, worse yet, would survive only by killing and taking what belonged to someone else. It was a new world with only two options: Kill or be killed.

Rodney Branch had no intention of being killed. He brought his right eye down to the scope and sighted the target. It was a hundred-yard, slam-dunk shot but he didn't have the heart to take it. It didn't matter. This guy was clueless, and he was destined to die, if not today, then tomorrow. If not here, then twenty miles down the road. But Rodney just didn't feel like shooting anyone today, especially some weak, ignorant city slicker who didn't know which end of the barrel the round came out of.

But, despite that, he couldn't let the man ransack his house. Rodney pursed his lips together and made a light kissing sound. Within seconds the hundred-pound German Shepherd was panting at his side. The old man smiled and scratched the dog's huge head. Rodney pointed down the hill, and the big dog's ears perked up. He growled softly. Rodney whispered in the dog's right ear, "Go down, Moses!"

The big dog took off racing down the hill straight for the intruder. By time the man saw him coming, it was too late. He raised his shotgun, but Moses lunged forward and parted the man's scalp with one savage bite, sending a sea of red blood spilling out onto the ground. The man screamed and dropped his shotgun. Moses backed up and lunged forward again, but the man had recovered and was already running back into the woods.

Rodney smiled up on the hillside. He let Moses play with the man for a while, then he whistled and the big dog came running through the woods and then back up the hill.

"Good boy, Moses! Good boy! Did you get the nasty man? Did you get him good?" Moses licked his master's face, and they both walked back down the hill to the house. Rodney stopped long enough to pick up the man's shotgun and examine it. It was a Benelli.

"Holy Moses! Can you believe this gun! I've always

wanted one of these!"

Rodney unloaded it and then walked toward the house. He laughed out loud. "We'll just hold on to it until the gentleman comes back for it. Wouldn't be right to steal it." He spoke directly to his dog now. "Thou shalt not steal! Right Moses?"

The old man and his dog plodded up onto the big porch. Rodney leaned the Benelli against the house and then sat down in the rocker with his rifle atop his lap. Moses took his place at the right hand of the master. Rodney started to rock slowly back and forth, back and forth, back and forth, scanning the tree line, waiting for the prodigal son to come home.

Five miles down the road, Dan and Jeremy came upon their truck, abandoned beside a corn field. The cap was open along with both cab doors, and much of their belongings were scattered on the pavement and in the ditch. Steam still rose up from underneath the hood where the damaged radiator hose had broken once again.

"Looks like that duct tape didn't hold, Dad."

Dan slowed to a stop about 30 yards away. He looked around cautiously, down the road and out into the corn fields on both sides. "Stay inside, Jeremy." When he got out of the truck and walked closer, the smell of gas was obvious. Dan unholstered his revolver, and then looked underneath the truck. He saw the wet spot on the pavement where they'd punched a hole in his gas tank and drained it dry. He looked into the back and saw the extra gas cans were gone as well.

"Can I come on up now, Dad?"

Dan holstered his pistol and motioned with his hand, and a few seconds later his son stood beside him. They walked to the front of the truck, and that's when they discovered Kate in the tall grass off the front bumper. Quickly, Dan ran to her and kneeled down in the grass. "Stay back, son." The woman was naked from the waist down, and it was obvious she'd been raped and abused before finally dying. Dan stripped off his t-shirt and spread it over her nakedness. Only then would he allow Jeremy to come forward.

His son fell down to his knees, vomiting out his stomach onto the Queen Anne's Lace and the Chicory weeds in the road ditch. A car pulled up, slowing as it drove by as all the occupants gawked in dismay. The driver saw the dead body and accelerated in a cloud of blue smoke. Traffic from down south had picked up the last few hours, and Dan knew the people were starting to leave the city in droves now. The need to get out ahead of them was urgent, because with more people would come even more bloodshed.

Dan's mind began racing, compiling a list of all the things they needed to do before the people who'd killed Kate or others like them came back. That's when he saw his wife's bloated and rotting body a few rows into the corn. He could hear the flies swarming around her. A breeze picked up and blew the stench over to the road where he kneeled beside Kate's dead body. The numbness set in with a renewed vigor.

While Jeremy remained on his hands and knees in the ditch, Dan walked over and wrapped his wife back up in the blankets. The stench was almost unbearable, and he fought against the spasms in his stomach and throat muscles. Dan walked over to his son and held him. As Jeremy cried in his arms, Dan kept a watchful eye. Five minutes later, he picked his son up and carried him back to the new truck and laid him inside the cab. For the next thirty minutes, Dan loaded what was left of their supplies into the bed of the new truck, then he carefully laid Kate and Debbie on top and slowly drove back to the cemetery.

CHAPTER 10

The Funeral - September 10, 8PM

DAN and Jeremy bowed their heads over the mound of dirt in front of them. The ground was hard, and it had taken them the rest of the day to dig three holes: one for Debbie, one for Kate, and a larger hole for the five rapists. Amazingly, only one person had stopped in to ask what they were doing. He was an old man named Joe who had been visiting his wife's grave every day for the past seven years. Dan hadn't known how to explain the seven bodies on the ground in front of them, so he'd just told the old man the truth. Joe had just nodded his head and made the sign of the cross on his chest. He'd even helped them dig, and now he stood beside them as they prepared to pay their final respects.

It was a cloudy day, looking like rain, so Dan wasted no time with his eulogy.

"Okay, God, we've got seven dead people here. One we loved. One we wrongly trusted. And five we killed." Dan felt a few drops of rain and continued on. "We don't really know what's going on in the world right now or why people are all of a sudden acting so mean but I assume you do." He hesitated and looked over at his son, who'd been crying the whole afternoon." I suppose people have always been like this, and it just took one little nudge to push civilization over the brink of civilized behavior. My wife, Debbie, that was Jeremy's mom, she kind of went astray there at the end, but we know she was sorry, and we'd like you to cut her some slack." He paused and looked up. Jeremy nodded to him."The other lady, Kate, she stole our truck, but I suspect she got more punishment than she deserved at the end. We ask that you give both Kate and Debbie special consideration on judgement day. After all, none of us are perfect." The fingers of his left hand were interlaced with the fingers on his right, and they tightened involuntarily when he prayed for the five rapists. "These other five strangers, well, we caught them raping an innocent woman, and I shot them all dead. If that's a sin, then I apologize, but please bear in mind these are hard times, and that I didn't enjoy it."

A long line of cars began passing by on the road, so Dan wrapped it up. "Okay, God, I guess that's about it, except we need to ask for your help getting to Michigan. We need gas and we should've been there by now, but things keep going wrong. We could use a break, so please protect us and keep us from evil. Thanks God. Amen."

Jeremy and Joe echoed with amens of their own. Dan reached over the mound and shook Joe's hand. "We gotta get heading east again, Joe, or we'll never make it." He looked down again, weighing his yet unspoken offer. "Are you sure you don't want to come with us? We've got room, and I really don't think things are going to be real safe here alone in a few days."

The old man smiled and looked over at his wife's grave thirty yards to the left. He didn't speak, but Dan understood and smiled in return. Joe reached out his hand to Jeremy, but the boy ignored it and rushed forward, embracing the frail, old man in a hug. "Thanks for helping me bury my Mom. I appreciate it." Joe hugged him back, then looked him straight in the eye. "You get on now with yer papa. He's a good man. And you do what he says." Jeremy nodded and Joe glanced over at Dan and added, "Why didn't you tell me you needed gas?" Dan just shrugged. As Joe walked away he called over his shoulder, "Go east a mile, and the third house on the left is mine. There's a five-gallon can of gas in my garage. Take the gas and the can. You're going to need it." Then the old man walked over to his wife's grave as if they'd already left, not bothering to wait for a response. The old man sat down on the grass and looked out into the alfalfa field across the way. It would need cutting again, soon, but he doubted his neighbor would bother. There were just too many things happening right now.

Dan walked over and got inside their new truck. He waited as Jeremy dropped to his knees and said his own private prayer. Amazing as it was, in the midst of all this death and hate, Dan was starting to like his son again. Jeremy finished up and walked over to the truck, all the while glancing over his shoulder every few steps. As far as he knew, he would never come this way again, and he knew this good bye was forever.

By the time Jeremy was on the seat beside him, Dan had already started the engine. He waved to Joe, but the old man wasn't looking, was just talking to his dead wife in the breeze as the rain started to come down harder. The truck pulled out onto the pavement, leaving the man and the cemetery to the grace of God.

᠊᠊᠊᠊

"What are you doing up there, Rodney?"

Rodney Branch was halfway up a wooden light pole, standing on the steel screen platform of his climbing tree stand just off the county road. There was a socket wrench in his left hand, and he almost dropped it when Sheriff Joe Leif called up to him from the ground. He'd been so focused on loosening the solar panel off the pole that he hadn't heard the patrol car pull up and stop.

"Hey, Joe, how's it going?"

The Sheriff was young in comparison to Rodney, middle-aged, well over six feet tall with a muscular build and black hair, just starting to grey at the temples.

Joe nodded as he spoke. "Fine, Rod, just fine, but you didn't answer my question."

The old man went back to loosening the nut that clamped the medium-sized solar panel to the pole. "Sheriff, I'm kind of busy right now, and this is dangerous work. Do you mind if we talk about this later?"

Sheriff Leif looked around uncomfortably to see if anyone was watching. "Rod I've got to tell you that martial law has been declared and my men have orders to shoot any looters on sight."

Rodney stopped turning the wrench. "Orders from who?" The Sheriff shook his head in exasperation. "From the Governor and the State Police that's who. I've got to maintain some semblance of law and order in this county until things get back to normal."

Rodney laughed out loud. "Joe, you know as well as I do that things aren't getting back to normal for a long, long time." Sheriff Leif lowered his head. He was getting a kink in his neck from looking almost straight up at the pole. In his gut, he knew the old man was right. Things were bad, real bad, and he was worried. The State Police had abandoned all the rural counties and moved closer to Lansing, Detroit and the other big cities in the state. Joe had communication with the Capitol, but not much information was filtering down to him. Right now, only three days after the blackout, his little county was an island and Lansing felt five million miles away. Most of his deputies were home with their families, trying to take care of them, and even if they'd been willing to patrol the roads, there was a severe shortage of gas for his vehicles, as shipments of everything, including gas, food, and parts, had ceased to flow into town, or anywhere for that matter.

The Sheriff came to a silent decision and moved off a few feet before sitting down on the grass in the ditch. He thought for a moment, then spoke. "Okay, Rodney Branch. You and I need to talk. I know darn well that you've been preparing for this thing ever since I was a kid, but now I need your help trying to salvage what I can and maintain some peace around here."

The old man responded by laughing again. He finished loosening the last nut and the solar panel dropped down and swung from the rope attached to Rodney's platform. He bent down, untied one end and started to lower the panel down to the ground. Joe stood up and walked over to catch it before it hit the dirt. "Thanks Sheriff." Rodney smiled. "I guess this makes you an accomplice."

Rodney came down a foot at a time in his climbing platform, and soon he was standing on the ground again. The Sheriff looked him straight in the eye. "I'm serious, Rod. I need some help. I was on my way to your house to talk."

Rodney loaded the solar panel into the back of his pickup truck, then sat down on the tailgate. "What kind of help?" Sheriff Leif sat on the tailgate beside him.

"To start with can you tell me what you're hearing on your short wave radio? You're the only one around here I know of who's got one."

Rodney reached into his shirt pocket and took out a pack of Camel unfiltered cigarettes. He shook one out and offered it to the Sheriff who quickly shook his head no. "Suit yerself." Rodney lit it up and took a long draw before exhaling the smoke above his head. "Seems to me a man has to die of something, may as well be cancer." The Sheriff didn't push him into answering. It would do no good. Rodney just sat there, smoking his cigarette in silence. When he was finished, he finally said something of substance.

"I'm hearing that Detroit is a dangerous place. People are dying left and right. The bad apples have taken over the barrel. Half the cops are either dead or AWOL and anyone who ventures out of their house is taking their life into their own hands." He crushed the cigarette butt out on the heel of his boot and stuck it inside his shirt pocket. "Yeah, right. You think Detroit was rough a week ago, it's downright lawless now. Lots of gunshots, law of the jungle taking over. Rape, pillage, plunder, you know, the usual, just lots more of it. Anyone still there in a month will be dead most likely."

He glanced over to make sure the Sheriff was still listening and to get an indication of his state of mind. "Flint and Saginaw are pretty much the same. The only place on the east side of the state that has any semblance of law and order is Dearborn."

That last statement caused Joe to perk up. "Dearborn? Why Dearborn?"

Rodney frowned. "Think about it, Joe. It's the biggest concentration of Muslims in the Midwest. Once law and order broke down, the Mullahs took over and declared Sharia Law. They were already organized before this chaos came down. This is an opportunity for them, and they won't waste it." Rodney hesitated, and looked over at his friend. "I expect they'll be coming this way sooner or later."

The Sheriff reached up and scratched his left cheek. "What for? There's nothing up here this far north?"

Rodney smiled and took out another cigarette. "That don't matter none. Nature abhors a vacuum, and anyplace that isn't organized and strong will suck them up like smoke in a chimney."

Joe shook his head back and forth. "I don't believe it. You never liked Muslims, but I just don't believe they'll leave the east side."

The sound of Rodney's laughter echoed out across the road. "Suit yourself, Sheriff." Then he looked him full in the eyes. "But what if I'm right?" Then he added. "You can even forget about the Muslims. maybe you're right. Maybe they won't come. But can you sit there and tell me the hordes in Grand Rapids, Lansing, and Detroit are going to stay bottled up while they starve and die of disease?" Rodney blew a cloud of smoke above his head to keep it out of Joe's face. "No way, Sheriff. Even those peace-loving, God-fearing Christians will spread out once they get hungry and people start shooting at them. There's a lot of people with guns in Michigan, and not all of them are as nice as you."

The Sheriff lowered his head and thought for a moment. "Yeah, I know. I've been thinking the same thing myself." He looked over at Rodney just in time to see him finish off the second cigarette. "So what do you think we can do about it?"

Rodney laughed again. "We? You're the Sheriff, not me." The younger man hopped down off the tail gate and turned and smiled. "You were born and raised in this county, and you fought for your country. No matter what other people say about you, I know you wouldn't let your neighbors die without putting up a fight."

Sheriff Leif reached into his front pants pocket and pulled out a gold-colored Deputy badge in the shape of a star. "Now raise your right hand and repeat after me, old man! I, Rodney Branch, do solemnly swear that I will support and defend the Constitution of the United States against all enemies, foreign and domestic; that I will ..."

Rodney clenched down on his teeth hard, grinding them together as he swore to himself. He didn't hear the rest of the oath, but he'd had it memorized for years. The Sheriff paused, waiting for Rodney to speak. Finally, the old man unclenched his jaw. "Why are you doing this to me, Joe? I'm an old man, and I just want to be left alone long enough for the kid to come home so I can die of old age."

The Sheriff smiled. He knew he had him.

CHAPTER 11

The Silence - September 11, 7PM

THEY were almost due west of Iron Mountain now, and Dan figured they had just enough gas to make it into Michigan and halfway to the Mackinac Bridge. But, after that, it was up to God.

It was about 2 hours before dark now, and they had pulled off the road onto a two-track deep inside the Nicolet National Forest. Jeremy sat on the bank of the small stream with his feet dangling down into the water while Dan slowly sipped on his creek-cooled Mocha Frappuccino. Several of them had broken, and, after this one, only three bottles remained. He felt a strange calm as the silence of the woods was broken only by singing birds and the wind blowing in the tops of the tall pine trees. Dan had always loved the thick, heavy smell of pine.

"Can I build a fire, Dad?"

Dan looked over at Jeremy and nodded. "Sure, don't see why not. We're so far back I don't think anyone will see it from the road."

Jeremy smiled and walked off into the woods looking for dead sticks and kindling, being careful not to hurt his bare feet. Dan had taught him how to build a fire way back when the boy was still Cub Scout age. Debbie had been furious, accusing him of teaching him how to "play" with fire. But, on this one occasion, Dan had defied her and taught him anyways. The next week Jeremy had burned down the neighbor's tool shed. There had always been so much he'd wanted to teach Jeremy, whom he'd always considered his son, how to shoot, hunt, fish, survive in the wild, but Debbie just didn't want him learning outdoor skills for some strange reason. He sipped his cold mocha and looked out into the pine boughs. It was odd and almost scary how quickly life could change. Three days ago Jeremy was screwing the neighbor girl and cussing out his father. Now, he was asking permission to build a campfire. The boy was scared, and he needed Dan more than ever. But what the boy didn't know, was that Dan needed Jeremy as well. This was no time to be alone.

A memory of his father stirred, and Dan remembered fishing with him as a boy. After all these years, he still missed him, almost to the point of tears. Dan brushed the memory aside. He assumed there were black bears over here on this side of the state, but didn't really know for sure. The fire was probably a good idea. It might scare them off.

He considered listening to the truck radio while Jeremy gathered wood, but decided not to. Although he was desperate for information, radio broadcasts were few and far between, and none of the big-city stations were even on the air. Once in a while he could pick up a small-town station operating on low power with a gas generator, but he expected this would last only until they ran out of fuel. Then the radio would go strangely silent. He suspected that television was a similar situation. In the end it didn't matter. The news these days was reduced to rumor, and if the rumors were true, then America was in deep trouble. Chicago was rioting and burning; there was no food; no clean water; no police to stop the killing and no firemen to put out the blaze. Civility, like a thin veneer, had been stripped away, leaving humanity at its basest level. Dan wondered *Is it law of the jungle now, kill or be killed, don't get involved in other people's business, protect what is mine at all costs? Is God still there, or did*

He turn out the lights on his way out of the galaxy? It was
as if America had traveled back in time two hundred years,
and each passing day was pushing them further back into the
dark ages.

Dan listened to the sounds of the woods now. There was
no noise, no clutter, no honking, no engines, no jets overhead, no voices, no radio.

The voice of man had been silenced, and only the God-
made sounds had survived.

Silence was a new way of life for Dan, and he found
himself thinking more and more about life and God and existence. Before the collapse there just hadn't been time to think
about where he'd been, where he was going, or even how
to get there, much less reflect on morality or the question of
right and wrong. But now … he had all the time in the world.

Dan put the bottle down on the bank beside him and
picked up the Bible again, letting it fall open randomly on
his lap. He closed his eyes the way he'd done as a child
and pointed to a verse on the page and read it out loud, half
expecting it to solve all his problems or give his stressed out
life some peace and direction. The verse read:

> *"If a man has sexual relations with a woman
> during her monthly period, he has exposed the
> source of her flow, and she has also uncovered
> it. Both of them are to be cut off from their
> people."*

Dan surprised himself by laughing out loud. Then he
thought to himself, *Okay, thanks God, important hygiene tip.*

"What's so funny, Dad?"

Dan turned around surprised and the Bible slipped from
his fingers and slid down the bank toward the stream. He
quickly reached out and grabbed it before it hit the water.
Jeremy dropped the wood in a pile and then sat down beside
his father. Dan smiled.

"Well, son, I was just thinking about how I've always

wanted to teach you things. You know, stuff about outdoor survival, shooting, hunting, cooking over a campfire, all the things your mother hated so much."

At the mention of his mother, Jeremy's face shadowed over, but then, just for an unexpected moment, he smiled.

"Do you remember that time I burned down the neighbor's shed?"

Dan laughed again. "Oh yeah. Boy did your mother ever ream me out for that one! And what about the time you tried to make gun powder and launched that home-made rocket through the living room window."

Jeremy nodded sheepishly. "Well, I wasn't aiming for the window. It just kind of popped up out of nowhere." He thought for a moment, reliving the past. "Mom sure was pissed off at that one."

The smile on Dan's face grew bigger. "Yup. I remember that day. I couldn't tell you this, because your mom would have killed me, but I was really proud of you for that."

Jeremy looked confused. "You were proud of me for launching a rocket through the window of our house?"

Dan shook his head as he talked. "No, son. I was proud of your ingenuity. You saw something you wanted and you went for it. You didn't know how to make a rocket, but you went on the internet and you read up and you figured it out all by yourself." Dan's eyes clouded over. "It was partly my fault anyways. I should have been there teaching you how to do it."

Jeremy lowered his head. "So why weren't you?"

Dan looked over and Jeremy raised his head. They locked eyes for a crucial moment in time. Dan pursed his lips. "Because I was stupid and selfish, son. All I could feel was my own pain and my own loneliness." He tossed the Bible down to his left. "If I'd been a real father, a better man, then I would have risen above my problems and focused on things I could change and good I could do. Instead, I just wallowed and you suffered for it. I'm sorry about that, and I wish I could take it back."

His son gazed out into the pines ahead. "Yeah, well, mom was a handful, wasn't she?"

Father and son laughed together. "No kidding, you can say that again. More than a handful. Your mom always reminded me of that Billy Joel song, *She's always a Woman*.

Jeremy asked innocently. "*Who's Billy Joel?*"

"Oh, just some old fart from the seventies who sang songs at a bar and played piano. He probably lived in LA, so he's most likely dead by now."

"Sing it to me."

Dan looked over skeptically. "Excuse me?"

"Just sing to me, Dad. Like you did when I was a kid."

The man thought about it for a moment, trying to remember the words. His Uncle Rodney had sang along with the cassette tape player while hoeing the garden. The memory came back and Dan started to sing slowly.

> *She can kill with a smile,*
> *She can wound with her eyes.*
> *She can ruin your faith with her casual lies*
> *And she only reveals what she wants you to see*
> *She hides like a child,*
> *But she's always a woman to me.*

Dan hesitated and glanced over at his son to see how it was being received. Jeremy seemed transfixed, so he sang some more. He couldn't remember the whole song or the right order, so he just closed his eyes and sang what he knew.

> *She is frequently kind*
> *And she's suddenly cruel*
> *She can do as she pleases*
> *She's nobody's fool*
> *And she can't be convicted*
> *She's earned her degree*
> *And the most she will do*
> *Is throw shadows at you*
> *But she's always a woman to me.*

Dan stopped singing. He couldn't remember the rest. He thought of his wife, and his eyes misted over.

"You got a good voice, Dad. I remember it when you used to sing to me at bed time. I liked it."

Dan looked up, surprised. "Really?"

Jeremy nodded. "Yeah, especially that song about the bright, golden haze on the meadow."

Dan smiled a bit. "Yeah, Rogers and Hammerstein, I like that one. My father used to sing that to me at bed time. Heck, he used to sing it all the time, He'd sing it and whistle it. He was happy when he wasn't thinking about my mom."

Jeremy lowered his head and dug at the ground with a small stick, throwing up black dirt between his legs. "She died when you were little, right?"

Dan nodded.

"And now my mom's dead too." He hesitated. "Does that mean we have something in common?"

Dan looked over and smiled. "It's more than that, son. We have a lot in common. I'm your father. You're my son."

Dan let the words sink in. There was a moment of clumsy silence. Then Dan stood up and walked over to the pile of sticks. "Okay, son, and now I'm going to teach you how to build a proper fire."

That broke the awkwardness of the moment, and Jeremy stood up as well, brushing the dirt and leaves off the back of his shorts.

"Forget it, Dad. You just watch the master, and I'll show you a fire to end all fires!"

Dan folded his muscled arms across his chest firmly. "So you think you can teach the old man how to build a fire?"

Jeremy copied his father, folding his arms across his chest as well. When the boy spoke, his voice was playful and almost happy.

"Think about it Dad. Who burned down the neighbor's shed? It was me, wasn't it? Not you. I say that makes me uniquely qualified to build a campfire, don't you?"

Dan let his arms drop, and for a moment the heaviness of the apocalypse melted from his shoulders.

"I got a better idea. Let's race. First person to get a fire going two feet high wins."

Jeremy mocked him. "Bring it old man!"

Dan yelled "Go!" and both of them set about scurrying for tinder and kindling, running, laughing, for a moment forgetting the chaos of the cities, the death, the loss, the mayhem.

And for a moment, the silence of the forest was filled.

CHAPTER 12

__Great With Child - September 12, 2AM__

SOME time before dawn, Dan was awakened by blood-curdling screams. He stirred inside the nether world that exists only between sleep and reality. At first he thought it was part of a dream, then it was real, then dream. The screams came again, and his eyes popped open wide.

"Dad, can you hear that?"

"Yeah, son. I hear it. Probably just a coyote. There's lots of them up here."

The scream came again, sounding more humanlike than before. "That's not a coyote, Dad. That sounds like a woman."

Dan pulled his knees up and rushed out of his sleeping bag. He laced up his boots and double-checked his pistol. "Stay here, son. I'm going to check it out." And then he stood up and raced off into the woods toward the eerie sound. The scream sounded again, sending chills up Dan's back, and he adjusted course slightly. As he got closer, he slowed his pace and tried to make less noise. When he got even closer, he could hear voices.

"Please, no!"

It was a woman's voice, and Dan was reminded of the five men he'd killed just a short time ago. He unsnapped the thumb break on his holster and slowly drew out the big,

Taurus revolver. The next voice he heard was a man's.

"Hold her down!"

And then another man, this one deeper and huskier. "Ouch! She bit me!"

Dan was startled at the sound of brush crashing behind him. He turned and pointed the gun just as Jeremy stumbled and fell at his feet. "Hi Dad."

Dan held his finger to his lips to quiet him. The two men kept talking.

"Hey! Did you hear that?"

"Yeah, it's just a deer. These woods are full of them. I used to hunt them when I was a kid. Just tie her hands back up so we can get her back to the cabin."

The woman screamed again, and was rewarded with a fist to the side of her head. She didn't scream again.

"Careful, Mike. Don't damage the merchandise."

Dan and Jeremy remained hidden in the bushes as the two men began dragging the unconscious woman off through the woods. They made a terrible racket. Jeremy spoke now in a whisper. "Dad, what should we do?"

Dan reholstered his pistol and thought for a moment. On the one hand, he was sure this type of thing was happening all over the country, so was it really a big deal that it was happening here too? After all, they couldn't save every woman. On the other hand … Then Jeremy broke his concentration. "We have to help her, Dad!"

Dan shot back a reply, surprised to hear himself say the words. "Yeah, right! Just like the last woman! The one who stole our truck and everything we own?" The hurt look on Jeremy's face caused Dan to feel ashamed. He softened a bit. "Cone on, Jeremy, we can't save everyone who's in trouble."

Jeremy nodded his head in the dimness of the coming dawn. "I know, Dad. I know we can't help them all." Then he looked his father full in the eyes. "But we can help this one." Dan's shame intensified as he looked down at the ground for a moment. The sound of the men dragging her

94

away was slowly fading into the distance. Another moment passed, another, and then another. "Dad?"

Dan looked over at his son and frowned. "Go back to the truck and wait for me there." Then he moved slowly off into the woods, following the sound of rustling leaves.

Two hours later Dan crept quietly back into camp. Jeremy looked up and saw the face of his father, smeared with black mud, like he was wearing a mask. His eyes were dark, opened wide, with a stare that scared him. He seemed like a different version of the same person. He looked like a Teddy Bear on crack.

"Put out that campfire!"

Jeremy immediately doused it with water. It hissed as smoke and steam rose up into the air and was lost in the tree-tops above. "What happened, Dad?"

Dan sat down on the bank with a heavy sigh. He felt so much older than he had three days ago.

"They have her in a cabin about a half mile from here. She's duct-taped to a chair now right beside another man. She looks very pregnant to me. I think she's in labor."

Jeremy's eyes opened wider. "Wow! Cool!"

Dan's eyes snapped back at him. "No! It's not cool! She's being held by three men, all heavily armed. Two of them are the same guys who stole the stuff from our truck and killed Kate. They've got my shotgun and my AR-15."

Jeremy squirmed on the bank beside him.

"What's an AR-15?"

But Dan ignored him. He was already deep in thought, making a plan, trying to figure out how to save the two strangers without getting himself killed. Jeremy sat there quietly. This man was different than the father he'd grown up with. He'd been somehow transformed into this Marine fighting machine, and it scared and awed him simultaneously.

༉࿔ ࿔༉

At the break of dawn, Dan was lying on the ground, covered in brush and leaves on a small hill overlooking the cabin. Out in front of him on the ground rested his fifty caliber inline ignition muzzle loader. He would have preferred his AR-15 with a thirty-round magazine, but they had stolen it from him. Now, he was reduced to relying on two hundred year old technology, albeit, significantly enhanced. With the fifty caliber Power Belt round and a double load of Pyrodex, Dan was deadly accurate out to two hundred yards. The big problem was reloading time and the huge amount of smoke the rifle gave off. He would get off only one shot. After that they'd know where he was, and it would take him almost a minute to reload.

As he lay in wait he thought about his son. It was time to teach him how to shoot, not just for his own protection, but for Dan's as well. It would have been helpful to have some flank security in this ambush, but without the proper training and equipment, Jeremy was more a liability than an asset. If he lived through this day, Dan planned on changing that.

Down below, Dan saw the front door of the cabin swing open and two men stepped outside. One of them carried Dan's shotgun, and the other clasped his AR-15. At a distance of one-hundred-fifty yards, Dan could hear their voices, but not make out the words. They both lit up cigarettes and stood on the porch laughing and talking. One of them leaned against the vertical support log on the wraparound porch. They were looking right toward Dan, but he knew they couldn't see him. Dan took some time to slow down his breathing and his heart rate. Then he slowly raised his eye up to the scope and settled in for the shot. The taller of the two men leaned the AR-15 against the cabin wall and took a leak off the porch. Dan took his time, just the way Uncle

Rodney had taught him, and two minutes later he began taking up slack in the trigger. The crosshairs rested squarely on the man's solar plexus. Oddly enough, when the blast rang out, Dan felt no remorse, no guilt, no sense of regret - only recoil. The smoke cloud rose up, obscuring the porch from Dan's view. When it cleared away, Dan saw one man standing and one collapsed on the wooden planking. That's when he noticed small pieces of bark flying off the trees around him. Dan moved behind the tree beside him as the man emptied all thirty rounds blindly into the hill side. Quickly, Dan began to reload. When the man ejected the empty magazine, Dan raised the muzzleloader and fired, this time hastily. The big lead slug hit the man low in the abdomen, knocking him to the floor of the plank porch. Dan reloaded again. By now the man was screaming for help as he bled out in the morning sunshine. Dan centered the crosshairs on the wooden door, waiting for the last man to come out. But no one came. He scoped the windows and saw the shades move off to the right. Raising the scope to his eye, he let the expensive Leupold optics gather in light and focus the shape of a man's head as he peered out the glass. Dan took careful aim, and slowly and gently pressed the trigger straight to the rear. The shot boomed out. The smoke rose up. The man fell down.

Dan remained on the ground another ten minutes, waiting for the man on the porch to bleed out and die. His screams died down, lessened and eventually silenced. It reminded Dan of times he'd been deer hunting and had accidently wounded animals. He always hated those times and suffered with the animal as they lay bleeding. But this time ... the ambivalence was gone. This was a different Dan Branch.

CHAPTER 13

**Unto Us ... A child - September 12, 7AM**

FOR the past four hours Jackie had been feeling contractions, but they were irregular and not real strong. She knew it was the stress that had caused her baby to come two weeks early. She also knew that unless she could get herself free from the duct tape and the chair that her baby would die; her husband would bleed to death; and she would die, not necessarily in that order.

She heard her husband moaning behind her and she pressed her head back trying to touch his own, but he'd slumped forward and was out of her reach. A week ago they'd been in the Dominican Republic giving aid and shelter to hurricane victims, and she'd been appalled at their living conditions and the corruption. Now ... she wondered ... was America any better off than Haiti? Had the only difference between America and third-world countries simply been money and power?

"Don! Stay with me honey!" She called over her shoulder several times, but he didn't respond. The gunfire on the porch had ceased, and she could hear birds chirping away outside. The man called Hector was laying on the wooden floor about six feet away. She knew he was dead because most of his head was gone. Jackie wondered what had happened. The other two men hadn't come back in from their cigarette, and she'd heard Hosea's screams start out loud and panicked, then listened as they'd dissipated into whimpers, and then quiet moans. She guessed he was dead now.

Hector was the one who'd beaten her husband over and over again without asking a single question. Over and over he'd punched Don until he'd lapsed into unconsciousness, and then he'd laughed and talked about raping Jackie and then killing her baby. All through the night the men had sniffed more and more drugs. It was like they didn't even need sleep.

A contraction came on again, starting slow, like a wave moving toward the beach, then it rose up as it hit the shallows, then cresting as it pounded onto the shoreline. Jackie heard someone screaming, then realized it was her and forced herself to close her mouth. The pain subsided and she could hear nothing but the birds outside, her own rapid breathing, and the slow, steady dripping of her husband's blood down onto the wooden floorboards. He would die soon. She struggled again at the duct tape, but it held her fast.

Jackie slumped her head forward onto her chest and prayed. "Dear God! Aren't going to get us out of this? Aren't' you going to save us? We dedicated our lives to you, and you reward us with torture, pain and death? Can't you at least kill us quickly?"

As if in answer, there was a scuffle on the wooden planking outside. Jackie looked up and saw a man peering carefully through the window. She couldn't make out his face, because it was all blacked over with something. She quickly thanked God that the man wasn't Frank, and then apologized for calling him a doubting him. Perhaps, this man was different. Perhaps, he would kill them all quickly. Her mind, her faith, her hope, in just a few short days, had been reduced to this thinking: that the best life had to offer was a quick and painless death.

Jackie looked up again and the man's face was gone

from the window. The dripping of Don's blood continued. A small field mouse scurried along the wall until it came to the brains spilled out and splattered on the floor. The little mouse stopped and sniffed. Jackie was surprised at the absurdity of her own thoughts. *I need to get some mouse traps. I can't have a mouse running loose in my cabin.*

Just then she heard a hand touch the doorknob, and Jackie watched as it turned. The mouse scurried away and disappeared through a small hole in the wall that she'd never noticed before. The door opened slowly, letting in light from the rising sun behind; it cascaded in swiftly, in streaks of light, making the blood on the floor shine bright red. The door swung open, and the man stood there outlined in brightness, his pistol pointed in, searching out the room for someone to kill. Jackie waited for the loud boom and the flash of the muzzle, but it didn't come. The man lowered his gun and took another step into the room.

The smell of death and blood and brains was all around her. The man walked in and stood over her, looking down. She wondered why he didn't say anything, why she didn't say anything. The man looked over at the dead body on the floor, then at her husband, then back at her. Finally, after what seemed like hours, he spoke.

"You okay, ma'am?"

Jackie started to weep. He was polite. He must be one of the good guys.

And then she felt the next wave moving toward the beach, surging, building, coming closer, and bringing with it pain, and suffering, and the inevitable promise of life or death.

❧　❧

Three hours later Dan placed his knees on the edge of the bed as he leaned over the woman with her skirt hiked up to her waist. The water had broken two hours ago, making the contractions stronger and eventually settling in at a steady once every five minutes. Now they were coming much closer together. Dan reached his hand in to feel the progress of the baby. The head was right there, ready to come out.

"Oh, Dad, that is so gross! How can you do that?"

"Just shut up, son, and get me that towel over there."

Dan moved his fingers around and tried to spread out the opening as best he could. He looked up into Jackie's eyes and smiled weakly.

"How's it going, Jackie?"

For some unknown reason, his smile infuriated her, and his sense of calm was driving her crazy. He'd been doing it for almost an hour now and she just wanted to reach up, grab him by the ears and scream into his face. *How do I look like I'm doing? Do I look okay to you? No! I'm trying to shoot a bowling ball out my vagina! So just shut up, wipe that grin off your face and let's get it done!*

But she didn't say anything.

"Okay, on this next one we're going to push, not real hard, just enough to get the baby's head so I can see it."

Jackie felt the next wave, and it was bigger and stronger than anything so far.

"Okay, Jackie. Go ahead and take a deep breath and push like you're having a bowel movement."

Jackie pushed. Jeremy peered over Dan's shoulder.

"Wow! Cool Dad. Look at that."

Jackie wanted to slap the boy. Instead, she pushed again and then stopped as the pain subsided.

"Okay, I can see the top of his head now. We're making good progress. Tell me when the next one starts and we'll try to get his head out."

Jeremy moved in closer.

"How did you learn to do this, Dad."

Jackie felt like she was on display at a museum.

"I saw it on The Learning Channel just last week."

Jackie's heart sunk. *The Learning Channel? My baby's*

life is in the hands of a one-hour TV special! She opened her mouth to say something derogatory, but pain wisely cut her words short.

"Okay, Jackie. Go ahead and push when you're ready."

But she was already gritting her teeth and bearing down.

"Whoa! Not so fast. You're going to tear! Softer, Jackie, keep control." Jackie let off just a hair, but the urge to push was just too strong."

Then the head came out just as the wave crashed on the beach.

"Okay! Stop now, Jackie!"

Dan held the baby's head in his left hand and reached down with his right to wipe away the fluid.

"Now give me the turkey baster, Jeremy! Now! Quickly, I have to have it!"

Jeremy fumbled with the rubber and plastic bulb, and dropped it on the floor. Dan reached down and got it himself. He quickly sucked the mucus and fluid out of the baby's nose. Almost immediately the little thing began to cry.

"Jackie, you have to push again. Just get one of his shoulders out."

Jackie felt her spirits lift with the sound of her baby's cry. "But I don't have a contraction."

"It doesn't matter, just see if you can push her out."

Jackie pushed, but nothing happened. She felt very weak, like she was ready to pass out. Then another contraction started to build.

"Okay, you need to push now."

The baby was screaming.

"I got the towel ready, Dad."

"You have to push, Jackie!"

Jackie ignored them both, waiting just a few seconds longer until the wave began to crest. She screamed and pushed. The baby slid out and Dan grabbed her with one hand on the head and the other on her back. She was wet and slippery and he almost dropped her to the floor.

"Don't drop my baby you idiot!"

"I need the towel now, Jeremy."

But Jeremy was watching in awe with his mouth dropped open.

"Give me the towel, son!"

Jeremy put the towel on the bed and Dan laid the baby inside it.

"She's the wrong color, Dad."

Dan didn't say anything. He quickly rubbed the baby's skin, getting off the wet, sticky slime. When he was done, he wrapped the baby in the towel and raised her up to Jackie's chest. She cradled her and wept softly to herself.

Dan returned to the woman's legs, hesitated, then quickly went to work. With a piece of monofilament fishing line, he tied off the umbilical cord and then with a pair of hair-cutting sheers, lopped it off.

"Dad, that baby's black!"

Jackie didn't say anything. She was too busy holding her little girl, kissing her and crying.

"Son, go outside and get the canteen out of my back-pack."

"What for, Dad? We got water right over there."

Dan snapped back at him.

"Just do as I say, son!"

Jeremy grudgingly left the cabin.

When the door closed behind him, Dan stood up and looked down on her.

"Listen, Jackie, you have a tear down there that I need to sew up, and I've never done it before. I'm thinking it's going to hurt a lot."

Jackie looked up at him with disbelief and laughed for the first time in days.

"So how many babies have you delivered before this one?"

"None. I helped deliver a calf once though."

She went back to loving her child.

"Then do your worst, farm boy. I'll try not to flinch."

Dan smiled, but she no longer wanted to slap him. Instead, she looked over to her husband, on the floor across the room. He was on blankets with a hole in his side put there by the man who'd just saved her life and the life of her child. She didn't know which would kill her husband quicker: the bullet in his side, or the color of her baby's skin.

CHAPTER 14

A time to kill - September 12, 2PM

"**DAD,** you need to stop shooting people all the time. At least until the ground softens up a bit." Jeremy stabbed his shovel into the hard dirt one more time and hit a root. The shovel's blade glanced off it, and the boy cursed under his breath. "Is one big hole good for these guys, or do we have to do three smaller ones?"

Dan sat off to the side with his feet hanging down in the newly dug hole. He couldn't tell if his son was serious or trying to be funny, so he gave him the benefit of the doubt. "Just the one hole today, son. These are all bad guys."

Jeremy picked up the hatchet and knelt down to chop away at the root. "So the rule is we bury good guys in good graves, and we pray over them, but the bad guys get one hole and no prayer?"

Dan grunted. "Yeah. I guess that's it."

Jeremy stood up and pushed hair away from his eyes. Dan noticed the boy needed a haircut. "So why do we have to bury these guys at all? They're pretty bad people, right?"

Dan stood and picked up his shovel again to dig. It was a good question in light of all that had happened in the past few days. "I think it's important to maintain a sense of dignity and respect for the dead, even if the dead are evil."

Jeremy went back to hacking at the root. "Sorry, Dad. I

just don't get it. Why don't we just dump their bodies a few miles down the road and let the animals eat them? After all, they were torturing Jackie and her husband."

Dan pushed the shovel into the ground and then drove it deep into the hard dirt with his right boot. "We don't bury them for their sake. We bury them to keep ourselves from becoming like them, son. Rules of decency are more important now than ever, because … well, because there's so much evil out there and it's important that good wins over evil."

Jeremy threw the root out of the hole and picked up his shovel again. "My Social Studies teacher, Ms. Maynard, would call that altruistic." He hesitated. "But, I guess it don't really matter all that much anymore. She lived in Eau Claire, so I'm guessing she's dead by now."

Dan kept shoveling, but thought his son's statement was sad. Even after all that had happened, he still couldn't believe that society was over. It had collapsed and now it was every man for himself. Three dead men were piled up not 10 feet away, and he and his 14-year-old son were having a conversation on ethics. Life had changed so fundamentally, so radically, and so quickly. He felt like he was just riding along on a river, out of control, just hanging on to a log in whitewater, and reacting to everything that was happening along the journey. But he had a feeling that every decision he made, to shoot or not to shoot, to kill or let live, to help or to hinder – each decision would contribute to either make him a better or a worse person. Dan knew that instinctively and wanted to teach it to his son, if at all possible. But the thing was, he really didn't know if it was possible, or wise, or even practical in a day and age where lawlessness was the law of the land. He stuck his shovel in the dirt and leaned on it.

"Jeremy. Look at me, son."

Jeremy stopped digging and looked his father full in the eyes. "Son, we may not survive the trip to Michigan. Or, if we do survive, then we could die soon after getting there. Life is pretty uncertain right now, and that makes everything we do today all the more important. Because, well, because we may not have a tomorrow." He reached over and touched his son's shoulder. "Jeremy, it was always true before, but we had life so easy that we didn't realize it. Now, more than ever, it's important that we do good in the eyes of God. Because we could be meeting Him face to face at any moment."

Jeremy nodded, but didn't have the words to respond. He looked down, then back up again. "Is that why you've been reading that Bible so much?"

Dan smiled softly and nodded. "I suppose so. Nothing like death to get a man thinking about life. And I suspect I haven't killed my last."

Jeremy bowed his head again, avoiding his father's gaze. "Dad, will I have to kill too?"

Dan wanted to lie to him. He wanted to scoop him up and bring him close. He wanted to tell him over and over again that everything would be alright and he'd protect him from the bad guys like when Jeremy had been younger. But this time he moved his right hand out and lifted his son's chin up so he could see his eyes. "Listen, son. Do you remember when you were younger and you kept telling me at bedtime there was a monster in your closet?" Jeremy nodded, his chin pressing down slightly on his Dad's fingers.

"Well, back then I told you the monsters weren't real, but now I can't say that. Because now they are real, and we're burying three of them right now. There are more monsters out there, maybe lots of them, and there's a pretty fair chance that some of them will need killing."

Jeremy turned away. A tear formed at the corner of his left eye,and he quickly wiped it away. "So I will have to kill someone?"

Dan went back to digging. "Tomorrow I teach you how to shoot. My life depends on it, and so does yours. But I promise that I'll get you back to Uncle Rodney's where things are safer and we have some friends to help look after us. That's the best I can do, son."

Jeremy nodded and went back to digging.

❧ ⸱ ⸱ ❧

Jackie Overton sat on the bed beside her husband, holding his hand and cradling their newborn daughter in her free arm. He was sleeping, and his hand felt hot. She let go of his fingers long enough to touch his forehead. It was burning, but not sweating anymore, and she didn't know what that meant. Her own head still hurt where the men had beaten her, and she was tired and sore from birthing, but all in all she was in pretty good shape, considering what she'd been through.

Jackie's hair was down now and properly brushed. It was long, straight and as black as midnight. Her eyes were dark and deep as well, a gift from her Lebanese mother. Jackie had spent the first years of her childhood in Beirut, living with a Muslim mother and a Christian father. The fact her parents had married was nothing short of miraculous, but that single act had taught Jackie more about unconditional love than anything else. Her father had been willing to die to consummate his love for her mother. Indeed, he had died for her mother, one night when their apartment was stormed by Islamist, who were infuriated that her mother had defied Islamic law by marrying an infidel and then spawning a Christian child. The other kids had called her an abomination that needed to be purged. The men had killed her father that night, beat him and cut off his head in the alley beside the apartment.

That same night other Christians had whisked her and her mother away to temporary safety. Within a year they were in America and living with her paternal grand parents. Jackie had grown to not only hate the Muslims who'd robbed her of a father, but all of Islam.

And now ... she looked down at her baby, her black baby,

and then to her husband, her white husband. She had cheated on a man who loved without bounds, and her guilt was worse than death itself. Of course, Don knew nothing. She had been discreet, and it had been a short-lived affair.

Her husband looked terrible. She looked over at the blood stains on the floor, then down at her daughter, suckling on her breast in complete comfort and calm. The baby was oblivious to the death and horror going on around her. That was the nature of babies, and they survived only by the grace and discretion of their parents.

Jackie had a terrible feeling her husband was dying. The man called, Dan Branch, had said he was gut shot. Such a cold and callus way to say it. He had attacked three men, killed them, and saved the life of her and her daughter, but one of the bullets had accidently hit Don in the process. The stranger had saved him and killed him all in one shot.

And now, as Jackie sat on the bed, waiting for her husband to die of infection, she wondered which would be worse: for her husband to die in his sleep before seeing his daughter, or for him to die after realizing his wife was a whore.

Either way, she also knew she was waiting for her own death. And it would be terrible. Once the man and boy were done burying the bodies, they would ransack the cabin, taking what they wanted and leave. But at least they would leave without harming her and her daughter. They were good enough people for that. Then … Don would die, and she would be alone again, helpless in a brutal world of evil men, unable to protect her daughter. But then again, what reason was there to grow up?

Her and Don had realized the nation's course. That's why they'd bought the cabin last year and why they'd fled Chicago when they had. The lights weren't coming back on. She knew that. And what made it worse, everyone else knew it too. Every person inclined to do evil was no longer restrained by the rule of law, leaving them free to rape, pillage and plunder as they saw fit. It was only a matter of time before they were found, just as they'd been found by these three men. And then … her and her daughter would die. Of course, that was the worst-case scenario, and if no one found them, they could starve or freeze to death here in the cabin, at peace with God in beautiful surroundings.

And then she could be with her parents again. She would show them her husband and her beautiful new baby, and they would smile, and laugh, and they would be happy again. Yes, happy again. Jackie found herself smiling. Then she looked back down at her dying husband. Yes, happy again, if he forgave her. But first … but first … not so happy. Her smile went away as she held her daughter and waited for her husband to die.

CHAPTER 15

Mr. Lechter and the Blind Man - September 12, 4PM

ACCORDING to those doing business with him, Jared Thompson was known as the Blind Man who kept Hannibal Lechter on a leash. Of course, *all that glitters is not gold and skim milk masquerades as cream.*

And Jared had made a living at masquerades - a very good living.

Jared was a very secretive man, and he had remade himself so many times that he sometimes woke up in the morning having to remind himself of who he really was, at least on that particular day. But most days he was just a blind man employing a very ruthless and competent assistant who just happened to think and sound like Hannibal Lechter. His assistant's real name of course was Sammy Thurmond, but no one feared and respected a man named Sammy Thurmond. So people just called him the Blind Man's Assistant.

Jared sat at the table now with Sammy off to his left standing slightly behind him. Two more of his men were in the background, just in case. But they didn't have names; they were simply mindless muscle, waiting to kill someone on his command. Sammy was the important one. He was devious, strong, and ruthless, just sort of evil; but the most important aspect of his character, at least to Jared, Sammy Thurmond was insanely loyal and protective. They were a good team. Jared made the plans, and Sammy carried them out - no questions asked. For Jared, it was a match made in heaven.

The door on the wall across from them opened up and three men in black suits walked through. They all carried submachine guns at the low-ready position. None of this bothered Jared; it was pretty standard in his line of work. Every day was a risk, and every second a gamble. He could die at any moment, but the important thing, at least to him, was knowing that should he die all his enemies would be captured and tortured before their deaths. He had paid a lot of money to arrange that deal. And he'd also hired someone else to supervise the torture and subsequent execution - just to make sure.

Jared Thompson was a stickler for redundancy.

Once the three machine guns were in place, a fourth man walked in and sat down across from Jared. This man was different than the others. He wore Arab garb, had a large nose and plenty of black and grey facial hair.

Jared didn't like the man, but he loved his money.

"You have achieved a great victory for Allah, may he be exalted."

Jared didn't say anything. He just nodded mutely, staring ahead blankly through his sunglasses, feigning humility to the Sheik across the table.

"The infidels have been humiliated and rendered impotent. We are grateful for your services."

Jared bowed slightly with his head. He knew this man couldn't be trusted, that the Sheik was a lunatic and considered Jared to be an infidel, deserving only of death or complete submission to Allah. But Jared didn't like Allah either - or his prophet Mohammed, or anyone else named Mohammed, Ahmed, Abdul, or any other ridiculous name of Middle Eastern concoction. Come to think of it, Jared didn't like anyone. He didn't even like himself, and a part of him, the innermost part, the part that only came out at night and in his dreams, was simply waiting impatiently to die. What no one else knew or understood was that all Jared's money, all his power, all his plans and schemes, were just a distraction from his own despair, simply a means to keep himself from self destructing for one more day.

"We have need of you again."

Jared thought to himself, *Of that I have no doubt. By yourself you are incapable of doing anything, even the most basic of things like taking a leak or making love to a woman. Everything has to be arranged for you, bought and paid for. You are a helpless man, kept alive only by the protection your money buys you. And it's not even your money. You stole it from your people, sold their oil and forced them to serve you. You are a despicable man.*

But on the outside, Jared nodded like a snake.

The Sheik motioned with his hand, and the man behind him produced a file folder. The Sheik slid it across the table. Jared opened it and studied it a moment. Jared ran his fingertips across the braille, quickly reading every detail. He smiled inside. They were so predictable. The dollar sign with a number followed by seven zeros made him laugh to himself. He wasn't doing this for the money. He had his own agenda. Besides, money was just paper now, in any currency.

But on the outside, Jared remained the nodding snake.

"None of this is a concern for you?"

Jared spoke for the first time.

"It's not a problem, sir. It will be done as you require."

The Sheik smiled and nodded triumphantly. In his mind, Jared was a traitorous infidel, willing to sell his own people into bondage, willing to rape, pillage and betray not only his country, but his heritage and remove all freedom from the land.

But Jared knew better. It was true that he'd brought on the thousand-year night with the help of his Muslim allies; it was true that anarchy was now loosed not only upon America, but upon the world; but what the Sheik didn't know, was that deep down inside, Jared Thompson had twenty-twenty vision.

Jared slowly and ceremoniously removed his sunglasses and looked deep into the Sheik's dark eyes. Then he looked into the face of the Sheik's three bodyguards, one at a time, registering the surprised look on their faces as the Blind Man met their gaze.

Jared nodded and Sammy Thurmond pressed a remote button in his coat pocket. The bullet-proof glass popped up, shielding Jared from the gunfire that erupted soon after. When it subsided, Sammy pressed another button and the bullet-proof glass lowered. The Sheik was slumped down over the table with a bullet wound to the left shoulder and the right arm. All of his body guards were dead, as were two of Jared's.

Jared looked into the man's eyes and smiled.

"I - I thought you were blind?"

Jared laughed.

"That's okay, I thought you were stupid. That's the difference between you and me. I was right, and you were wrong."

The Sheik's eyes filled with terror and confusion.

"But why? Why would you do such a thing? We made you rich!"

Jared stood up and produced a pearl-handled nine millimeter pistol from his coat pocket. He aimed it across the table straight into the Sheik's face.

"Because you're impolite. And I don't like you."

Jared pulled the trigger. The Sheik's head jerked back and then slumped forward again.

"Besides, I'm a patriot, and I won't let foreigners come into my own country and take it over."

He glanced back at Sammy who immediately stepped forward. Jared placed the pistol in his hand and walked out of the room, stepping over dead bodies all the way to the door. He stopped at the exit and glanced over his shoulder.

"Bury the Muslims at the pig farm outside of town. Have

our men cremated. It's only right."

Sammy remained expressionless as he nodded compliance.

"I never liked that man. He is so impolite!"

Jared left the room.

CHAPTER 16

A Slice of American Pie - September 12, 8PM

"*HE'S* dying from infection, and there's nothing I can do to stop it. He needs a hospital."

Tears welled up in Jackie's eyes, but she refused to let them fall in front of Dan Branch. She would wait and cry alone later on. But what he asked next surprised her.

"Where's the nearest hospital from here? How far away is it?"

She looked up at him...puzzled. "Why do you ask?"

Dan leaned back and made eye contact with her. He knew she hated him; it was obvious by the way she glared at him; but to ask a question like that she must think him a heartless brute. He sighed and maintained his calm demeanor. "Because we need to get him to a hospital or he'll die for sure. They have to operate and clean out the infected organs and then pump him full of antibiotics. There's still a bullet in there too that has to come out."

Jackie thought to herself, *Yes, a bullet that you shot into him*. But she didn't say it aloud. She knew it was irrational, that Dan Branch had saved them, but he hated him for it and would never forgive him. She mumbled softly. "Eagle River has a hospital. It's a 40-minute drive from here."

Dan looked down for a moment. Forty minutes worth of

fuel, 80 minutes for the trip, not to mention the added danger of traveling to a city in this chaos. And most important of all…Eagle River was in the wrong direction. Dan looked over and saw Jeremy studying him. He was reminded of his talk with his son earlier in the day. He recalled his words vividly and painfully. *Now, more than ever, it's important that we do good in the eyes of God. Because we could be meeting Him face to face at any moment.* He cursed himself inside for hesitating to do the decent thing.

"We'd better get going then. He won't make it until morning." Dan stood up beside the bed and walked toward the door. "I'll make room in the truck bed for him. I'll have to drive easy but fast. Time is important."

Jackie's mouth dropped open and she looked at him in disbelief. *Why was he doing this?*

"Jeremy, I need your help."

They both walked out the door to the truck. Once out of hearing, Dan turned and faced his son. Jeremy was the first to speak.

"Are you sure this is a good idea, Dad?"

Dan didn't answer right away. "No, I'm not sure, but I do know it's the right thing to do. I shot that man, so I need to try and save him. It's cut and dried."

Jeremy lowered his head. "I thought you said the cities weren't safe?"

Dan reassured him. "Eagle River is small. It should be okay." Then he started walking to the truck. "I want you to stay here with Jackie and the baby. They're going to need a man to protect them."

Jeremy opened his mouth to argue, but Dan held up his hand to cut him off. "It's decided. The baby is newborn and Jackie will have all she can do just to keep the baby alive. She's going to need help. I can make the drive alone, but you're needed here."

Dan stopped at the truck and opened the door. He reached behind the seat and pulled out the Winchester Model 1800 shotgun. He quickly showed him how to operate it before handing the firearm to his son.

"Never point it at anyone you don't mean to kill. And anyone who tries to hurt you, Jackie or the baby has to die. Understand?"

Jeremy swallowed hard before answering. "Yes, sir. I'll do my best."

Dan forced a smile then moved to the back of the truck to drop down the tailgate. Ten minutes later, the wounded man was loaded into the truck bed and Dan was ready to roll.

Jackie walked out onto the porch and stood there holding the baby. She wanted to cry, but she would do it later. Dan walked over to Jeremy and hugged him tightly against his chest. "Protect the women and children. That's your job now."

Jeremy squeezed him back, and nodded his head. He was trying to be brave.

"Just hurry back, Dad. We need to get to Michigan."

Dan glanced over to Jackie and nodded his head. "I'll do my best, ma'am. Watch my son, please."

Jackie lowered her head, but didn't answer. Dan turned and hopped into the pick-up truck and drove off down the two-track to the main road.

Jeremy stood and listened until the sound of the truck's engine was faded and gone. He wondered if he'd ever see his father again.

❧ ❧ ❧

Thirty minutes into the drive, Dan noticed more and more houses, so he knew he was getting close. He'd have to stop and ask directions, and that thought unnerved him. He knew strangers would not be taken too kindly. He reached down and hit the "search" button on the radio, looking for a station that might give him some intel, but no such luck. There were very few cars on the road and the few people he did see outside were armed to the teeth.

Suddenly, the radio came alive with a tired, slow voice.

"This is Danny Dixon, the voice of Eagle River's classic rock. We'll be broadcasting for five minutes every hour on the hour as long as the fuel lasts. Sorry folks, no music today. In the immortal words of Don McClean *I went down to the sacred store, Where I'd heard the music years before, But the man there said the music wouldn't play.*

The man's voice quivered a bit before going on. "Now ain't that the saddest words you ever heard?"

There was silence for a moment. Dan remembered the lyrics to the classic rock song *American Pie*. He had never understood them, but they had intrigued him nonetheless.

"So the music won't play today, but maybe tomorrow, the good Lord willing. But for today, I have a list of do's and don't's from the Eagle River Community Emergency Response Team."

The DJ then rattled off a list of precautionary instructions on boiling water, on eating spoiled food, how to go to the bathroom without polluting the city, and the list went on. Dan half listened. He had *American Pie* stuck in his head now and it wouldn't go away.

> He was singing, "bye-bye, miss American pie. Drove my chevy to the levee, But the levee was dry.

Dan started humming at first, then he broke into song. It was crazy, and he knew it, but for some reason he just couldn't stop.

> Them good old boys were drinkin' whiskey and rye And singin', "this'll be the day that I die.

"And now for the news."

Dan immediately stopped singing and listened to Danny Dixon.

"There is no contact at all from Madison. It is rumored

that the Capitol building burned to the ground last night, but it can't be confirmed. Martial law was declared, but no one knows if the Governor is even alive. Citizens with Ham radios have reported that all the major cities are being looted and burned by hungry and angry mobs. The Eagle River Chief of Police has asked that anyone with prior military or law enforcement experience report to the city hall as a volunteer. You will be briefed and trained for duty.

"The Eagle River Fire Chief has imposed a ban on indoor cooking as many cities have already burned down, and the Chief has no way to put out the fire.

"As to the rumors of foreign invasion on the West Coast, well, those are just rumors and no one knows what to believe anymore. Just be careful with those firearms and conserve your ammo just in case.

"Okay, well that's all the time I have. I'll fire up again in 55 minutes for an update. Have a good night, and God bless Eagle River."

The voice cut off and was replaced with static, leaving Dan more lonely than before. The song flashed into his head again.

I met a girl who sang the blues
And I asked her for some happy news,
But she just smiled and turned away.

Up ahead Dan saw the flashing strobes of a city police cruiser and a fire engine, so he slowed down. As he drew near, he saw a dozen men behind cars with shotguns and rifles all aimed at him.

And in the streets: the children screamed,
The lovers cried, and the poets dreamed.
But not a word was spoken;
The church bells all were broken.

Dan kept his hands on the steering wheel and let the truck

roll to a stop, all the while wondering, was this the last train to the coast?

֎ ֎ ֎

Jeremy watched as the little baby sucked on his mother's breast. A week ago he would have been embarrassed or even chuckled and made a derogatory comment at the sight of a woman's bare breast, but in light of all that happened, Jeremy no longer felt trite. The sight of a mother feeding her baby seemed as natural to him as anything he'd ever seen.

"How come your baby's a different color?"

Jackie flinched inside at the question. This boy was so blunt, not in a rude way, because she sensed that he wasn't trying to hurt her, just that he was curious and really wanted to know. The boy's only fault was lack of boundaries and no sense of social appropriety. She measured her words before speaking.

"I made a terrible mistake."

Jeremy nodded. "Yeah, that's what I figured." He shrugged his shoulders. "It had to be that. What else could it be, right?"

Jackie looked at him and halfway smiled. *On the other hand, his raw honesty was somewhat refreshing when juxtapposed to the verbal games that most adults played. If this boy was thinking it, then he was saying it.*

She just nodded her head and looked back down at her baby.

"My mom made lots of mistakes like that too. It killed my dad, hurt him real bad." He hesitated and looked down at the floor. "I guess it killed her too, in the end that is."

Jackie looked up again. "Your mother is dead?"

Jeremy nodded. "Yes, she died three days ago of a drug overdose."

She shifted the baby in her arms, allowing the child to get a better grasp on the nipple. "I'm sorry to hear that, Jeremy."

121

"We buried her yesterday in a cemetery a ways back." He rubbed his eyes briefly. "It was the best we could do."

Jackie smiled softly. "At least you still have your father."

Jeremy smiled. "Yeah. I do. If you have to have a dad, then I guess he's the one I would choose. He's saved my life twice already since this all started."

Jackie shifted her gaze. She seemed suddenly more interested. "Yes, I guess we have that in common then. He saved my life too, and the life of my baby. How did he save your life?"

Jeremy shrugged his shoulders. He was holding the shotgun in his left hand with the stock end resting on the floor. He leaned it up against the wall in the corner. "He's just always there for me, even before all this happened. I knew I could count on him, even when I cussed at him, abused him, you know, all the things that kids my age do to parents just cuz we're screwed up and angry."

Jackie remembered her teen years and nodded in agreement.

"And then he shot those five guys the other night who were raping a woman in the cemetery."

Jackie's eyes got big. "He shot five men? I mean five men plus the three men he shot today?"

Jeremy nodded. "Yeah, it's really weird. We keep running across people that are being hurt, and the only way to save them is for Dad to shoot somebody."

Jackie's brow furled and she couldn't help but think, *What manner of man is this who kills eight men in three days? And is he going to kill me too?*

"But they were really bad dudes, and they needed killing. Dad saved that woman, then she stole our truck and all our supplies, so we had to chase her down, then we found her dead on the side of the road along with mom's body. We took them back to the cemetery and buried them. An old man helped us and then gave us 5 gallons of gas to make it here. He was a good man, but he stayed there and prayed over his wife's grave. He was a nice old man and I hope he's okay."

The boy shrugged again. "We're trying to make it to Dad's Uncle Rodney's house in Michigan. Dad says he's more prepared for this than anyone else in the world. He raised my dad after his parents died. We have that in common, because both my parents are dead too. Dan is really my step-dad, but he feels more like a real dad than anyone I ever known."

Jackie was looking up now and they locked eyes for a moment.

"He's one of the good guys, Jackie."

Jackie nodded and then looked back down again. She fumbled with the baby as she changed breasts and then continued the feeding.

Jeremy kept talking, and Jackie just listened. He talked about his mom cheating on his dad, not once, but many times. He talked about shooting a rocket through the kitchen window, about a girl named Tonya, and a dog he'd had named Elijah that had been run over by a car. A few times she thought he would cry, but he quickly changed the subject and ended up smiling and even laughing in some places.

After a half an hour, she started to like him. And then an unusual thing happened. Jackie talked too, not just a little, but a lot. She shared about her husband, her childhood, the murder of her father and even about her affair with the Haitian refugee.

An hour later, when they were both all talked out, Jackie laid the sleeping baby on the bed and cooked some food. It was nothing fancy, just a can of Dinty Moore stew and some bread and butter. They both ate in silence, but it was now a graceful silence. In her mind she wondered, *Where is my husband? Is he alive? Will he forgive me? Will my baby live?*

They both finished eating. The boy walked out onto the porch and stared into the night, waiting for his father to return.

Jackie went back to the bed and lay beside her new baby.

Now that she was finally alone, she held the baby and she cried.

❧ ❧ ❧

"I want you to keep you hands where I can see them, and very slowly exit the truck."

Dan assumed it was a police officer talking to him, but he couldn't see anyone because the blinding search light from the police cruiser was in his eyes. Before getting out of the truck, Dan unholstered his big pistol and put it on the front seat beside him. Then he opened the door and raised his hands above his head. His heart was pounding in his chest beyond his control.

"He's got a gun, George!"

Dan heard the accusation, but was quick to correct them."

"No, my holster is empty. I left my pistol on the seat in the truck. I don't want any trouble. See, look at it."

Dan turned to the side so they could get a good look at his empty holster.

"Easy, men. The holster's empty."

A big man in a police uniform stepped out from behind the car and walked slowly toward him. He stopped six feet away before speaking again.

"State your business, stranger."

Dan squinted in the bright light and tried to shade his eyes with his left hand.

"I got a man in the truck bed. He's hurt real bad, and he needs a doctor. I just want to get him to the hospital here."

For a moment there was no answer. Dan felt naked in the light with so many guns pointing at him, but he had no choice but to endure their skepticism, at least for now.

"What's your name and where are you from?"

"I'm Dan Branch. I live in Menomonie over near Eau Claire, but I'm headed to my home town in Northern Michigan to ride this out where I've got friends and family."

The police officer took a step closer. The man's head blocked the light so Dan could finally get a good look at him. His hair was black and grey, but it was all messed up and his face was streaked with blood and dirt. He had a feeling that something bad had happened here.

"What kind of injury?"

Dan hesitated.

"He's been gut shot. Him and his pregnant wife were attacked about 40 minutes from here. She's okay, but he needs surgery and antibiotics."

The man was quiet for a moment, and when he spoke again, his voice was cold and emotionless.

"You need to turn around and head back out of town. No one can enter. It's for our own safety. Orders of the Mayor."

Dan looked at him in disbelief. How could this happen in only four days time?

"But...he'll die."

The policeman's voice wavered a bit now, but his face remained stern.

"Sorry. I got my orders. No one gets into town for any reason. No exceptions."

Dan took a step forward.

"Stop!"

The police officer drew something from his waist. Dan assumed it was a gun, so he froze in place.

"What's wrong with you guys? Are you just going to let a good man die when you have the means to help him? I'll leave him with you and I'll wait here if you want. Just help my friend. Please."

Dan watched the inner struggle move like a spasm across the cop's face.

"Listen, friend, I don't like this any more than you do. But this is a dire situation. We've already shot and killed a dozen men in the last two days, and every last one of them claimed to be the good guys. But they weren't. We let them in, and they murdered and raped the Mayor's wife and daughter. We're not trusting anyone again, so you need to turn around and leave while you still can."

A sudden wave of anger filled Dan as he took another step forward. The Taser darts sprang out and lodged in his chest sending 50,000 volts pulsing through his body. Dan collapsed immediately, writhing in pain on the pavement.

"Daniel, go check the bed of his truck and tell me what you see."

The cop was standing over him now, and every time Dan tried to get up, he pushed the Taser button again. After three times, Dan stayed down."

"He was telling the truth, George. The man back here's been gut shot. Don't look none too good, either."

"Check his pulse."

There was silence for about thirty seconds. Dan just lay there unmoving. Finally, Daniel yelled out.

"He's dead, George. No pulse and no breathing. He's still warm though and hasn't stiffened up. Must be pretty recent."

"Okay then. Open his cab door and unload his pistol. Then bring me the bullets and help me get him back inside his truck."

The man did as he was told, and soon handed 5 four-ten shotgun shells to the cop. The cop smiled and placed them in his pocket.

"Must be carrying a Taurus Judge. That's a mean gun."

He looked down at Dan, then latched on to his right arm and lifted him to his feet. Dan was surprised at how powerful the man was. The other man, Daniel, lifted him by the other arm and they both drug him to the cab.

The police officer pinned Dan up against the truck door and looked him straight in the eye from just six inches away.

"Can I trust that you'll never come back here again?"

Dan was weak and wobbly, so he didn't answer right away. The cop stepped back and hit the Taser trigger again. Dan spasmed and fell to his knees. But this time he was mad. He reached up and ripped out one of the darts and lunged

126

forward, falling down around the man's ankles. He felt a kick to the groin and doubled up on the ground, but still reached out to the cop's pant leg. Now both men were kicking him. He felt the officer's baton crash against his head and face several times. Finally, he covered up with his hands, absorbing the blows, hoping just to survive.

> *And the three men I admire most:*
> *The father, son, and the holy ghost,*
> *They caught the last train for the coast*
> *The day the music died.*

As he lapsed into unconsciousness, the sound of Don McClean's singing laughed inside his head without remorse or mercy.

They tossed Dan's body into the truck bed and drove him out ten miles before stopping by a hayfield. They parked the truck and the cop took one last look at Dan and the dead man before shaking his head. In his mind, he couldn't help but think, *So this is what we do with good people now. How did it come to this?*

Then he reached into his pocket, pulled out the five loose four-ten shells and threw them on the floor of the truck bed. He said out loud. "Don't come back, Dan Branch from Menomonie. You may be one of the good guys, but if you do, we'll have to kill you. And we're the good guys too."

The officer turned and walked back to his cruiser where Daniel was waiting.

"Get out of the driver's seat, Daniel. This is my car."

Daniel moved over and the cop got inside and drove away, leaving Dan Branch to the night.

CHAPTER 17

A Time to Heal - September 13, 10AM

JEREMY had moved two chairs out onto the porch, and he and Jackie were waiting there when Dan's truck lumbered back in and coasted to a stop. He was slumped over the steering wheel with his face down. Jackie held the baby close while Jeremy ran forward to the truck.

"Dad! Are you okay? I waited up almost all night long!"

The boy reached the cab and looked in just as Dan raised his head and turned. What Jeremy saw caused an adrenaline dump into his bloodstream and his heart to pump faster.

"Oh my God! Dad, what happened to you?"

Jackie stood up and walked over still clutching her baby. When she saw Dan's swollen and bloody face, she ran back into the cabin. A moment later she returned with a wet rag. Jeremy already had the truck door open, and Dan had fallen out onto the dirt driveway.

"Roll him over on his back, Jeremy."

Jeremy complied while she checked his pulse and his breathing. She noticed his left eye was swollen totally closed and the right eye was open just a slit. Jackie shook her head, wondering how he'd even managed to drive back.

"Get me a bowl of water and another towel from inside. We have to clean him up and see how bad it is."

It took ten minutes to wash up Dan's face and to get him inside on the bed. Jackie removed Dan's shirt and saw the mass of bruises there. She thought to herself, *It will be a miracle if no ribs are broken.*

She disinfected the cuts on his face with iodine and Dan came to briefly. He looked up through one eye and saw Jackie hovering over him. When he spoke his voice was raspy and labored.

"I'm ... sorry."

A clouded look came over Jackie's face, and she jumped up and ran back out to the truck. When she reached it, she looked into the truck bed and saw the stiffened, discolored body of her husband. His eyes were open and lifeless, staring out at nothing.

Back in the cabin, Jeremy heard her scream again and again. The baby awoke and she cried too. Dan coughed and some blood ran down his chin. Jeremy wiped it away with the rag as he cried along with Jackie and her baby.

But to Dan, it was all a foggy haze except for the pain in his face and his chest. He passed out again, leaving his son ill-equipped to deal with the chaos and pain around him.

Jeremy, who only five days before, had been worried about acne, Twitter, Facebook, and Hotmail, stared out blankly, trying desperately to cope with this harsh, new world.

⤳ ⤳

Jeremy's shovel hit the dry, packed earth and glanced off a stone, landing harmlessly to one side. Jackie had asked him to bury her husband beneath the oak tree to the left of the cabin. To the boy that meant only one thing: lots of roots. But he didn't have the heart to refuse her. She was already in enough pain, so Jeremy dug and hacked his way through the roots and dirt while she stayed inside to take care of the baby and his father. It was a wise division of labor.

The blisters on Jeremy's hands had popped several days ago and were already turning into calluses. He sat down on the edge of the hole with his feet hanging down inside. From experience, Jeremy knew that most of the roots would be at the surface, so once he got down a foot or so into the yellow sand, the ground would get softer and the digging would become easier.

Jeremy didn't like this new life of his. It seemed stressful. But the more he thought about it, the more he had to admit that the old life hadn't been that great either. He'd gone from a drunken, carousing mother with an overbearing stepfather to a dead mother and a stepfather who kept shooting people. And the worst part was, Jeremy had to bury all the bodies.

He took a long drink of water from the milk jug beside the hole. Fortunately, there was a hand pump well beside the cabin that gave them fresh water. Apparently Jackie and her husband, Don, had purchased this cabin for the sole purpose of living without electricity. Jeremy couldn't help but wonder what type of person would do something like that.

He looked over at Don, wrapped in a blanket beside him, and nodded his thanks. Jeremy wondered, *Why don't I feel weird sitting next to a dead guy?* He put the jug of water down and pulled his Blackberry out of his front breast pocket. He turned it on and waited for it to power up. There was no signal - again. Then he pushed the button on the right side to view his pictures and videos stored inside. He pulled up and played the video of him and his mother. On the screen, he watched as his mother hugged him, and he tried to pull away. He remembered that night explicitly. She'd been a little drunk and was trying to hug him in front of other people. Jeremy had stopped liking that about four years ago. But now…he would do anything to have her embarrass him just one more time.

He thought about his stepdad, laying inside on the bed, swollen and bleeding, wondering *Is my dad going to die as well?* He didn't know. Jeremy just knew that five days ago was a million miles away, and that he didn't even feel like the same person. He felt older.

He listened to his mother's voice over and over on the Blackberry as tears welled up in his eyes but refused to flow. Finally, the video stopped playing and his Blackberry shut down for good. It was useless with dead batteries. The boy felt like crying, but then he looked over at the dead body beside him and laughed out loud. What good would it do to cry? In the face of all the death and change, crying seemed like a senseless act.

He jumped back down into the hole and started digging again, and two hours later he was done. As carefully as possible, he drug the body down into the hole. He winced as it crashed down and landed headfirst. He heard the neckbones crack. As quickly as he could, he straightened out the body and tucked the blanket edges back in where they belonged. He was glad that Jackie hadn't seen that.

Five minutes later Jackie came out holding the baby in her arms. She stood over the hole, not crying, not talking, just standing.

"I'm sorry, Jackie. I wish we had a box or something." That was all that Jeremy knew to say. He wanted to console her, but he was a teenage boy with limited social skills and life experience. The truth was, Jeremy was growing emotionally numb. What he didn't know was that Jackie was growing numb as well. The two of them stood over the hole looking down at the blanketed body.

"Dad says good people should get words said over them and a prayer. Do you want to say something?"

Jackie kissed her tiny baby girl. "I'd like to be alone with him for a minute, please."

Jeremy nodded. Inside he was relieved, and quickly went back in the cabin to check on his father. Jackie stood over the grave alone now. She allowed herself to cry for a minute or so, then shut off the tears as if on command, as if they flowed from a spicket deep down inside her.

"I don't know what to say, honey. I wasn't counting on all this. I just want you to know that I love you, despite what I did. I know you must realize by now I cheated on you, and I feel terrible about it. I deserve to be in the hole instead of you. I know that, and I'm so sorry. Please forgive me, honey. It was the only time I did anything like that. I don't understand why I did it, but I'm going to have to figure it out. I wish so much I could get your forgiveness, but I guess I'll just have to live with the guilt. Lord knows I deserve it."

She looked down at her baby, the black-skinned, Haitian little girl baby, and allowed the tears to flow once more, and she spoke through sobs.

"I wanted to share parenthood with you, Don. I wanted to have *your* baby. Instead, I had to pretend, all through the pregnancy, that my baby was yours, when I knew in my heart she wasn't. It doesn't make me love her any less, it's just…I wish she was yours so I could have a part of you to hold and love forever. But, instead, I have the baby of a man I never knew and met only once. I deserve this."

She bent down carefully and scooped up a handful of yellow dirt and tossed it onto the blanket. Then she walked back inside the cabin.

A few minutes later Jeremy came out and filled in the hole.

Northern Michigan - September 14, 8PM

It had been a week now with no word from his nephew, and Rodney was beginning to worry about him. The plan had always been clear. When he sent the message, Dan was to beat it back here to Michigan as fast as he could. Something must have gone wrong. And that's why Rodney was loading up his Ford F-250 and heading out just before nightfall.

He knew it was dangerous, perhaps even foolhardy, but…

he felt he had no choice. Everything around him, all the preparations, he hadn't done for himself, but for the kid. So, even though his chances of success were slim to none, he figured a slim chance was worth taking. Besides, a slim chance was a million times better than no chance.

"Where in God's name did you get a Thompson submachine gun?"

Rodney was jolted out of his thoughts by Sheriff Leif's question. He just smiled and threw the cigarette butt onto the ground.

"Do you really want to know, Sheriff?"

Joe Leif gave him his best "why-do-you-do-this-to-me look" before sighing. He changed the subject.

"So what's in this black case here?"

"A fifty caliber BMG hunting rifle."

"A hunting rifle? What can you hunt with a fifty caliber?"

"Anything within fifteen hundred yards."

Joe shook his head in despair. "God help us all. You are such a felon! I'll never be re-elected if this gets out."

The old man lit another cigarette and took a heavy pull on it. "I wouldn't worry about that if I was you. Don't think they'll be many elections going on for quite some time now. But, tell ya what. If there is, I'll vote for you a hundred times if you like."

Joe shook his head back and forth in exasperation. "God help us all!"

They finished loading up, and then got in and drove off just before dark. If all went well, they'd reach Menomonie by morning, and then they'd know his nephew's fate. Rodney had welded steel pipes on the front bumper and steel plates around the cab, bed and tailgate. The extra weight would ruin his gas mileage, but Rodney had installed an underground diesel tank years ago and had filled it up over a week before the blackout. This mission would not fail for lack of fuel.

Rodney looked in his rear-view mirror and saw Moses

standing on the porch, watching them drive away. He felt a sense of excitement, knowing he was driving into a world of unknown danger, knowing that he might die on the roadside from a stranger's bullet. So many unknowns, so much had changed. There was nothing he could be sure of save one thing: *I'll bring my boy back or die trying!*

When the truck faded from view, Moses lay down on the porch and placed his head on his paws, nestling in for the long haul.

That night, Jackie and Jeremy ate together in silence. Jeremy didn't know what to say, and Jackie had no intention of talking. Dan and the baby slept quietly in the background.

After a dinner of canned stew and bread, Jeremy washed the dishes without being asked. The dishwater was cold, but he put in extra soap to ward off the germs.

When he was done, he walked over and sat down beside his father. He stayed there looking at him for a half hour, then went out onto the porch where he sat on the wooden planking with his legs dangling off and his forearms and chin resting on the railing. He recalled the fire-building contest he'd had with his father and smiled involuntarily.

"What could you possibly have to smile about, Jeremy?"

Jackie had come outside without him knowing it. Jeremy looked over his shoulder and the smile went away. "You're a real glass-half-empty kind of girl aren't you?"

"What?" She looked at him in amazement. "Did you just refer to me as a girl?"

The boy smirked to himself. "You heard me. Did I stutter?"

Jackie walked up to the railing and looked down on him. "Anyone ever tell you that you can be a real snot sometimes?"

Jeremy made an adolescent farting sound by pursing his

lips together and pushing out air and spit. Jackie ignored the gesture and forced herself to focus. A few seconds later she spoke again.

"I just wanted to tell you thank you."

Jeremy looked up surprised.

"What for?"

She sat down on the porch beside him.

"For burying my husband."

Jeremy turned back to look into the woods.

"No big deal. I bury a lot of people now."

She looked into the woods too.

"Well, it was a big deal to me. So, thanks. I owe you one."

The boy reached up and scratched the peach fuzz on his face. "Is my dad going to make it?"

She looked over at him as if surprised. "Well, yes, of course he is. All the wounds are superficial, no broken ribs that I can tell, no internal damage. Unless he gets an infection, then he should heal up just fine. I'll keep bathing him with soap and disinfecting the wounds to make them heal faster."

A half smile came to Jeremy's lips.

"Okay, then, guess we're even."

The woman looked off to the left of the cabin at the mound of dirt.

"Can you make a wooden cross for Don tomorrow?"

Jeremy thought about it for a moment and then nodded.

"Yeah, sure, no problem." Dad taught me how to lash sticks together with rope. I can do it."

Jackie's curiosity got the best of her despite all she'd been through the past week.

"So what is your dad like?"

Jeremy shrugged.

"I don't know. I used to think he was just a normal, pain-in-the-butt dad until a week ago."

Then he told her all about the ball bat and how Dan had

smashed his stereo and punched him in the face. She laughed spontaneously.

"Hey! It wasn't funny!"

Jackie covered her mouth to stifle it.

"I'm sorry, I just got this image and I couldn't help myself. You know you had it coming, right?"

Jeremy turned his face away so she couldn't see him smiling.

"Maybe." Then he added. "I used to be a bit of a jerk, back when I was a kid."

Jackie suddenly saw the sadness in his statement. *Back seven days ago when he was still a kid.*

"Did your dad really kill all those people?"

Jeremy nodded, but was quick to defend him. "He had to. It was kill or be killed. I never knew he could do things like that. He was a Marine ya know." Then he looked thoughtful for a moment. "I was lucky he didn't kill me that day in my bedroom."

Jackie listened and fifteen minutes later he was still talking. Finally, when he paused, she interjected.

"Your dad sounds like a good man, a capable man." She went silent. Jeremy noticed.

"What's wrong?"

Jackie shook her head. "I was just wondering…what do you think he's going to do to me and the baby?"

Jeremy frowned and started to answer just as the baby began to cry inside the cabin. Jackie hopped up quickly and called out over her shoulder as she walked back inside.

"There's some rope in the tool shed along with a bunch of other stuff that Don put in there. You should check out all those boxes in there. He stocked up on all kinds of things. We should inventory them."

Jeremy nodded and then she was gone. He thought for a moment. His dad was right. Women don't make any sense. He called them an enigma. He stood up and walked out to the tool shed to take a look. It was good to know that his Dad would be okay.

Menomonie, Wisconsin - September 15, 4AM

"Are you sure this is the right place, Rodney?"

The Sheriff pointed his flashlight on the door knob as Rodney wiggled it and then moved off to check the windows and then the back door.

"Hush up, Sheriff. We wake the neighbors and we're liable to eat some buckshot!"

They had driven straight through without stopping. The reserve fuel tank had served them well, and they'd eaten MREs while driving and relieved themselves in Coke bottles. Once, near Eagle River, they'd run into a road block, but quick thinking had taken them down a side road and around the town. Everything else was quiet. Now they both stood outside Dan's house. It was locked up tight with no sign of life inside.

Rodney let out a deep sigh as he unzipped his pants and urinated on the lawn. Sheriff Leif walked over to see what he was doing.

"What are you doing, Rodney?"

He finished up and shook it off. The Sheriff heard the zipper come up and shook his head in disgust. "Can't you at least go behind a tree?"

The old man ignored him and walked over to the sliding glass doors off the side deck. He stepped up onto the wooden planking and pushed the gas grill to one side. After grabbing the door handle firmly, he lifted up hard and muscled the glass door out of the track and carefully set it on the deck leaning against the vinyl siding.

"Rodney that's breaking and entering."

Rodney laughed. "Only if I get caught."

Joe Leif followed reluctantly, all the while thinking, *If he gets caught, then I get caught too.*

Once inside the house, Rodney went straight to the basement stairs and walked on down. "Shine that flashlight over here, Joe." The beam lit up a wooden book case on the cement block wall. Rodney felt around the edge until he found the latch. He swung the book case out, revealing a row of four olive-drab, metal wall lockers. The doors were unlocked. He opened them and found all the lockers empty.

Rodney smiled.

"He made it out of town."

Joe stepped up beside him.

"How do you know?"

He pointed at the empty lockers.

"He took all the gear with him."

"How do you know it wasn't stolen?"

Rodney shook his head from side to side. "And you call yourself a cop. There were no signs of forced entry, Joe. Looters tend to break things when they're in a hurry."

The Sheriff nodded. "Yes, I suppose you're right. So what was inside the lockers?"

Rodney turned and headed back up the stairs, talking as he went. "Oh, nothing much. Just the essentials."

For the first time since leaving Michigan, Joe Leif laughed out loud. "For you that could mean an Abrams Tank and a dozen Stinger missiles."

"Absolutely! The right of the people to keep and bear arms shall not be infringed."

When they reached the top of the stairs, Joe hesitated. Rodney stopped and turned around. "What's wrong, Sheriff?"

"You don't actually have a tank back at your place do you?"

Rodney smiled and toyed with the lawman just for fun. "Of course I do, Joe. I bought the M1 Abrams Tank do-it-yourself-kit off Ebay three years ago, but I just haven't gotten around to putting it together yet."

Sheriff Leif laughed nervously. "You don't really have a

tank … do you?"

Rodney picked up his pace and walked out the side door. He put the door back in its track and walked over to the truck with Joe close on his heels.

"Let's turn some miles, Sheriff. I want to find some place to hide out before daylight. We'll get some sleep and then make the mad dash back when it's dark again."

They both crawled up into the cab of the F-250, fired up the diesel engine and headed back for Michigan. All the while, Rodney wondered *Where are you kid. Why didn't you get home?*

The Cabin - September 15, 8AM

Dan woke up that morning and immediately tried to get out of bed. He rolled out onto the floor and screamed with excruciating pain. Jeremy and Jackie rushed over from the breakfast table and helped him back onto the bed.

"Dad, you can't be getting up yet. You're all broken up inside."

Dan tried to talk, but the pain was too great. His chest was a mass of bruises and his face felt like it was on fire. He lay there unmoving, hoping to die just so the pain would stop. It was then he realized he was breathing too fast, so he purposefully slowed it down, taking longer, slower, steadier breaths.

Dan closed his eyes for a moment, and when he opened them Jackie was over his face, her long, midnight hair cascading over her shoulders and hanging down on his chest. He looked at her with his one, good eye, and couldn't help but notice how attractive she was. Inside, he winced. Here he was, on his deathbed for all he knew, recently widowed, stranded away from home during the apocalypse, and he was still noticing good-looking women. His Uncle Rodney had told him it was the Branch family curse. Dan couldn't argue

139

with him.

"Just relax, Dan. You're hurt pretty bad, but you'll heal up if you just stay relaxed and let your body do its job."

Her voice was soft and soothing. Jackie lifted his head up, placed two capsules in his mouth and poured water down his throat. He took as much as he could but then choked.

Jeremy looked at his Dad's swollen and bruised face, trying to smile, but couldn't.

"It's okay, Dad. We're going to take care of you. Just go back to sleep."

Dan closed his eyes, and the world became fuzzy and dark. He could hear their voices, but had no idea what they were saying. Then the voices faded away, and his world went once more black.

"Is he okay, Jackie?"

She nodded and then walked back to the table. Jeremy followed her. "Yes, he'll be fine. I've been giving him Tylenol with Codeine."

"What are those?"

Jackie smiled. "Something that will make him feel a lot better than you and I do at this moment."

Jeremy nodded his understanding. "Oh, you're giving my dad drugs."

She sat back down at the table and picked up her spoon again. "No sense in letting him feel all that pain. Nothing gained there."

Jeremy watched as she took a bite of her ground wheat cereal. Don had stocked three hundred pounds of Red Wheat in the pantry along with a grain grinder and a host of other food. No matter what else happened to them, they would have plenty to eat. But, already, Jeremy missed ice-cold Mountain Dew and pizza. Wheat just wasn't quite the same. He felt like he was at a health food camp for senior citizens. Most of all, Jeremy missed junk food: good old fashioned refined sugar, BHA, BHT, Monosodium Glutamate, and partially hydrogenated vegetable oil. They were the building blocks of every growing teenager.

"I thought you didn't like my dad?"

Jackie stopped her spoon right before her next bite, then placed it back in the bowl. "What gave you that idea?"

Jeremy looked over at his dad as he talked. "I saw the way you looked at him after we buried Don. You hate him. You think it was his fault that your husband died. But I don't see it that way. He almost died trying to save your husband's life."

Jackie considered denying it, but then shrugged. "Since when did you become so astute?"

"I'm not astute. I don't even know what that word means."

Jackie couldn't help but smile. "In this case it means you can see inside people, know what they're thinking and feeling."

"So I was right? Cool. I'm not used to that."

It was still too close after her husband's death, the birth of her illegitimate child, and the end of the world as she knew it to tell for sure, but she saw all the signs that she might someday like this young boy.

"I'm sorry, Jeremy. I know what the facts are, but my feelings don't always agree with reality."

Jeremy nodded. "Yeah, I know how women can be. Dad says they don't make much sense and they can drive a man insane."

She looked at Jeremy, then over to Dan, then back to Jeremy again. "Your dad said that about women?"

The boy nodded.

She took another bite of her wheat, placed her elbows on either side of her bowl atop the table and grimaced.

"No more Tylenol with Codeine for him then."

Jeremy smiled and took another bite of his wheat.

"I hate your cooking, Jackie."

She nodded. "I know. Me too."

The baby cried. She got up and brought her over to the table to nurse her. Jeremy watched as she bared her breast and the baby latched on.

"I'm supposed to turn my head away and complain how gross that is, but…I don't know, things like that just don't seem important anymore."

Jackie nodded. "I know what you mean. Things like wholesale death and destruction just have a way of cutting through all the superficial crap and reminding people what's important in life."

Jeremy nodded. "Well, I don't know what superficial is, but you might be right about the crap part. Life is pretty crappy right now. But, if my dad gets better and we make it back to Michigan, then…I just might have a shot at figuring out what life is all about."

She looked up from her nursing and smiled slightly. "Keep it up, kid, and you just might grow into a man."

He ate the rest of his cereal without talking. His spoon clanked into the glass bowl. Jeremy looked at her, then down at her baby. "You mind if I ask a personal question?"

Jackie's face began to cloud over. "I don't know. What's the question and I'll tell you?"

"How come your baby's black?"

Jackie turned her head away and frowned, considering the question for a moment. "My baby's black because I cheated on my husband and lived to regret it. I screwed up. I hurt him, and I feel pretty bad about it. I should be dead in that hole outside, not him."

Jeremy leaned back in his chair and shrugged. "I don't know. Maybe we should all be dead in that hole. I screwed the neighbor girl and she was only twelve years old. I didn't love her or anything. I just wanted to use her. That's worse than what you did, because I'm only fourteen. You're old and it took you thirty years to get this bad. I got bad in half the time it took you."

Jackie looked over at him, not knowing what to say. She

could see he was serious and it saddened her.

"What can I say. We're all bad. We've all sinned."

Jeremy nodded in agreement.

"Yeah. We've sinned. But, I wonder, about God, what's He going to do to us. Can He forgive us?"

Jackie thought about it for a moment, finally realizing there was more depth to this boy than she'd first realized. "Yes, I think God can forgive us. He's a pretty big guy." She paused. "But I wonder. I think God will forgive us, but can we forgive ourselves?"

Jeremy brushed the hair out of his eyes and then met her gaze. For a moment, he was silent.

"Maybe all this world falling apart stuff is God's way of cleaning us up and giving us a second chance."

Jackie looked up. "You think so? I'd like that."

He stood up and took both their bowls to the sink.

"Well, I forgive you, Jackie."

Suddenly, she wanted to cry, but she held it in.

"I forgive you too, Jeremy."

There was silence save the sound of dishes being laid in the sink.

"I'll do the dishes. You just keep feeding the baby."

And that was the last time they talked about sin.

CHAPTER 18

RODNEY was driving east about twenty miles from Eagle River when the large, White-tailed buck jumped out in front of his truck.

"Watch out, Rod. Got a deer up there."

The old man responded by stepping on the gas pedal, and the truck lurched forward, pushing Sheriff Leif back in the seat. He reached forward and dug his fingernails into the dash board.

"What are you doing, Rodney?"

The deer turned its neck and looked into the big truck's headlights. It was the last thing he ever saw. There was a big thump, and the truck lurched a bit. The deer careened off to the side and landed thirty feet off the road unmoving.

"Just testing the integrity of my new steel bumper system."

Joe let go of the dashboard. The imprints of his fingernails were still there.

"You ruined my dashboard, Sheriff."

Joe tried to smile.

"If you keep that up I might lose control and soil your leather upholstery as well."

Uncle Rodney laughed out loud. "That's good, Joe.

You're starting to loosen up and get a sense of humor. You take life way too seriously."

The Sheriff moved his head over to the left to look at the speedometer.

"How fast are you going?"

Rodney was still grinning.

"We're making good time. I want to get back into Michigan before daybreak."

Joe frowned. "The speedometer says we're going ninety-eight."

"Oh, that. Well, the speedometer's busted."

"Really?"

"Yeah. It broke when I hit that deer back there."

Now Joe was smiling. He was silent for a moment.

"So, what do you think happened to your nephew?"

The smile on Rodney's face faded away. He thought a bit before answering. "My gut tells me he's okay."

Joe looked over at him. Rodney's face looked dangerous in the dimness of the truck's console lights.

"I don't know, my friend. It doesn't look good."

Rodney nodded to himself.

"Don't worry. He's okay. I can feel it in my gut."

Joe didn't agree with him, but he relaxed back into his seat in silence. Several minutes later they saw flashing strobe lights up ahead as they come upon the outskirts of Eagle River. Joe leaned forward in his seat.

"That's the first law and order we've seen since we started. It's encouraging."

Rodney cast him a sideways glance.

"Maybe."

The Sheriff didn't like Rodney's tone, but he let it go. "Better let me do the talking on this one, Rod."

He slowed the truck down and coasted to a stop about twenty yards in front of the police cruiser. The big searchlight turned on and lit up every crevice of the truck cab blinding them.

"I say we put pedal to metal and blow clean through. We'll make the U.P. before dawn."

But Sheriff Leif was already halfway out the door.

"Just stay put, Rodney. I'll have us out of here in no time flat."

As Rodney watched from inside the cab, he saw Joe walk forward, then stop, then raise his arms above his head and turn around. Two men came out and removed his pistol from his side, then put him down on the pavement. As the Sheriff was being handcuffed and led away, Rodney quickly formed a plan.

Two more men came out from behind the barricade with pistols drawn. They approached Rodney's truck from the driver's side. He waited until they got within fifteen feet before hitting the accelerator. As he drove by the old man quickly opened the door, knocking them both to the pavement. He spun the wheel and the truck slid around pointing him back west. Gunfire erupted from behind him, and he heard the clanks of lead on steel plates. Two minutes later the strobe lights were no longer visible.

Rodney glanced down at the speedometer and let up on the accelerator. Five miles out of town he pulled the truck into a cornfield. He drove down the fence row, then pulled into the corn. The stalks fell down by the hundreds as he hid the truck deep inside the field. He shut down the truck and listened to the engine cool.

He thought about the Marine Corps, about his time in Vietnam. The smart thing to do was get on the road and beat it back to Michigan. But…one thing kept coming back to him, haunting him, reminding him of deeds long gone. He said it out loud, as if the saying gave it blood and bone and flesh.

"No man left behind."

Uncle Rodney was already forming a plan.

Eagle River - September 16, 10AM

Sheriff Leif paced back and forth in his jail cell like a caged animal. He couldn't believe they were treating him this way. After all, he was part of the brotherhood. He was a county Sheriff for pete's sake. What happened to professional courtesy? When he'd first seen the strobe lights of the roadblock, Joe's first thought had been *I'll just show them my badge, talk to them, and they'll escort us through town.*

But that hadn't happened. Not even close. He'd been handcuffed and thrown into the back of the cruiser. Then after Rodney had taken off, they'd hauled him out and beaten him with batons before taking him here. He told them he was a Sheriff from Michigan but they laughed and took his badge, his wallet, everything. And now he was waiting for the Chief of Police to come in and question him. Normally, he'd be confident about his outcome, but Rodney's hasty retreat had lessened his chances of talking his way out of this mess. *I can't believe Rodney just left me like that!*

He heard footsteps coming down the hall and two people laughing. When he saw the Chief of Police, his heart fell. The man's eyes had that look, like Barney Fife on steroids.

Sheriff Leif smiled and reached his right hand through the bars in an attempt to shake the Chief's hand. The Chief just stood there, looking at him with a penetrating gaze. Inside, Joe was a little confused. He'd never been treated this way before, certainly not by law enforcement. He'd always been afforded the respect of his badge and his office. But this man…he could tell…this man respected no one.

"My name is Sheriff Joe Leif from Northern Michigan. My friend and I were on our way back home when your people stopped us."

The Chief said nothing.

"You've no doubt seen my badge, my ID, my Glock 22. I'd be appreciative if you'd just drive me to the state line so I can hitch a ride home."

The Chief's icy face broke into full-out laughter.

147

"Why, sure, Mr. Leif, we'll take you all the way to the bridge if you like. I'm sure this is a big misunderstanding, and we'll have you home in your warm, safe bed by night-fall."

Joe's smile dropped to the floor and bounced around on the concrete until lying lifeless and still.

"Why are you doing this, Chief?"

"Because I can." He turned away for a moment, and when his face came back around, his eyes were full of hate and rage. "I'm doing this because I have no proof of who you are! I'm doing this because people from Chicago and Milwaukee have been invading this town for days now, stripping us bare and even killing some of us! Eagle River is a closed town. Nobody gets in and nobody gets out."

Joe pursed his lips together but said nothing.

"It's my job to protect the good people of Eagle River. I owe nothing to you or anyone else who visits. You should have drove around us. We're an island in a war zone, and we have to protect ourselves."

Joe involuntarily took a step back. He thought for a moment. "I'd like to do that now, Chief. I understand your concern, and I'd just like to get back home so I can protect the good people of my county as well."

The Chief's eyes appeared to soften, just a bit.

"You don't have to give me back my badge or even my gun. My partner's probably waiting for me a few miles down the road. Please, just let me walk out of town and you'll never see either of us again. Please."

The Chief moved his left hand up to his chin and stroked it gently in thought.

"As a County Sheriff and fellow Law Enforcement Officer, you are deserving of professional courtesy. I'll let you go, and I'll even give you back your gun and badge. But first I need to verify who you are. When communications are restored, and your story checks out, then I'll send you on your way."

A rush of adrenaline surged through the Sheriff's bloodstream. First he was afraid, then the fear was quickly followed by anger.

"You can't hold me here! The communications may never come back on. It could be years! I haven't done anything! If you keep me here then I want a lawyer! I want to be charged!"

The Chief's face began to turn red, and it didn't stop turning. Joe could see the man's jaw clench and his teeth grind together. When Joe stopped talking, the Chief very calmly said.

"As far as I'm concerned, martial law has been declared. Your civil rights are on hold. The Constitution no longer exists. For the foreseeable future, I am the law. I make the rules. You will stay in that cell until I say you leave. And if you cause any trouble, I'll personally take you to a secluded woods and put a bullet in your head."

He hesitated and then smiled.

"You're not in Kansas anymore, Sheriff. This is my town. Get used to it." And then he turned and walked away.

Joe felt dizzy and light-headed and had to sit down on the bed to keep from falling over. Suddenly, he had the distinct feeling that he would never leave this place alive. He'd made fun of Rodney for believing that society wouldn't recover, that law of the jungle reigned. But now...he wished he'd never gotten out of the truck, Rodney should have run the roadblock. But how could he have known there was a crazy man in charge of an entire town? Ten days ago the Chief would have been committed to a mental hospital, but now he was in charge.

Joe lay down on the bed and curled into the fetal position.

☙ ❧ ❧ ☙

Eagle River - September 17, 2AM

The city jail was easy to find. It was the only building for blocks around with lights. Rodney had already checked out the big, diesel generator in back. It wasn't guarded. In fact, he didn't think anything was guarded. These people were so confident and sure, they had become very lax in their security. Arrogance was a flaw which he had every intention of exploiting.

Several hours ago, just after dark, Rodney had started his long hike in from the cornfield. There were few lights on so finding the lit-up jail had been easy. There was a police cruiser parked in front. He knew it was functioning,because he'd watched it pull up and the police officer walk inside. Rodney crouched down and ran up to the car. He peered inside and saw the keys still dangling in the ignition. He shook his head from side to side in disgust. *Man, these people were stupid.* He opened the door and took the keys and gave them a toss into the bushes nearby. Then he crept around the edge of the building to where the diesel generator blared away. He pulled out his big Leatherman and opened the wire cutters. With one snip the wires were cut and the night became deathly quiet.

Rodney pulled the night vision goggles down over his eyes and lit up the night. He moved right up to the front door and walked in. Once inside, he could hear voices.

"Damn it, Jerry, I thought I told you to refill the diesel generator out there!"

Another man answered. "I did. I think I did anyways. Where's the flashlight? I can't even see my hand in front of my face."

The first man bumped his shin on a desk and yelled in pain.

"There's one out in the cruiser. Let's go fetch it and get the lights back on."

It took both men the better part of a minute to find the door and leave Rodney alone. He stood pressed against the wall as they walked right past him within arm's reach. The old man couldn't help but smile. It would be so easy to kill them both. He quickly moved down the hall all the way to the back. There were only three jail cells, and Joe was sleeping in the last one. Reaching down into the right cargo pocket of his camos, Rodney pulled out the CTS-M-14 thermite grenade and placed it on top of the door lock. Without waking Joe, he lifted up his night vision goggles, pulled the pin and stepped back to a safe distance. Rodney knew from experience that it would reach four thousand degrees Fahrenheit and burn through over a half inch of steel in less than twenty seconds. The show was about to begin.

Sheriff Leif was deep in the bowels of a sadistic nightmare, dreaming that he'd been captured by an evil feudal lord and imprisoned below the keep in his rank dungeon. He was chained to the wall, and festering sores covered his body, oozing out puss and blood. In the dream he had a long beard, suggesting that he'd been there for many years. He was skinny and naked and covered with filth. The stench was unbearable.

As he sat there with his bare back against the stone wall of his cell, the jailer came forward with a torch burning pine pitch. The light was bright and hurt his eyes. They quickly adjusted and he watched as tiny drops of flaming pitch fell to the dirt floor and extinguished. In the light of the licking flames, he saw the face of his tormentor.

"I am the law. You have no rights. Now you will die. I have decreed it."

The Eagle River Chief of Police threw the torch inside his cell onto a pile of blankets and rags. Rats scurried into the corners as the blaze burned higher. The light blinded Joe's eyes, and the heat grew intense. He screamed in his dream, over and over again, all the while pushing himself up against the wall in an effort to escape the heat.

When Sheriff Leif woke up, he heard a man scream, but quickly realized the voice was his own. The moment he opened his eyes, he saw the intense light flashing off the brick wall in front of him. He felt the heat on his back. Then the light quickly ceased and he heard the cell door come open with a metal clank.

"Let's get out of here, Joe."

He turned and saw a man dressed in camo with big goggles over his face. He smiled, knowing that it could only be one man in the world. He quickly jumped up and hugged the old man.

"You came back for me!"

"Shhh, be quiet. They probably already heard you screaming. We got to beat feet out of here before they block the front door. Here, put on these goggles and these black cover-alls. Joe worked fast and soon both men were walking for the front door. Just as they reached it the door burst open and the flashlight beam poured in blinding them both.

"Don't move or we'll shoot!"

Rodney pulled Joe to the side just as bullets sprayed into the space they'd just occupied. They were on the floor now and Rodney reached into his left cargo pants pocket and pulled out two M67 fragmentation grenades.

"It's time to make a new door. Get behind this steel desk. Push over that filing cabinet in front of us."

Joe complied and Rodney tossed the first grenade out the front door. "Better close your eyes and plug your ears." The grenade landed and rolled down the steps before exploding, sending shrapnel across the face of the building. The second M67 landed near the far wall. After exploding, Joe felt the night air come inside and looked over at what used to be a far wall. Rodney unholstered his Colt 1911 and fired several rounds through the front doorway as they jumped up and ran through the hole in the wall.

They were outside now, running to the bushes. It was

pitch black again but with night vision they could see like it was high-noon. They heard voices behind them and the night was filled with a dozen gunshots as the captors fired blindly into their own building. Joe was terrified, but Rodney laughed as he ran. They reached the drainage ditch where the gear was stored, and both of them fell down in a clump. Rodney was breathing in gasps like he'd just finished a marathon run.

"I need a cigarette really bad."

Joe looked back but could no longer see the jail cell. The gunshots were still ringing out in the night.

"Here, put on this backpack and carry this rifle."

Joe looked down at it. "Is this an AR15?"

Rodney scoffed. "Not a chance. What would I do with a sissy gun like that? This here's a full auto M16A1. You got ten thirty-round mags in your pack there."

Joe pushed the goggles back on his head but could see nothing, so he put them back down again.

"Where in the world did you get a Vietnam-era M16? And don't tell me on Ebay because I know better."

Rodney smiled. "I got it in Vietnam of course. I was a supply sergeant my last six months in-country. I got a lot of stuff like this. Yup, it's old, but I took good care of it. It fires almost every time."

Rodney jumped up and started moving again.

All Joe could think was *Almost every time?*

❧ ❧ ❧

Four hours later they were back inside the F-250 and touring down the road at ninety-five miles an hour. Sheriff Leif looked over at the speedometer and frowned.

"Can't this thing go any faster than this?"

Rodney pushed down on the gas pedal. They stopped for nothing, and four hours later they rolled to a stop in Rodney's driveway.

Moses jumped up and ran out to greet them, barking all the way. Joe looked over to Rodney and said.

"Okay, that trip was educational."

Rodney smiled and lit up a cigarette. He looked up at the clear, blue sky before releasing the smoke from his lungs.

"Yes, I found it…invigorating."

Joe looked at him with questioning eyes.

"Doesn't it bother you in the least that we may have killed or injured some police officers back there?"

Rodney took a puff off his cigarette and then flicked off the ashes. "Well, if you're asking me if I feel any remorse, then, yes, sure. I feel bad about it." He thought for a moment, then knelt down to pet Moses. "But I'll tell you what bothers me more. We drove into Wisconsin to help my nephew, and you were beaten, arrested, and thrown in jail without due process. Your God-given rights were taken away, not by thugs, or gang members or bullies, but by people who used to uphold the law."

Rodney threw his cigarette down and ground it into the dirt with his boot. "I like you, Joe, but you best reach around and pull yer head outta yer ass and smell what's going on in the world. Things are different. Things have changed. This is a whole, new world, and yer gonna have to choose sides. Yer gonna have to ante up and take a stand for what's right."

Rodney started to walk away, but then stopped and turned around again. He pointed his finger at Joe and started to shake it fiercely. "When cops turn bad, their life is forfeit. And that's the way it should be. This is not anything new. The rule of law has collapsed before. Sometimes the good guys turn bad. Sometimes the strong oppress the weak. There's nothing new here. The only big question to answer isn't how I *feel* about it, but what am I going to *do* about it!"

Sheriff Leif let him walk away. He stood there stunned. He couldn't believe he was hearing these words from his friend. But then he thought about it as he walked to his car and started to drive away. He remembered the hateful look on the face of the Eagle River Chief of Police. He'd seen that look before, but it had always been on the face of a crack-head or a drunk or an armed robber...one of the bad guys. But he'd never seen that much hate and arrogance in a law enforcement officer. It was like the world had gone collective crazy, like the thin veneer of civilization had been stripped away leaving the basest traits that humanity had to offer.

As Joe drove home to his wife and kids. he couldn't help but wonder. *What is going to happen to us? What life have we left my kids?* The Sheriff thought about it long and hard, but in his heart, he knew that Rodney was right, at least most of what he'd said. And the one thing kept coming back to him over and over and over again.

The only big question to answer isn't how I *feel* about it, but what am I going to *do* about it!

He thought about it all the way home, trying desperately to form an answer to the impossible question.

CHAPTER 19

The Great White Invasion - October 25, 6PM

IT had been over a month since Dan had coasted back into the cabin driveway, beaten, bruised and battered. Jackie had nursed him back to health, but they hadn't really formed a friendship. Dan avoided talking to her whenever he could. Neither Jeremy nor Jackie understood the way he ignored her. They had even discussed it once while Dan was out taking a walk, but came to no conclusions.

"Okay, Dad, I got the last of it loaded into the truck. Anything else you want me to do?"

Dan walked past him and continued on into the cabin. "I'll get that heavy nylon tarp, then we can cover everything up. No sense taking any chances with the weather. Looks like it might rain tonight."

Despite the rocky start at the cabin, with Dan killing three men, then Jackie's husband's death and Dan's injuries, they had neither heard nor seen another human in over a month. Apparently, Jackie's dead husband had chosen the hideaway site well. They were a long way's off the road, and more than fifty miles away from a town of any size. Just to be sure, Dan had instructed Jeremy to camouflage the end of the drive with brush and to cut down the mail box. Dan came back with the tarp, and the father and son spread it out over the truck bed and tied it down.

Jackie watched the two men from inside the cabin, holding her little baby, wondering whether she was doing the right thing. They had invited her to come along, and Jeremy had insisted when she'd balked. The boy was turning out to be quite a sweetheart, and they had become good friends. He was very good with baby Donna as well, changing her diapers, holding her so she could rest, and whatever else was needed. From what he'd told her of his past, Jeremy had become a much better person after the lights went out.

But his father...she didn't know about him. He was such a stoic, always frowning at her, seldom talking at all. For some strange reason, Dan Branch both aggravated and intrigued her.

She looked down at the baby and smiled, then looked back out the window. She caught Jeremy grinning at her as he waved.

Once the truck was all set, they came in and sat down at the table for a dinner of canned beef, canned green beans and biscuits. As usual, Dan said nothing.

"Good biscuits, Jackie."

Jackie smiled, then looked over at Dan. He saw her staring as if she expected him to say something. Dan just grunted and went back to his meal. He thought about her as he ate. *That woman is always looking at me. She hates me. I know she does. I don't blame her either. I killed her husband. One night she'll slit my throat while I sleep.* That's what he was thinking, but he said something completely different. "Yes, the biscuits are good. Thank you."

She nodded and took a bite of her food. The fading light from outside filtered in through the window, lending an elegant shine to her jet-black Lebanese hair. Dan noticed how it cascaded over her petite shoulders and on down to her chest. He didn't hate the woman, but everytime he looked at her, he was reminded of her dead husband, the man he'd wrongly shot. Jackie made him cringe, and filled him with guilt.

"What's that stuff on your hair, Jackie?"

She smiled and looked over to Jeremy. It's scented olive oil. Don had it imported from Lebanon. I like it because it reminds me of my homeland"

Jeremy nodded while he shoveled on another fork-full of beef. "Cool. I like it. It smells nice." He looked over at Dan. "It sure smells nice. Right Dad?"

Dan looked up from his food, and hesitated before responding. "Yes. It smells nice."

Jackie narrowed her eyes, wondering to herself, *why does this man hate me so? I've done nothing wrong to him.* The baby started to cry, so she pushed her chair back and went to the other side of the room to feed her. Dan turned his head away as she bared her breast, and the baby latched on.

"That's pretty cool the way you do that, Jackie. Without your breasts Donna would probably die."

Jackie smiled. "It's the old-fashioned way, but I suspect all babies will be breast-fed from now on or not at all." She looked over and saw that Dan had turned his chair slightly to face the other wall. She thought for a moment before speaking with a waver in her voice. "Is there anything else I need to get ready before we go to bed tonight, Dan?"

Dan answered without looking over in her direction. For some reason, he always felt very uncomfortable when she fed the baby. He didn't understand it, because it seemed like the most natural thing in the world. "No. I think we've got it all covered. We should probably get to bed early though, so we get good sleep and an early start at first light."

Jackie reached down and softly stroked Donna's black hair as she nursed. Her hair was black and coarse, but not kinky. The baby's skin was dark, but had an olive hue to it.

Everyone finished eating, then Jackie and Jeremy did the dishes while Dan cleaned his gun. For the past week, ever since Dan had been able to move around, he'd been teaching Jeremy how to shoot a long gun and a pistol. Fortunately, the boy turned out to have a natural talent for it. Once the dishes were done, Dan spread his sleeping bag out on the couch and crawled down inside it. Jeremy spread his bedding out on the floor a few feet away, while Jackie took the bed with the baby inside a box beside her.

The cabin was all one, big room, and Dan hated the close proximity to Jackie and her baby. Dan pulled the sleeping bag over his head and rolled over away from her direction.

No, he didn't hate her, but he didn't like her either. In fact, just looking at her made him furious. That fact aggravated him, because he didn't understand it and couldn't control it.

Once snuggled in bed, Jackie opened up her Bible and read to herself Psalms chapter 46 by the light of an oil lamp. Then she contemplated the first few verses.

> *1 God is our refuge and strength,*
> *A very present help in trouble.*
> *2 Therefore we will not fear, though the earth*
> *should change And though the mountains slip*
> *into the heart of the sea;*
> *3 Though its waters roar and foam, Though the*
> *mountains quake at its swelling pride.*

It had long been one of her favorite passages. It calmed her, reassured her, reminded her that no matter what happened to her, God would be there, even in the face of oppression, pain of loss and hopeless odds. God would be there, and she would claim any promise He was willing to offer her. Ever since Don had died, she'd spent more time reading the Bible and praying. She'd even read some with Jeremy, and the boy seemed genuinely interested in God.

Jackie didn't realize it, but she looked stunningly beautiful in the faint lamp light. She slowly closed the Bible, followed by her eyes, as she prayed softly to herself so no one else could hear.

"Dear God. You are my refuge and my strength. Please protect me and protect my baby." Then she blew out the oil lamp and rolled over in the cold, lonely bed.

A few yards away, Dan Branch peeked out from beneath the sleeping bag, watching her every move. And he wondered to himself, *Why do I hate her?* And then, *Why ...* But he never finished the thought.

He rolled over and fell asleep, cursing all women under his breath, and cursing himself for what he was feeling.

Dan woke up first at 6AM and dressed himself quietly in the dark, pulling on his boots last of all and then walking outside. He was shocked to see nothing but white. The wind was howling through the trees with the snow blowing almost parallel to the ground. It was coming down so hard and fast that he couldn't even see the truck parked thirty feet from the porch. He stepped off the wooden planking and sunk to his knees in cold, wet snow. He cursed out loud. Then he stepped back up on the porch and waited there for five minutes, getting a feel for the storm and calming himself down. He thought to himself, *Even if we make it out to the main road, we'll never make it home.*

With stooped shoulders weighted down like lead, he opened the door and walked back inside, leaving the cold and wind to do its worst.

"But this won't last for very long, will it, Dad?"

Dan moved the oatmeal around in his bowl without looking up. He didn't answer.

"Dad?"

Dan glanced up as if hearing his voice for the first time that morning. "What?"

Jeremy looked over at Jackie and then back to his father again. "I said, this isn't going to last for very long is it?"

Dan grunted. "I don't know, son. Probably not. This is a pretty early snow, even for this far north. We'll need a warm front to melt it off though, since there won't be any snowplows to clear off the roads."

Jackie broke her silence for the first time that evening. "But what if it doesn't melt? What if we're stuck here all winter long? We don't have enough food to eat, and we don't have enough wood to burn for heat. Winters are real long up here."

Dan was quiet as Jeremy looked over expectantly to his father, waiting for an answer. Finally Dan folded his hands together and placed them under his chin before responding.

"Well, I guess we have to plan for the worst. I wasn't expecting this to happen, but now we have to deal with it." He ran his fingers through his greasy, blonde hair before finishing. With no hot and cold running water, he only washed his hair and bathed every other day. The Branch family had always been gifted with greasy skin and hair.

"Let's wait a few days to see what happens. If it warms up and thaws off, then we'll plan on heading back to Michigan before the next storm hits. If it stays cold, then Jeremy and I will cut wood with that old handsaw and axe in the shed out back. It'll be hard work, but it has to be done or we'll freeze to death."

Jeremy interrupted him. "What about food, Dad?"

Dan nodded. "Not a big problem. There's that stream a ways off where you and I first camped. It leads to a pond where we can fish. There's also plenty of game here, rabbit, deer, and whatever else we can shoot. A couple of deer, and we should be set for food until spring. We can supplement it with the grain and the canned goods and all the other food that…" Dan hesitated a moment before continuing. He swallowed hard. "With all the other food that Don and Jackie stockpiled here. We'll be a lot better off than most people this winter."

Jackie nodded and looked down at her baby and chanted

her silent mantra *God is our refuge and strength, a very present help in time of trouble.* She repeated it over and over and over again, as if the words held power and could save her and her baby. Inside, she cried, but she swore that no one would ever know her tears.

❧ ❧ ❧

A Day of Risks - November 18, 6PM

It had taken almost four weeks of back-breaking, bone-chilling work, but the wood was cut, split and stacked all around the cabin. There was a large, White-tailed doe hanging in the pine tree beside the cabin as well. Dan had put it up twenty feet to keep it away from any wildlife that might take an interest. The snow had not stopped, in fact, it had intensified, and, after a few days, Dan realized that winter was here to stay.

"I'm going to attack Madagascar from South Africa, and I'll be rolling three dice."

Dan looked up and his mouth fell open. "Are you nuts, son. I outnumber you four to one! You're going to lose!"

Jackie looked over at the "Risk" board game of military conquest and smiled. She loved watching them both play. She enjoyed witnessing their tantrums, their testosterone-fogged displays of manliness that served only to jade their tactical decisions. Jeremy was extremely aggressive, attacking in a kamikaze-like rage that sometimes worked, but always left his father frustrated and sometimes angry at his wanton display of foolish aggression. Dan's style of play was more calculating, like a chess player he thought out every move, always having a mission, an objective, always attacking at the right time and defending when needed. He was a very good tactician. But he had one weakness. Dan was predictable.

"I think he can take you, Dan."

Dan ignored her, but Jackie continued. "Let's face it, Dan.

You're a lousy roller and Jeremy is lucky. You don't have a chance."

Dan looked over at her. She was nursing the baby again, right there in front of him. The baby's eyes looked over at him, mocking him as she suckled. All Dan could think was *Breast feeding really sucks!* He had begun to talk to Jackie a little more over the last few weeks as if he'd become desensitized to her presence. Because, let's face it, the cabin was small and it was cold outside. She was always there, every place he turned, so he had been forced to deal with her and his own feelings.

"I suppose you think you could beat me too?"

Jackie smiled tauntingly. "In a heartbeat, old man!"

Dan grated his teeth together and pursed his lips tightly. "I'm not an old man. I'm only 34."Jackie and Jeremy both laughed out loud. "Well, you're the oldest man for miles around as far as we know." Jeremy agreed by nodding his head up and down.

Dan thought for a moment, trying to regain his composure. *Why did he hate this woman?*

"Okay, Jeremy, let's clear the board and start over, and we'll see if General Jackie is all talk or whether or not she can run with the big dogs."

Jackie smiled and whispered softly, "Woof! Woof! Bring it on, farmboy."

They quickly set up the game and began to play as the wind and snow raged on all around them. The fireplace glowed with red-hot coals and gave off extra light to help out the two oil lamps on the table beside them. Dan quickly conquered Australia and began collecting two extra armies per turn. He then used Australia as a launching pad for his military offensive. But something strange happened. Jackie fell back, absorbing his attacks, slowing his offensive, and then Jeremy countered with his usual and customary kamikaze attacks to his flank. Dan destroyed his son's armies, leaving him all but defenseless. He planned on finishing him off the next turn, but Jackie handed in a match and used the extra armies to drive him back into Australia. Dan, who had never lost at "Risk" before, was now fighting for his life.

And every time Jackie attacked him...she smiled.

Two hours later, Jackie made her final roll and won the game. Dan was both shocked and impressed.

"How did you do that? I've never lost before."

Jackie smiled slyly. "What a coincidence, neither have I."

"I can't believe that, Dad. You got beat by a girl!"

Dan's eyes flashed angrily. "Oh shut up, son. She beat you first."

"Yeah, well, she beat you second. This girl is good!"

Then Dan looked over at her, his face taking on a grave look. "Seriously, Jackie, how did you do that?"

She thought for a moment. She so much wanted to bring him down to size, but figured he'd already suffered enough.

"I'm from the Mideast. War is in our blood, in our genes. It just comes natural to me."

Dan accepted her explanation with a nod of his head. "Okay, makes sense. I'm really impressed."

But Jeremy wouldn't let it go as he howled out loudly. "My Dad, the mighty Marine, vanquished by a Lebanese, breast-feeding Mommy!"

Dan's face clouded over again, as he slid back his chair with a screech on the wooden planking. "I need to get some fresh air."

As he walked out the door, Dan pulled on a wool coat. He didn't like wearing it, but Jackie had offered it to him. Since he'd brought no winter clothing, he'd had no real choice but to accept it. Dan wore the same size as her now-dead husband, but he didn't feel right wearing the clothes of a man he'd killed.

As the door shut behind him, he walked over to the edge of the porch and leaned against the four-by-four column and looked up at the full moon. His breath steamed out, billowed, and then was carried away by the icy-cold breeze. The snow had stopped and the wind had died down right after night fall as it often did. Dan felt the ice seep down into his eyes and his bones. He thought about his Uncle Rodney, wondering if he would ever make it back there. He thought about everything that had happened in the last three months, amazed that his life could turn so quickly and so radically. Dan sucked in the ice-cold air and held it in his lungs for a moment before letting it out. Closing his eyes, he tried desperately to get a handle on all his conflicting emotions, but he just couldn't sort them all out.

Just then the door swung open with a creak and Jackie walked over to him, the snow screeching underneath her boots. She stopped beside him and looked up at the moon.

"It's pretty tonight."

Dan nodded uneasily.

"I needed some fresh air too. I love Donna, but sometimes I just need to get out of the room. It's like I'm on duty with her twenty-four seven and it wears me out."

Dan said nothing and, as usual, it drove Jackie crazy. She glanced over at her husband's grave. There was a four-feet high wooden cross jutting up through the snow. She knew his body was down there in the frozen ground. *How long had it been? Only two months? It seemed like years.*

"Jeremy told me about his mother, Debbie, your wife. I'm sorry it all happened the way it did." Dan looked up into the moon, but said nothing. "It must be painful...and confusing for you."

Dan nodded. "It is what it is."

Jackie laughed softly and pulled the lapels of her coat together to block out the cold.

"What's so funny?"

"It's you, Dan. It's you. You're so stoic, so tough all the time, never letting anything out. Never talking. Always pretending like nothing phases you, like you're superman or something."

A hint of a smile turned up on the left side of his mouth.

"No, I'm not superman."

"No?"

"Of course not. Superman would've kicked your butt in Risk."

Jackie smiled.

"Dan Branch, was that humor coming out of your mouth?"

But Dan didn't answer, so she quickly changed the subject. She pointed out to the woods as she talked. "So, what do you think is happening out there, beyond the woods, in the big cities I mean?"

Dan thought for a moment. He looked down at his boot and kicked some packed snow off the porch and into a drift. "Millions of people are dying. They're starving. They're freezing. They're dying of sicknesses that used to be cured with a doctor's appointment."

Jackie nodded. "I know you're right. How many do you think will die?"

Dan shrugged his woolen-covered shoulders. "I don't know, maybe seventy percent the first winter."

Jackie's eyes narrowed. "That many?"

"It's not just the cold and hunger and sickness. There's also people being murdered out there wholesale. The weak are being slaughtered by the strong to acquire what they have. The strong will survive and the weak will die. Our society has always been an artificial one, unsustainable over the long haul. Sooner or later it had to come to this."

Jackie looked over at the side of his face. "Why do you say it was inevitable?"

Dan looked back at her and their eyes met. "Because people are selfish, and they can always be counted on to do what's in their own best interest. I don't know how the lights went out, and maybe we never will know, but I can bet you one thing: it probably had something to do with greed and power."

For a moment, Jackie could say nothing, then she surprised him. "You've just talked more to me in the last two minutes than you have since we met."

Dan shifted his feet uncomfortably on the snow-covered wooden planking. "I - I don't know what to say to that."

Jackie laughed, her eyes shining like obsidian in the moonlight. "That's because you're a man, Dan Branch. And real men don't *talk* - they *do*."

Dan looked off over to the right, away from her. She felt him slipping away, so she talked fast before he left completely.

"I want you to know that I don't blame you for my husband's death. Sure, yeah, I did at first, but I'm over that now and we have to move on without it. You and I are going to be trapped together in that little cabin for the next four months, so we need to talk to each other or I'll go stir crazy." She paused. "So…can you please tell me…why do you hate me so much?"

Dan shifted his legs so the left was now over the right as he leaned against the column. He wasn't expecting the direct approach. "I didn't know you could tell."

She smiled softly. "Dan, I'm a woman. Of course I can tell."

The moon looked down on them both, wondering how long it would take them to get it all out in the open. He was in no hurry. The moon had all night.

"I don't hate you. I don't think. But I don't like being around you. Makes me feel uncomfortable. You remind me of my wife." He kicked the toe of his boot into the porch again.

She seemed surprised. "Really? May I ask why?"

Dan hesitated, unsure of himself. "Because you cheated on your husband, so I identify with him."

Blood rushed up to fill Jackie's face and she slumped over the railing as her head filled with dizziness.

"I - I." But she couldn't finish her words. Tears filled her eyes and ran down her cheeks unopposed. Then her nose began to run. She turned off to the side, so he wouldn't see the unladylike display.

Suddenly, Dan felt like a jerk.

She sniffed a few times and then wiped her nose on her sleeve. Dan turned away to give her privacy.

"I suppose I deserved that…and more."

Dan said nothing. He just let her talk.

"Don was a good husband. He provided well, and he was very kind to everyone. He deserved better than me."

The anger that welled up in Dan confused him, but he seemed helpless to stop it.

"So if he didn't deserve it, then why did you do it to him? What would possess a woman to do that to a man who was good to her?"

Jackie said nothing at first. She'd been asking herself the same question for almost a year now. *Why did I do it? Why did I betray the only man who ever loved me?* When she answered him, she surprised even herself with the sudden clarity of her response.

"Because in a moment of passion, I acted out of the weakest part of my character."

She continued to sob, but quieter now.

"So what does that exactly mean? You only did it once? It surprised you? The devil made you do it?"

Jackie steeled her resolve and turned off her tears. Dan noticed the change and was intrigued by it.

"No one made me do it. *I* did it. I'm responsible for it. I hurt the man I love. He was good to me, and I betrayed him. I have no defense, and I accept full responsibility."

She started to cry again. "There! I'm a bad person! Are you happy now? I deserve to be disrespected and abused. I know that and … I welcome the pain."

Dan's eyes squinted together as he looked at her in wonder. "Are you serious? You really feel this way?"

Jackie nodded, but couldn't speak through the tears. Dan grunted and kicked some snow off the porch into the drift.

"Heck, I guess you're nothing like my wife then. She laid with lots of men, and never felt bad about it. I don't think guilt was in her." Dan looked out at the blowing snow. "No, you're not like her. Truth is, if she'd been more like you, I would have forgiven her and we could've moved on and made a happy family."

Dan's voice wavered in the cold. "But she wasn't like you. She felt no remorse."

Suddenly, Jackie stopped feeling sorry for herself and focused on the man beside her.

"I'm sorry, Dan. I know you're a good man. I can tell by watching you, and by things that Jeremy says. You didn't deserve what she did, and I hope you know it wasn't your fault." She stopped for a moment to think, then went on. "Sometimes people just do bad things. I did a bad thing. I take responsibility for it, and now I have to live with what I've done."

Dan looked over at her, but his attitude had suddenly changed. His anger had faded, and been replaced with a small measure of respect.

"God will forgive you for it. He always does." He hesitated for a moment. "All of us need a little forgiveness right about now. At least you didn't kill anyone."

Jackie raised her head up and looked over at him. Their eyes met. Dan pointed to her nose and said. "You're dripping." She turned away to clean it off, then turned back again.

"It wasn't personal, Dan, what your wife did. She was broken inside."

Dan nodded. "I know that. Doesn't make it any easier though. I'll get over it."

Suddenly, she wanted to rush over and hold him, like she was holding a child just fallen and skinned on the playground. But…she couldn't. So she just nodded. Then he surprised her.

"I want you to know that I respect you for being honest

with me, and for your heart. You have a pretty heart. Our God is a God of second chances."

The twinkle began to come back in her eyes.

"Thank you, Dan."

"You're welcome. Like you said, we've got to get along in the cabin all winter long, so we best be honest with each other from the get-go."

Jackie looked out at the snow. "Isn't it odd how you can start a conversation, or a day, or anything, really, with one perception, like, *this day sure sucks*, and then, in a flash, with just a few words, the whole thing can go from blackness to light, from sadness to something so much better."

Dan hacked up some phlegm and spit off to one side. Jackie grimaced.

"Oh, I don't know. You're making me nervous now."

A soft smile traced Jackie's lips. "Nervous? Why? I'm the one who just went to confessional."

Dan smiled softly himself.

"All women make me nervous. Especially…women that look like you do."

Jackie thought for a moment, trying to decipher his words. And then it dawned on her, and she was surprised. "Dan Branch, do you think I'm attractive?"

Dan turned and looked at her angrily. "No, of course not! You shouldn't say stuff like that."

She smiled again. "Then what kind of woman do I look like that makes you so nervous?"

Dan turned and spit again to his right into a bank of snow. "You're not entirely ugly."

Jackie looked over at her husband's grave and then back at Dan. *This is too weird for me.* Dan seemed to read her mind.

"Anyways, we shouldn't be talking about it since my wife just died and your husband too, and he's lying right over there underneath that tree, probably listening to every word we're saying."

Jackie nodded. "Yeah. I suppose you're right. It's still grieving time for me and for you too. But…" She looked out at the pure, white snow, sparkling like diamonds in the night. "If I don't have some adult conversation for the next four months I'll go totally crazy. I'll make a deal with you."

Dan looked over uncomfortably. "What deal?"

"If you promise to try and talk to me more, then I'll promise to start looking less attractive."

Dan looked down at the snow, trying and failing to stifle a smile. "Well, now, I guess that's an offer I just can't refuse."

The baby started crying, and Jackie turned and walked back inside without saying another word. Dan was getting cold, but he didn't want to go back in yet. He still had some analyzing to do. Inside, the baby quieted down, and he could hear Jeremy talking to her. He wondered what they were saying. He thought about his dead wife, how she'd cheated on him so consistently, how she'd killed herself. He thought about the nine men he'd killed, knowing that he might be required to kill again. Dan thought about the condition of his heart. He knew, deep down inside that he was changing, that things like that couldn't happen to a man and not change him, either for the better or for the worse. And he wondered…*what is happening to me. Am I getting better, or am I getting worse?* And then it occurred to him. *Maybe I'll ask Jackie.*

The man part of Dan was confused. *Why do I feel so close to her now? Where did my anger go?*

After one, last look at the moon, he whispered out loud to no one in particular. "And I'm not getting old!"

Dan Branch trudged clumsily back inside the warm cabin. But outside on the porch, the moon kept glowing down on the new-fallen snow, making it shine, making it glisten. In the cities, hundreds of miles away, the snow covered the corpses while a different moon shown down. But here…out here …away from it all, the night was beautiful and pure.

CHAPTER 20

"I don't know, Joe, aren't most people alone these days?" Rodney crushed out the cigarette on the snowy porch with his boot before blowing the cloud of smoke up and away from the Sheriff who stood beside him.

"I suppose so, but I wanted to stop by and invite you over for Christmas dinner anyways. I know Marge and the kids would like seeing you. This is a holy day, ya know."

Rodney gazed out at the treeline as if looking for something. Joe Leif saw him staring and followed his gaze on out to the woods. "Still no word from the boy?"

The old man shook his head from side to side. "No way he'd let himself get caught out in this winter, especially if he had the young one with him. He's still comin' though. He'll make his move after the thaw."

Joe nodded. "So you think he went north or south?"

Rodney laughed. "That boy's too smart to go anywhere near Chicago right now. He went through the U.P. Probably still holed up somewhere." He spit off to one side into the deep snowbank. "He'll be here in Spring."

The Sheriff no longer wore his uniform, except on official business, and he only drove his police cruiser when he had to. Today he was dressed in insulated coveralls and riding a snowmobile to conserve gasoline. He always pulled a small sled for hauling things and people through the snow as well. In the Spring he would be on a quad or a horse, depending on the petroleum situation. Joe hesitated for a moment before attending to official Iroquois County business. Then he just spit it out.

"So, what kind of talk are you hearing on the Ham Radio?"

Rodney chuckled to himself. "I wondered how long it'd take you to ask that."

Joe smiled. "Just doing my job. Well, and I can't help but be curious myself about it. You hear anything from the major cities?"

The old man brushed a six-inch layer of snow off the porch railing and then leaned his forearms down on top of it. "Not a word, Joe. I gotta tell you though, only an idiot would be broadcasting from inside the cities right now. Anyone with a Ham radio would have to have one big-assed antennae, and that's a dead giveaway. Most Hams were smart enough to get out the first few days."

"So you've heard nothing?"

Rodney pulled a Marlboro red hard pack out of his breast pocket and shook out another cigarette. He offered another one to Joe, but the Sheriff shook his head. "I didn't say that."

Joe waited patiently as the old man took out his Zippo and lit up. Then he asked again. "So, what'd you hear?"

"Talked to a guy near Jackson a few days ago. He saw about two hundred inmates moving down I-94 west towards Kazoo. They were raping, killing and eating everything in their path. They were organized and extremely effective."

Upon hearing this, Joe brushed away more snow off the railing and leaned down closer to the old man. "So, do you think we have enough posse to take them out?"

Rodney looked over at him and laughed. "Why in the world do you keep calling them the posse? Ya know darn well they're the militia! We've organized and trained four hundred citizens to defend this county and you insist on calling them posse."

Joe smiled. "Well, technically they are posse. I swore them all in as deputies just like I did with you. What difference does it make?"

"Well, none, I suppose, at least on a practical level. I just think you still got that political correct bug up yer ass that says the word "militia" is a bad thing."

Joe couldn't deny it, so he redirected the conversation. "You never answered my question. Can we take them?"

More smoke exhaled and was carried away on the sub-zero breeze. "Yer darn right we can take 'em. We can take on a thousand guys like that."

Joe smiled, reassured by the assessment.

"But those inmates from Jackson Prison are the least of our worries, Sheriff. I doubt they'll even make it this far north. It's too hard to keep that many scum in line for more than a few months. I doubt they'll go any farther than Grand Rapids. Then they'll run into some rival gang, maybe bigger and meaner, then they'll fall apart or mutate into something else altogether."

The old man stopped talking, and Joe was forced to wait while Rodney took his sweet time organizing his thoughts. A bright, red Cardinal landed on a tree branch a few yards away. Joe watched it for a moment until Rodney continued.

"Remember when I told you about Dearborn last fall?"

"Joe nodded.

"Well, word on the airwaves is they got organized. They were pretty smart about it too. They got themselves armed to the teeth, then they took over all the warehouses in the Detroit area. They got supplies up the wing wong, and they're giving food to anyone who converts to Islam."

The Cardinal hopped off the branch down to a rock where Rodney had spread some seed and began feeding.

"So why is that such a bad thing? No more anarchy, and people who need food are getting it in an organized fashion. I got no problem with that. It could be a lot worse you know."

Rodney took one last drag off his cigarette and then threw it down on the porch before grinding it out with his boot. "You need to read up some on Islam, my friend. It's not the religion of peace that the old media used to tout. Islam in its truest form has always been a religion of conquest, almost from its inception."

Joe questioned him further. "How so?"

"Read the history. It's in their own book. You don't understand radical Islam. It was founded by one man, a man with self-serving interests, and he spread his power and influence by conquering others. Muhammad claimed to be God's prophet, therefore, anything he said was considered equal to that of God. Did you know that Muhammad had 23 wives and concubines? One time he wanted to marry the wife of his step-son, something that was forbidden by Islamic law, so he simply claimed to have received a revelation from Allah that it was now lawful for him to take her as his wife. His step-son, who was a good Muslim, wanted to please the prophet, so he immediately divorced his wife so Muhammad could bed her. On another time, Muhammad, the great prophet of Allah, married a 6-year old girl, then consummated that marriage when she was only 9 years old. Joe, you need to understand Islam for what it really is. Allah is not the god of Judaism and Christianity. He is not the god of love and tolerance."

Rodney looked out at the treeline again, scanning it for any movement. "Nope, he ain't full of love. He ain't Santa Claus. But he sure is comin' to town."

Joe didn't speak for almost a full minute. He just soaked it all in, not wanting to believe it. "But what about the government? They can't do anything once the state or the feds get up and running again."

Rodney laughed out loud. "Pie in the sky thinking, my friend. Pie in the sky."

The Sheriff zipped up his coveralls to ward off the chill he was feeling. "God almighty, I hope you're wrong about this."

The old man nodded his head. "Yeah, me too. I got a bad feelin' though that I ain't." Then he looked over at Joe and their eyes met. "We need to meet with the other Sheriff's around us and form an alliance. It's the only way we can be strong enough to fight them all off. Right now we're a lone wolf, and a wolf all by himself can't survive. He needs the pack to hunt and thrive."

Joe shoved his hands down into his pockets and let them warm for a few seconds. "This is a heck of a thing to be talking about on Christmas."

Rodney smiled and then burst out laughing altogether.

"Hey, I almost forgot. I got presents for you."

Joe smiled and shook his head. "I didn't get anything for you, Rodney. To tell you the truth, I didn't even think about it."

Rodney stepped inside the door and then walked back out with an olive drab ammo can. There was a red bow tied around the handle. "It's 500 rounds for your Glock."

Joe laughed and his eyes got moist. Rodney stepped back in the house and reappeared with a case of MREs with a smaller gift-wrapped box on top of it.

"The MRE's are for your whole family. There's a lot of good stuff in there. This here box is a thousand rounds of 22 caliber for your son."

He stepped back inside and reappeared one more time with a duffel bag. He dropped it down on the porch with a thud. "It's full of canvas, denim, and cotton for Marge. I know she sews, and this stuff will make some pretty sturdy clothes for all of you." Then he laughed. "And from what I can see you lost a bunch of weight and need some new trousers."

The Sheriff stepped over and hugged the old man. Rodney's arms remained at his side for several seconds, then he reached up and grudgingly returned his friend's hug. Finally, he said. "Hey, Sheriff. Break it up. I don't want the neighbors to get the wrong idea."

Joe laughed and stepped back. "You don't have any neighbors, Rodney." They both loaded the presents onto the snowmobile sled, and then Joe put on his helmet and waved as he fired it up and drove away through the snow.

Rodney stood in the snow, with the ice-cold wind blowing straight through his old bones. He raised his hand and gave a slight wave. He mouthed the words "Merry Christmas" before walking back inside to sit by the fire and finish cleaning his shotgun.

Christmas - December 25, 9AM

"Merry Christmas, Jackie."

Dan Branch led the beautiful, Lebanese woman by the hand out to the porch. She was blindfolded, and when they stopped on the snow-covered planking, Dan reached behind her to remove the dish towel from her eyes.

When she looked out at the bright snow, it took several seconds for her eyes to adjust to the brightness. Then she saw it, and gasped out loud, reaching up with her hands and covering her mouth. "Oh Dan! It's beautiful!"

There, in the snow in front of her was a shoveled path that led from the front porch all the way out to her dead husband's grave. The walls of the path had been carved through five-feet-high drifts. Jackie stepped down off the porch and into the path. She could barely see over the top of it.

"Dan, it must have taken you hours to do this!" Dan stepped down beside her and was surprised when she threw her arms around him, hugging his chest. Her face brushed against his cheek, and he shivered when he felt her skin and smelled the scented oil in her hair.

"So you like it?"

She smiled and he could see tears running down her cheeks. "Like it? I love it! It's the best gift I could ever have." She brushed the tears away. "Sorry, I didn't mean to do that in front of you."

Dan cocked his head to one side and took a step back away from her closeness. Still, even after a month of talking to each other about personal things, she made Dan shiver whenever they were close. Deep down inside, he wished she felt the same way. He thought it odd that he could feel that way just over three months after his wife's death. He still loved Debbie, and he knew Jackie still loved Don, but... their love was different. Jackie had so many fond memories of Don, and she talked about them often. Dan listened to her almost every day. Sometimes she cried; other times she managed to hold it back. But there was always a twinkle in her eyes when she spoke of her husband. It wasn't that way for Dan. When he thought of Debbie, there was always pain, regret, and remorse, always thoughts of her other lovers, and the image of her kissing the man from Eau Claire, and sleeping in his bed. It was different, much different, and Dan envied Jackie the feelings and memories she treasured. Yes, he envied her pain.

"Come walk with me."

Dan seemed surprised when she reached back her mittened hand and grabbed onto his own. He hesitated, so she pulled him along as they walked out to the grave. Dan stumbled along behind her, feeling like he was intruding into another man's bedroom. It felt awkward.

" I so much wanted to come out here and visit him, but the drifts just got too big for me. It must have taken you forever to dig this out."

In truth, Dan had been digging all night long as she slept. It was the only way he could surprise her. After all, the four of them lived together in a small cube, so there were no secrets.

"Did Jeremy help you?"

178

"No. He was sleeping."

She stopped and turned around. Dan almost bumped into her. "You were out here all night long digging in the dark? For me?"

Dan smiled and the shivers started to overwhelm him. "It's only because I feel sorry for you. It's your ugliness. I did it out of pity."

She immediately pushed him down in the snow, then jumped on top of him, smearing a handful of cold powder in his face. Dan screamed and then laughed. He rolled over and pinned her down in the snow in a perfect wrestling reversal. Their faces moved closer together; their breath came out in steamy puffs, mingling, rising, and rolling away as one.

Dan looked into her dark eyes. She looked back. Their smiles faded, slowly at first, then abruptly. Her hair had fallen out of her stocking hat and cascaded out onto the white snow, lending the perfect black and white contrast. Dan felt his heart beating like the engine of a race car. Then he saw her lips form into a frown.

Dan mouthed the words "I'm sorry. I didn't mean to…" He rolled off of her and onto his back in the snow. She remained there beside him, looking up at the white overcast of the winter sky. Jackie reached over and grabbed his hand again. This time her mitten was gone, and she removed his leather glove, gripping her fingers into his palm and squeezing tight.

"I mean it, Dan. This is special to me."

Dan nodded his head in the snow.

"I know. That's why I did it. I feel like I know you now."

Jackie rolled over onto her side, placing her right hand onto Dan's chest. She gazed down into his eyes. He loved her perfect olive skin. "What are we going to do, Dan?"

He lifted his head and rolled over to face her.

"I don't know, Jackie. But it's ten below zero out here and I feel like I'm burning up inside."

Jackie moved closer and kissed him lightly on the lips. It

was a brief kiss, a loving kiss, but he could still feel the heat of her passion through it. "I'm burning up too, Dan."

She repeated the question. "What are we going to do?"

He thought for a moment, then he blurted out the craziest idea that came to his mind. "Let's go ask Don."

Jackie's eyes narrowed for a moment, then they brightened. "That's crazy!"

She jumped up and pulled him to his feet, then dragged him stumbling behind her all the way to her husband's grave. When they both stopped, Jackie looked over at him and beckoned for Dan to start.

"No way! I'm not going to start. He's your husband!"

She smiled back. "Yes, but you're the one who shot him."

Dan's face screwed into a frown. A few seconds later he relented. "Okay, fine. I'll do it."

He looked back to the cross in front of him. It was made of Red Cedar, and the bark was beginning to peel off about halfway down the main beam.

"Okay...okay. Yes, I can do this."

Dan cleared his throat. "Hi Don. Merry Christmas to you." Don didn't answer. He just lay there quietly, taking it all in. Jackie nudged him to continue. "Tell him how you feel, Dan."

Dan looked over at her like a puppy waiting in line to be drowned in a bucket of water. "Jackie this is crazy." She responded with a frown and shoved out her lower lip. Dan looked at the grave, then back at her, then back at the cross again.

"Okay, here it is, the thing is, Don. I fell in love with your wife. I didn't mean to, but we got stranded here in this cabin together, and then you died...well, technically, I killed you, but that's what happened, and there's nothing I can do about that now, so it's water under the bridge. But the thing is I love her and there's nothing I can do about it and it's driving me crazy, so...I was wondering ...would you mind terribly too much if I married your wife?"

Dan saw Jackie collapse to the ground out of the corner of his eye. He reached over and caught her while she was still on her knees. Then he knelt down beside her.

"Are you okay?"

She was crying now, with full-blown tears and wailing like a siren. "That's the most romantic thing I've ever heard. You just asked my husband for my hand in marriage."

Dan looked over at the cross, then back to Jackie and nodded. "Yeah, okay, I guess that's true." For a moment the silence was broken by the sound of Don rolling over in his grave, but neither Dan nor Jackie could hear it. They were too busy staring into each other's eyes.

"I love you, Dan."

"I love you, too, Jackie."

Then Jackie looked over at the cross and asked her husband point blank. "Don, is it okay with you if I marry Dan?"

There was no answer, save the howling of the winter wind.

"I'll take that as a yes."

Jackie turned back to Dan and fell into his arms. They embraced on their knees before the cross, then kissed in the polar wind, feeling only warmth and love. Hand in hand, Dan and Jackie rose up and walked back to the cabin.

Mercifully unaware, Don's dead corpse remained frozen under the ground.

One Hour Later

"Dad, this is crazy! Are you sure you want to do this?"

Dan nodded enthusiastically. "Of course I'm sure, son. I thought you liked Jackie."

"Well I do. Of course I do. She's fantastic! And I love the baby too, but, this just seems too weird for me."

Dan scoffed at him and waved with his hand. "Are you kidding me, son. This is nothing compared to what I did an hour ago."

"Do I want to know, Dad?"

"What?"

"Do I want to know what happened an hour ago?"

His father smiled. "Ask me again when you're eighteen."

Jeremy bent his head down and placed it in both palms.

"Dad! I don't want to hear any of this! What are you wanting me to do?"

"We just want to get married, son. There's nothing wrong with that. We're both consenting adults. We love each other, and we're both available. This is cut and dried."

Jeremy raised his head and yelled back the most obvious thing he could think of. "But we're in the middle of the wilderness and there's not a pastor for miles around!"

Dan smiled. Jeremy took a step back and started to shake his head from side to side in protest. "No way, Dad. No way!"

Fifteen Minutes Later

"Do you, Jackie Lynn Overton, take this man, Daniel Edward Branch, to be your lawfully wedded husband, to have and to hold, from this day forward, for better, for worse, for richer, for poorer, in sickness and in health, until death do us part? If so, please say, 'I do'."

Jackie looked into Dan's eyes and said "I do."

The fourteen-year-old boy turned from Jackie over to Dan and repeated the same phrase for his father. Dan immediately said "I do".

"You have declared your consent before the church. May the Lord in his goodness strengthen your consent and fill you both with his blessings. What God has joined together, let no man tear apart. Amen. You may kiss the bride. But try not to gross me out."

Dan and Jackie stood in front of the cross once more, turned toward one another and fell into a warm embrace. They kissed long and hard until they were interrupted by the sound of a baby's cry.

"Dad, I think the baby's hungry. We better get back inside and feed her. Besides, it's cold out here."

Dan turned and gave his son a hug. "Thank you, Pastor."

Jeremy shrugged his shoulders and threw a handful of rice as they walked back toward the cabin. He followed them, complaining all the way. "Please, God, don't send me to hell for this. My Dad made me do it."

CHAPTER 21

The Honeymoon - January

T_{HAT} same night, Dan moved off the couch and into Jackie's bed, where they consummated their new marriage all night long. Jeremy, who had moved up from the floor to the couch, was forced to plug his ears and press the pillow tightly over his face with the covers pulled way up like a shield.

Finally, after several hours of nonstop intimacy, They paused and listened to the sound of Jeremy snoring just a few yards away.

"He's really being a good sport about this don't you think?"

Dan smiled. "Yeah. He's growing into a pretty, good kid." Then he rolled onto his right side and propped his head up with his right hand. The moon reflected off the snow and came into the small window over their bed, shining through the frosted pane. Dan reached over with his left hand and caressed Jackie's skin softly. "I feel like we've been stranded on this desert island with no hope of being rescued. But, truth is, I don't want to be rescued anymore."

Jackie moved closer to him, placing her right hand on his side. "Neither do I, be rescued I mean. I just have a feeling that we're better off here than most others. It's got to be really bad out there. I almost feel guilty. I mean, here we are with enough food, with warmth, with family. We're safe here while others are dying."

Dan thought for a moment. "True enough, all of it. But I have to tell you, honey. Next year may not be this easy. If we stay here, our food will run out, and we have no way of replenishing it. But if we make it back to Michigan, then we have a whole community of friends to help us out. Uncle Rodney has been stocking up for decades, because he saw all this coming."

Jackie's brow furled slightly. "But…how do you know he's still there?"

Dan laughed out loud, but she quickly shushed him. "You'll wake the baby!"

He placed his hand over his mouth in an attempt to stifle his laughter. "I'm sorry, Jackie, it's just that you don't know Uncle Rodney. The man's too tough and too mean to die. I guarantee you when the last man falls to the ground on this green earth, then Uncle Rodney will be there to dig the grave. He's a stubborn, old coot."

Jackie's frown gradually turned into a smile. "You really love him, don't you?"

Dan nodded. :After my dad died, Uncle Rodney took over. He raised me and made me who I am. I owe it all to him."

"Is that part of the reason you're so set on going back there?"

Dan smiled. "Just a part of it, honey. I wouldn't drag you and the baby all the way through hostile, strange territory if I didn't believe it was worth the risk."

She moved her hand off his side and down onto his stomach where she ran her fingers through the hair on his abdomen. "But…what if he doesn't like me?"

Choking back more laughter, Dan answered her right away. "Of course he won't like you! He doesn't like anyone! But he will feel sorry for you and take you in, if for no other reason, than you're so butt ugly!"

Jackie started to beat on his chest and Dan rolled over and laughed out loud. "You beast! Why do you say such things?"

"I'm sorry, but I was a Boy Scout, and I cannot tell a lie."

She stopped hitting him and he pulled her close. Jackie reached up and kissed his throat while she whispered. "I was a girl scout you know."

Dan feigned disinterest. "That's nice."

"You should have seen me in that short, little uniform skirt."

"Really? I loved those skirts. Do you still have it?"

Jackie reached down and caressed the inside of his thigh. Dan immediately rose to her expectations. She smiled. "Oh my! Is your little boy scout saluting me?"

Dan grabbed her and pulled her closer. "I hope you understand I won't be able to walk in the morning."

She opened her mouth and kissed him fiercely, then bit his lower lip tenderly. "Join the club. Now shut up and do your worst, farm boy."

And he did.

January 7, The Long Winter

"But I want to know more about your Uncle Rodney. Tell me about him."

Dan smiled first, then his face grew tense as he thought about it. Finally, he sighed out loud. Both of them were on the couch. The baby lay on the bare, wood floor on a blanket, playing with a spoon. Jeremy was outside, splitting wood, his intermittent blows of the axe to oak could be heard as tiny thunderclaps inside the warmth of the cabin.

Jackie played with the ends of her black hair and pulled both legs up on the seat cushion underneath her bottom. She remained silent, intrigued by his facial expressions, wondering what could be so complex about Uncle Rodney that would cause Dan to react this way.

"Uncle Rodney's not easy. I don't know that I ever understood him."

"Well, that's okay. I didn't ask you to explain him. Just paint me a word picture. Start with his physical appearance, and then just expand from there."

Dan's smile slowly returned. This was one of the things he liked about Jackie. She could open him up, look down inside him, see all the screwed up things, and still find something useful.

"I suppose I could do that." He paused and his eyes looked up to the bare rafters as if he was seeing a picture not inside the room. "I haven't seen him for years, but even back then he seemed old. Probably in his seventies by now. His hair was grey and white last time I saw him; it was long, down past his collar. It was usually greasy but combed back out of the way. Uncle Rodney always wore flannel and denim. Always. Even in the heat of summer. The man knows what he likes. He has a purpose about him that I envy, because I wish I had a handle on my life, my purpose, what I'm supposed to be doing."

Jackie's eyes perked up and she listened to his monologue more closely.

"But ... at the same time ... that man scares me."

Jackie cocked her head to one side.

"Really? How so?"

"Well, he's just so cock sure of himself all the time, so capable. Just watching him walk, even though he's old, you get the feeling like you don't want to mess with him. You can tell by looking at him that he's the top of the pecking order. And that's confusing too, because by so many other world standards, he's at the bottom rung of life."

Jackie reached over and softly scratched Dan's neck, just below the hairline. She'd been cutting it for him since they'd been here.

"He's a poor man, lives in an old house built into the side

of a hill. There's a swamp on one side and the hill in back and to the east. His house is cluttered, but everything else about his personality is highly organized. Once he makes his mind up to do something, then nothing can stop him. He never gives up. He's resilient, indomitable, stubborn, and above all … tenacious."

He stopped for a moment as if to let the last word sink in. *Tenacious*.

"Those sound like pretty admirable qualities, honey. Is there anything you don't like about him?"

Dan laughed out loud. "Yeah, sure. There's lots I don't like about him. He's resilient, indomitable, stubborn … tenacious."

Jackie smiled with him. "Okay then, so your Uncle Rodney is complicated?"

Dan nodded.

"Well, then it looks to me like the apple didn't fall that far from the tree."

Dan gave her a confused look. "You think I'm complicated?"

Jackie moved closer to him, letting her feet swing back out and onto the floor again until they came to rest again on the edge of the blue, baby blanket. "Honey, I *know* you're complicated. It's your defining characteristic." She kissed him on the mouth, with her right hand behind his head, scratching his neck like she would the fur on a puppy dog.

After a few seconds, their lips separated. Dan looked uncertain. "Okay, so, is that good?"

She nodded enthusiastically. "Oh yeah. I like my men stubborn, and resilient and most of all … tenacious!"

She released him and bent down to pick up the baby. They both looked at Donna's face, into her deep, black eyes, and Dan touched her cheek with his callused, thick fore finger.

"I feel like I could stay here forever."

Jackie nodded her head in agreement. "Okay, then, let's

do it."

Dan got up and threw another piece of oak onto the fire. Sparks popped up and rose into the chimney. He stirred it with the poker, looking into the red and yellow-hot coals as if being consumed by them. Jackie broke the silence again.

"Okay, so what's bothering you now?"

He smiled and looked off to one side so she couldn't see his face.

"Come on, farmboy! Tell me what' you're thinking! I married you so now I own you. You have to tell me everything. No secrets!"

Dan tried to change the subject. "Why do you always call me farm boy? I was born and raised in the north woods."

Jackie narrowed her eyes at him. "Are you trying to dodge my question?"

She knew him so well after just a few short months. It was unnerving. He played with her some more.

"Okay, lady. You tell me why you call me farm boy, and I'll tell you what I'm thinking."

She smiled. "Okay, but you have to promise to tell me what you're thinking. And not just this one time, but every time I ask you. Agreed?"

Dan pondered her proposition for a moment, and thought to himself, *If I go along with it, then I'll have to tell her anything and everything I ever think. On the other hand ... it could lead to some really nice "snuggle time" later on. But, of course, he couldn't tell her that.* It was an easy answer.

"Yeah, sure. Agreed. So why do you call me farm boy?"

Jackie leaned in closer before answering. "Have you ever seen the movie *The Princess Bride*?"

Dan nodded. Yeah, sure. Who hasn't?"

"Well, do you remember at the beginning when Buttercup was harassing Westley by constantly asking him to fetch her water, or fetch me that cup, things that she could have gotten herself?"

Dan nodded. "Yeah, I remember. I only saw it once. I

liked the swordfighting scenes."

"Well, then the grandfather, played by Peter Falk said this. I've got it memorized:

That day, she was amazed to discover that when he was saying "As you wish", what he meant was, "I love you." And even more amazing was the day she realized she truly loved him back."

Dan thought for a moment, trying to remember the first time she'd called him farmboy. And then it came to him.

"I remember the first time you called me farmboy."

As she pulled her baby closer to her, she smiled. "Oh really? I'm flattered. I don't remember. When was it?"

Dan reached over and brushed the baby's black hair on the right side of her head. He'd never seen a baby with so much hair before.

"It was just before we delivered this little baby. You were screaming in pain, and not very appreciative I might add."

Jackie's eyes softened as her whole face lit up. "You remembered the first time. You really do love me don't you?"

Dan didn't answer her. He just stared into her eyes. Jackie reached over and placed her free hand behind his head and pulled him closer. "Kiss me, farmboy!"

Dan answered her quietly as he moved closer.

"As you wish."

CHAPTER 22

The Winter of Our Content- February

AFTER their dubious, nontraditional wedding, Dan and Jackie, fell into a winter lull filled with routine and work. They woke up everyday at dawn, usually via baby Donna who now served as their alarm clock. Dan would build up the fire, while Jackie nursed the baby. Then both Jeremy and Dan would grind enough wheat for the day. Jeremy used an old mortar and pestle, which was cumbersome and slow, while Dan fashioned a larger, more efficient grinder from two grinding wheels he'd found out in the shed. Every morning, their breakfast consisted of wheat porridge, leftover venison from the night before and unleavened wheat bread toasted over the fireplace.

After breakfast, Jackie cleaned up while Dan and Jeremy either split wood or hunted wild game. Dan showed his son how to fish from the fast-flowing stream that ran past the cabin using grubs and insects found inside rotting logs. The hardest part was breaking through the ice, which was usually achieved by smashing logs over the surface. They found if they broke the ice every day, it remained thin in one spot. The fish they caught were small, either Dace, Trout, or Shiners, but they were tasty, nonetheless, and were a welcome change from a steady diet of grain and red meat.

Jeremy soon discovered he had a natural talent for hunting, once Dan taught him the basics, and soon Dan left most of the hunting and fishing to his son.

For lunch they had meat sandwiches, supplemented with a can of beans or corn for variety. Afterwards they played with the baby, talked, and sometimes napped.

Dinner was always cooked in the large, cast iron kettle that hung in the fireplace. Jackie surrounded the kettle with small, hand-shaped loaves of baking bread. Inside the kettle, she added whatever the hunters provided for her. As a result, the cabin was always filled with a mouth-watering aroma of cooking meat, sauce and vegetables. It wasn't unusual for the kettle to contain a mixture of fish, squirrel, rabbit, and deer simultaneously. To the kettle, they added dried beans, sometimes rice, even cat-tail roots that Dan and Jeremy dug up from around the shallow pond. As long as there was ample salt, Jackie remained confident she could scare up a meal that filled their bellies and had a semblance of flavor.

After the first month, even Jeremy admitted her cooking talents were improving.

The last of the candles and kerosene soon were used up, but Dan discovered that deer contained a waxy tallow of fat beneath their hide that would burn just fine, even though it didn't smell the best.

At night, they played Risk, and Jackie usually won. Throughout the long, winter weeks, Jeremy became less aggressive in his playing style, while Dan became more adventurous. By the end of February, Jackie was still winning, but the games were much, much closer.

Some nights, Dan taught Jeremy about infantry tactics and basic strategy. Jackie listened closely as Dan talked about the proper way to set up an ambush, how to move silently through the leaves, and demonstrated fire team hand signals. Using the old, Army Ranger Manual that Uncle Rodney had sent to Dan many years ago, all three of them became proficient in a myriad of outdoor survival skills as well as battlefield tactics like flanking maneuvers and how to dig in and hold the high ground.

All three of them read the manual from cover to cover several times during the winter, and Dan quizzed them weekly on what they were learning.

Through it all, Jackie gained a new understanding and appreciation for Dan's mindset. He was a very careful and calculating man, not afraid to take a calculated risk, but neither would he take a foolish gamble with human life. He was a capable military man with an indomitability and resilience that just wouldn't quit. Jackie grew to feel safe under his wing and worked hard to gain his respect and to please him.

Dan was diligent about watching his new soldiers, examining their choices, analyzing their personalities, and finding out exactly what they were likely to do in any given situation.

To round it all out, Dan taught Jackie how to shoot a pistol and a long gun. She turned out to be an excellent shot, especially at long ranges. Most of their shooting was dry fire, so as not to give away their location. But Dan believed that some measure of live fire was necessary for sighting in and for confidence building.

Always, at night, just after dinner, Dan would read from the Bible. Then, Jackie, who had graduated from Bible College, would then explain what she believed the scriptures meant. She was impressed that Dan was able to relinquish the leadership role to her during that time. But the bare truth was, Dan didn't know much about the Bible, and Jackie did. Dan caught on fast and asked probing and insightful questions. He was an impressive student. She was especially happy with Dan's prayers. They were lacking in pretense and very down to earth, as if God was really there listening to them, and He was a real person. More than ever before, her faith came alive during the dead of this winter.

Jeremy and Dan fell in love with baby Donna, and spent many hours playing with her. During these times, Jackie enjoyed fading to the background and just watching the two men play with her child. By the month of March they had become a cohesive, intimate family and military unit, ready to fight and die for each other on a moment's notice.

By winter's end, they were prepared for the newly formed tooth, fang and claw world that featured a world without lights. Oddly enough, all three of them were happier than they'd ever been.

March 6, The Second Power Failure

"Jeremy! Why did you do it?"

Jeremy looked down at the ground but said nothing.

"Do you realize what you've done? We can't get home now!"

Every day for the past four months, Dan had started up the truck and let it idle for five minutes just to keep the battery charged up. He wasn't a mechanic, but he knew that harsh, cold was rough on a car battery, and that it would likely go dead if he didn't. If that happened, they would likely never make it back to Michigan. So he was furious when he saw Jeremy's cell phone plugged into the power inverter and the ignition switch turned on. That morning, he turned the key, but nothing happened. The battery was drained.

"I want an answer, Jeremy! Why were you even bothering to charge up your cell phone when there's no service anyways? That's the stupidest thing I've ever heard of!"

Tears welled up in Jeremy's eyes and his face turned red as he stomped off the porch and ran into the woods through the snow.

"Get back here, son! Don't you …"

Dan felt Jackie's grip on his sleeve.

"Don't Dan. Let him go."

Dan looked at his wife like she was crazy. "Don't you understand what he's done? We can't leave now. We're stranded."

Jackie nodded. "Yes, I understand, but the cell phone was important to him."

Dan looked perplexed. "Why? It doesn't even work."

Jackie moved closer, cradling the baby in her left arm and putting her other around Dan's shoulder.

"The camera in his phone works, and all the pictures of his mother are in the memory. It's the only thing he has left of her. He watches them everyday when he thinks no one is looking."

Dan took a moment to let it all sink in. "But … why didn't he tell me? He could have plugged it in while I run the truck everyday?"

Jackie cocked her head to one side. "Really, Dan, come on now. He's a man, and men just don't do well with tender feelings. Anger, yes, a man can do anger, but not remorse, not sadness and a sense of loss." She hesitated. "Your son is grieving, and it embarrasses him."

Suddenly, Dan felt like a jerk. His head slumped down, and he moved off the porch and into the snow after his son. The snow drifts had been melting, and Dan was getting anxious to head back home. Now, it appeared, that was all in jeopardy, unless he could think of something to recharge the battery.

But first … his son.

He found Jeremy sitting on a large shale rock by the pond.

"Hi son."

Dan moved up behind him.

"Can I sit down with you?"

He could hear the boy's sobs over the steady peal of the north wind.

Jeremy didn't answer, but he hadn't expected him to, so he just spoke his peace.

"I'm sorry, son. I screwed up back there. I shouldn't have yelled."

No response from his son.

"Jackie told me about the pictures of your mom on the cell phone. I didn't know or I would have offered to recharge your phone every day while I started up the truck."

Dan reached into his pocket and pulled out the phone and handed it to Jeremy. Jeremy reached his hand out and took it without turning his head.

"I didn't know you had those pictures. I'd like to look at them myself."

Jeremy spoke for the first time.

"Yeah, right. You don't even think about my Mom anymore. You're too happy with Jackie."

Dan thought for a second before talking.

"I think about your Mom everyday, son. I still love her, and I miss her. I miss her smile, her laugh, and the way she used to hold me." He paused, as if thinking. "And I miss her smell too."

Jeremy turned back to him. "You mean the Jasmine scent she always wore?"

Dan nodded. "Yep. And even the Ivory soap she washed with. It always had a very clean smell, and it reminds me of her."

Jeremy nodded. "Yes, I remember that soap. She always tried to get me to use it, but after I turned eleven, I just wouldn't do it anymore. It was baby soap." Jeremy tightened his lips together as a tear ran down his cheek. "I wish I had used the soap now. It was important to her."

Dan nodded. "Yeah, she tried to get me to use it too. I told her it wasn't manly enough for me." Dan put his hands into his coat pocket to ward off the cold. :There are a lot of things I regret, Jeremy. Those are things I have to live with."

Jeremy looked over to him. "But how could you still love her even after all the things she did to you?"

Dan turned out into the cold, facing the wind as he pondered the question. "Hmm, that's a good question. I've had a lot of time to think about it these past few months. I have to admit, that I was really mad at your Mom for a long time, but...after a while, anger just loses its draw on a man, ya know what I mean?"

Jeremy nodded.

"She did some pretty bad things though, Dad. I mean, she's my Mom and I'm still mad at her myself. So how could you possibly not be mad at her?"

Looking out over the frozen pond, Dan tightened his arms around his torso in an effort to hold in the warmth.

"I think the trick is to understand nature. Nature abhors a vacuum, and you can't just not hate someone. You have to put something in its place. So, in order to not hate your Mom, I have to love her instead. Every day I pray to God that He will forgive her and give her a second chance. I think the only way to stop hating someone is to start loving them."

Jeremy thought about it for a moment.

That sounds like a pretty good way to handle it. I might try that too. So, do you think God will do it, give her a second chance I mean?"

Dan shrugged his shoulders. "I don't know, son. I would never presume to know the mind of God. He pretty much does what He wants to all the time. And I don't begrudge Him that. He did create us all, so I suppose that gives Him the right. But the way I figure it, there's no harm in me asking for the favor. God gives people second chances all the time, so why not your Mom too?"

A tiny smile moved onto Jeremy's face. It went away suddenly. "So, are you still mad at me?"

Dan laughed out loud. "I sure am, but I won't stay mad for long. You know I love you."

Dan reached over and hugged his son. Jeremy hesitated, but then returned the gentle gesture.

"Are you going to punish me?"

Dan was surprised to hear the question. It seemed so absurd after all that had happened in the past 6 months that his son still worried about a little thing like that. It was almost as if he wanted a consequence for his action. So Dan gave it to him.

"Absolutely. You're grounded from television for a week."

Jeremy laughed out loud now too, and soon they were both laughing together.

"Let's take a look at those pictures on your phone. I would love to get a gander at your Mom again."

Jeremy powered it up and both men began viewing the photos and the video clips of their old family. When they were done, Jeremy asked the obvious question.

"So, Dad, how are we going to get home now?"

Dan looked into his son's eyes before answering, as if measuring the boy's mettle.

"Well, son. I have a few ideas, but I'm going to need your help. It might be dangerous."

Jeremy didn't hesitate. "That's okay. Everything we do now is dangerous. I know that. But you can count on me. I'll do whatever it takes. I won't let you down, Dad."

Dan turned to face his son. "Okay then, son. Here's my idea, and you can tell me what you think."

The two men talked on the rock for thirty minutes. The wind died down a bit as the sun came out briefly from behind a cloud. When they were finished, they walked back to the cabin as one.

CHAPTER 23

The Plan Comes Together

DAN and Jeremy started by removing the battery and bringing it inside the cabin to warm up. Then they cleaned off the cables to make sure they were getting a good connection. Once the battery was warm, they hooked it back up and turned the key. The engine turned once, but wouldn't start up. In the end it just clicked as if mocking them.

"Dan, honey, wouldn't there be a few abandoned cars on the main road? We could take batteries out of them until we found one that worked."

His hand moved up to his chin as he thought.

"Maybe, but any car on the road right now has been there since the first snow. That means it's been sitting idle for months and is deader than the battery we have here."

Jeremy piped in. "So how do we usually handle this?"

Dan was quick to answer. "We go to the store and buy a new battery or we get a jump start from someone else. Or we could plug in a battery charger to recharge this one."

"None of that's going to work, Dan."

Dan grunted at his wife, still deep in thought. The baby started to cry and Jackie rushed over to get her off the floor. She was rolling over now and even crawling a bit. The baby was quick to laugh and smile, and was fast becoming the most popular entertainment in the cabin.

Dan turned to face the window. Just then the sun broke from behind a cloud and streamed into the cabin. The days were getting longer now, so things were warming up, and they were seeing the sun more and more, which was a welcome change.

Suddenly, Dan smiled.

"What are you thinking, Dad?" Jeremy smiled too. "Jackie, Dad's got an idea!"

Jackie rushed over with the baby in her arms. "What is it, sweetheart?"

He looked at her and reached his hand out to the window, The sunlight landed on his skin.

"We use the sun, Jackie. It's simple."

Jackie looked perplexed. "Dan, we don't have any solar panels or anything to build them or even know how to build them if we did."

Dan reached out and grabbed her by the shoulders. He turned his wife to look him full in the face. "Sweetheart, you and I may not have solar panels, but the Wisconsin Department of Transportation has thousands of them."

Dan and Jeremy looked up at the wooden pole. The lone solar panel was hanging above them twenty feet off the ground. It was small, but big enough to trickle charge the truck battery. They'd walked through the snow for five miles before finding this one, always giving houses a wide berth, not willing to take the chance on a hostile resident, determined to protect his home.

"How we gonna get up there, Dad?"

Dan looked around. Both of them were wearing snow camo made from bed sheets, and were barely visible against the backdrop of snow. "We need us a ladder."

"But we don't have a ladder, dad. All we got is a few tools

and this twine."

There was a sound off in the distance. Dan took the hat off his ears so he could hear better.

"That's a snowmobile! Quick, get off the road. We need to hide in the swamp!"

"But, Dad, we could flag them down and get help."

Dan ran for the swamp, yelling over his shoulder as he went. "Follow my orders! Now!"

Thirty seconds later the snowmobile raced by on the highways, kicking up a plume of white snow in its wake. The man was dressed in a snowmobile suit and helmet with some type of long gun strapped over his back. Neither of the men spoke until the machine was long out of sight and the engine's drone faded away.

"Why didn't we get his help, Dad?"

Dan turned toward his son. "We'd better talk."

They both sat down on a log. Dan unslung the AR-15 from his shoulder and leaned up it against the log. Jeremy did the same with the Winchester shotgun.

"We don't know who that guy was, Jeremy. He could have shot us, then followed our tracks back to the cabin and then killed Jackie and Donna."

Jeremy's face clouded over. "Why would he do that, Dad?"

"To get the things that we have, son. That's the way things work now. Yeah, sure, a year ago we would've flagged down the first person to pass us and they would have helped. But this is a whole, new world we have now, and you know how dangerous it is, right? I mean, you saw the last guys we met. We had to kill them before they killed us. That's the way it is now."

He could tell that Jeremy didn't want to believe him, so he continued. "Listen, son. I know this is tough to take, but think of it this way. Do you know why we didn't stop at that house back there to ask for help?"

Jeremy shook his head from side to side, then took off his white stocking hat to run his fingers through his hair.

"Not really, Dad. I would've stopped for help. Not all people are bad now, just like all people weren't bad before the lights went out. Some people are still good. Look at us - we're still good. Right?"

On the one hand, Dan admired his son's ability to look for the best in people. On the other hand, it might get them all killed.

"We no longer have the luxury of trusting strangers, son. We can't do it. If we trust the right people, they'll maybe help us, but ... if we trust a bad guy ... we could all die. From now on, we trust no one except each other until we have evidence to trust another."

Jeremy looked disappointed, but nodded his head in compliance. "Okay, Dad. I trust you."

Dan smiled. "Okay then, here's what we do."

After explaining it to him, Jeremy used a small bow saw to cut down three saplings about four inches in diameter. It took a full hour, but he was finally able to cut ten cross pieces which Dan quickly lashed onto the other two saplings to form rungs. Within two hours they had a fairly sturdy ladder which they promptly leaned up against the power pole.

Before making his way up, Dan gave his son final directions. "Your job, son, is to steady the ladder. Don't let me fall. If I get hurt, we won't make it back before dark and we'll freeze out here. If the snowmobile comes back, hide in the swamp again until he leaves."

A look of concern came over Jeremy's face. "But what if he doesn't leave, dad?"

Dan's face grew stern. "Under no circumstances are you to come out of the swamp. If something happens to me, get back to Jackie and the baby and protect them. Do you understand?"

Jeremy didn't answer.

"I said - Do you understand!"

Reluctantly, his son nodded in response.

Leaning his AR-15 up against the pole, Dan began making his way up the ladder, slowly, and very carefully. Jeremy did his best to hold it steady, but the ladder wiggled back and forth against the pole. It would have been hard enough with an aluminum ladder, but it was especially dangerous with lashed-together sticks.

Finally, Dan made it to the top. He tied the rope around his waist and then around the pole. Next, he took off his gloves and pulled the Crescent wrench out of his front pocket. He closed up the wrench to about half and inch diameter, then placed it on the nut for final adjustments. At first, the nut wouldn't break free. It was on tight. The wrench slipped off twice, threatening to strip the head, but on the third try, the nut finally broke free.

"How's it going up there, Dad?"

Dan looked down and smiled.

"Good son, just three more nuts and I can lower it down to you."

Dan removed the next nut with no problem. Then he tied another rope around the ladder rung and onto the metal bracket of the solar panel. Just as he started to loosen the third nut, Jeremy yelled up to him.

"Hey, dad, can you hear that?"

Dan's pulse quickened. It was the high-pitched whine of snowmobile engines approaching.

"Get in the swamp, son!"

Dan started to untie the rope, but his fingers were numb from working the cold, metal Crescent wrench. He looked down and Jeremy was still there.

"Hurry, dad!"

"Get in the swamp, son!"

Dan looked out and saw the two snowmobiles approaching from the west, each was pulling a sled. He tried to stay calm as he worked the knots loose, but it was no use. His hands were just too cold. The snowmobiles stopped below him and both men dismounted. Dan looked down for Jeremy, but he was no where in sight.

"What are you doing up there, stranger?"

Both men had removed their helmets and were smiling up at Dan who had no choice but to cling helplessly to the ladder.

"Oh, just hanging around I guess."

One of the men laughed out loud. "Well, looks to me like you're stealing county property."

Dan hesitated. He didn't trust the man's tone of voice, or the look on his face.

"Well, actually, I think I'm stealing state property, but I reckon they won't be using it for a while so it's okay."

The man's smile went away.

"Well, partner, you reckoned wrong. Ya see, my friend and I are planning on taking every solar panel off this stretch of road for fifty miles in both directions. It's a business venture you might say."

Dan glanced out into the swamp hoping that Jeremy was running away to safety. He thought to himself *how am I going to get out of this mess*.

"Listen guys, I can appreciate a good business deal, so let's strike a deal right now."

The taller man appeared to be in charge, and his smile grew even bigger until it spanned the full width of his face. Then he laughed out loud.

"Now, son, what could you possibly have that we want?"

Dan pointed down at the AR-15 leaning against the power pole. "Take my rifle in return for this one solar panel and leave me unharmed. That's all I ask."

The two men looked at each other. Finally they both burst out laughing.

"Get the man's rifle, John. I'll take care of this guy."

The other man picked up Dan's AR and walked it over to his snowmobile. He placed the rifle inside the sled began to lash in down with a bungee cord.

"Thanks for the rifle, partner. But we can't let you have the solar panel. It just wouldn't be good business."

Dan looked around, thinking desperately, wondering how

to get out of this mess. He was tied to a pole, twenty feet off the ground, hanging by a rickety ladder. Dan realized that he was about to die.

"Out here, my friend, possession is nine-tenths of the law. And the way I see it, we possess the rifle, the solar panel and we possess you."

He walked up to the ladder, placed his right hand on a rung and started to shake. Caught by surprise, Dan fell off the ladder and the rope around his waist hiked up under his armpits, before quickly cinching tight around his lungs and cutting off his air supply. Dan hung there while both men laughed below.

After thirty seconds without air, Dan began to gasp and choke. The men laughed even harder.

"Look at him up there, John, swinging off that rope like a monkey."

The man directly below the pole lifted up his coat and drew a 45 caliber 1911 pistol from his holster before aiming it at Dan, swinging helplessly on the rope.

"I feel merciful today, stranger. We can't just leave you up there to die a slow and agonizing death." The man's trigger finger eased back as he centered the front sight on Dan's head. He timed his trigger pull with the swaying motion of Dan's body.

BAM! The man dropped his forty-five into the snow as the shotgun slug tore into his chest. Red blood sprayed out onto the white snow as the other man looked on in shock. Jeremy's shotgun barked out again, this time shredding the rope tied to the pole, releasing his father for the 15-foot drop into the snow. The other man ran towards the snowmobile and the engine quickly fired up. Just as he began to speed away, several shots rang out, sending the man sprawling into the snow. One shot to the man's head with Dan's Taurus revolver had quickly done the job.

Dan turned in the snow and pointed his revolver at the first man down, who was now bleeding out in the snow just a few feet away. As Jeremy walked out of the swamp, Dan took the rope off his torso and caught his breath.

By time they reached the man, he was almost dead. A red, bubbly froth was coming out his mouth, and he coughed it out onto the snow. Jeremy looked down and tears welled up in his eyes.

"I'm sorry, mister, I didn't want to do that."

The man looked up at him, and the crow's feet around his blue eyes wrinkled as he squinted up at Jeremy. He uttered his final words through his bloody gasp.

"You're … a … boy?"

Then the life in his blue eyes went out like the flame of a candle. Jeremy's shot had gone under his right armpit, through both lungs, then partially blowing off his left arm at the elbow as it left his body.

Dan was proud of his son's shot, and relieved at his survival, but he didn't say anything at first. Then he heard whimpers and looked up at his son. Tears flowed freely down Jeremy's cheeks. He walked over and hugged him with his left arm.

"He was going to kill you, dad. He would shoot you for a gun you were going to let him have for free."

Jeremy looked into Dan's eyes. "Why?"

Dan shook his head. "There's evil in some folks. It just happens."

He squeezed his son hard.

"But you saved my life. That's what matters."

He turned his body and they both hugged as the snow began to drift lazily down.

An hour later they made their way back to the cabin in the snowmobiles. The new snow covered their tracks behind them.

CHAPTER 24

Decision Point

JACKIE had been shocked to see two men drive up on snowmobiles. In fact, she'd met them at the door with a pistol aimed at their heads. Only when Dan saw the gun pointed at him did he think to take off his helmet.

"Oh, Dan! You're back!" She let the pistol come down and rushed off the porch where he scooped her up. They held each other for several seconds while Jeremy looked on clumsily.

"Let's get inside honey. The snow's coming down pretty hard now."

"Where did you get these snowmobiles?"

Dan pointed back to Jeremy as he spoke. "Son, go ahead and throw a tarp over the sleds to keep the snow off the new gear. Then come on inside and we'll talk."

Once inside, Dan told her everything that had happened. She was relieved that Dan was okay, but her first concern was for Jeremy.

"That's going to mark him, Dan. It will change him."

Dan nodded. "I know. It's sad, but he's strong. He'll be okay. Besides, he'll have to just reason out that he had no choice." Dan looked over at the door, expecting his son to walk through at any moment. "These are hard times, and hard times make for hard men. But it is what it is. We're going to be seeing a lot of things we wouldn't normally see from now on." He shook his head sadly. "Normally I wouldn't be driving a stolen truck, and I certainly wouldn't take two snowmobiles that didn't belong to me. But … I don't know, Jackie. The rules are all screwed up now. I have to figure out what's right and wrong, and I have to do it in the context of keeping my family alive. I feel like … well, like I want to know what's right and what's wrong, so I can do right, but the lines are blurred now."

Dan looked like he wanted to cry, so Jackie leaned over and pulled his head into her shoulder. The baby was playing on the blanket by the fireplace. Outside, they could hear Jeremy moving things around in the bed of the pick-up truck, looking for the tarp.

"I know, Dan. But I have confidence in you, in your judgement and in your sense of right and wrong. We'll figure it out together, but in the meantime we need to pray about it, and maybe God will help us decide some new rules that keep us on the right path." She hesitated. "What do you think?"

He pulled his head up and smiled at her. "I think I married the right woman."

Just then Jeremy stomped the snow off his boots and walked through the door. As soon as he walked in, Jackie got up and walked over to hold him. Jeremy just stood there, like a rock, not sure how to respond to her.

"It's okay, Jeremy. You did the right thing. You shot a bad person, and you saved your dad's life in the process. You had no choice." She put her palms on either side of his face and moved his head down so his eyes met hers. "I would have done the same thing, Jeremy. I would have killed those men to save your father. They were bad people, and they needed killing. Think of how many other people they would have killed and hurt before someone else stood up to them and put an end to it."

Tears ran down his cheeks. Jackie wiped them away and smiled softly. "In bad times like this, Jeremy, people either get better, or they get worse. You are becoming a better person. You were forced to defend the people you love against a bad man. You did good, son."

The tightness in Jeremy's face lessoned. She'd never called him "son" before, and it made him feel good.

Dan walked over and the three of them embraced for a few seconds more. Then they sat down for bread and venison stew.

"First, let's look at the pros and cons of both ideas. We'll list them out on paper, then analyze them before we decide what choice to make. Sound good?"

Jeremy and Jackie both agreed. Jackie held baby Donna over the table toward Jeremy.

"Here, Jeremy, hold Donna so I can take notes."

Dan sat at the head of the wooden table with Jeremy on his left and Jackie on his right.

"But first, I want to read you both something. It's from Ecclesiastes chapter 4, verse 12. It very simply says '*Though one may be overpowered, two can defend themselves. A cord of three strands is not quickly broken.*'"

Jeremy looked down at the wood as he held the baby. His father looked over at him. "Son, without you today, I would have been overpowered. I want to publicly thank you for saving my life."

Dan hesitated while Jeremy just nodded his head softly. Then Dan continued. "We are the three strands, and we are bonded together through our love of God and our love of each other. No one is going to stop us from getting back home. This family stands together as one cord, strong, loyal, and, if need be, fierce."

Dan held his right hand out onto the oak wood table top in front of them and kept it there. Jackie looked him in the eye and smiled before placing her own hand atop her husband's. Jeremy looked at them both, one at a time. Then he reached out slowly with his right hand

and completed the cord.

For the rest of the meeting they talked freely about the pros and cons of two plans: Do they wait for the thaw and drive back in the truck? or, Do they go now in the snowmobiles? It was a tough decision, because there was so much risk involved in both methods.

Jeremy argued for waiting and taking the truck.

"It will be warmer, and more comfortable for the baby and Jackie. We'll be able to haul more food and equipment too. We've already got it started back up by jump starting it with the snowmobile battery. It's a brand, new truck and not likely to break down. With the roads dry of snow, it will take less time as well. And what happens if we take the snowmobiles and a warm front moves in and melts the snow? We'd be dead in our tracks."

Jackie countered quickly with an argument of her own. "But the same thing could happen with the truck. A blizzard could come and snow us in. We'd be stranded for days in the cold."

Jeremy interrupted her. "Yes, but only for a few days. With snowmobiles we'd be stranded until next winter when the snow comes again."

Dan nodded. "That's a good point."

But Jackie wasn't done yet.

"The snowmobiles are smaller, they're all-terrain vehicles and we won't be restricted to roads. With the truck we'll have to drive through dozens of towns, and some of them are likely to be hostile. The snowmobiles can drive through the woods, open fields, across frozen swamps, you name it."

Dan reached up to scratch the beard on his chin. He'd let it grow out the past few months. His hair was blonde, but his whiskers had a reddish tint. It made for an interesting face. He chimed in.

"What happens if we get to the Mackinac Bridge

and it's blocked with stalled cars? With snowmobiles we could snake our way through, even zip across on the ice in the straits if it's still cold enough."

Jackie made one, last point. "And what about gas? The truck gets less than 20 miles per gallon, and a snowmobile gets more than double that. Truth is we only have enough gas to make it halfway back with the truck. Where would we get the rest of the gas? We can make it all the way with the snowmobiles."

Jeremy shook his head back and forth. He clutched the baby tighter to his chest. "It's too cold for the baby."

Dan nodded. "That's a good point, son." He paused for a moment. "On the other hand, if we run out of gas halfway there, we're stranded in the cold as well."

He glanced over at Jackie. "Honey, make a list with two columns detailing the benefits and disadvantages of each. Then we'll look at it and decide."

It took Jackie only five minutes, and when she was done, the list looked like this:

Truck	
Benefits	**Disadvantages**
Provides warmth & shelter	Gets us only halfway
Transports more food & supplies	Confined to roads
Doesn't rely on snow.	May not be able to cross bridge
Will travel faster.	May get stranded in blizzard

Snowmobile	
Benefits	**Disadvantages**
Gets us all the way	Will be cold for baby
off-road to avoid trouble	Carries less supplies
Can't get snowed in	Must have cold & snow
Will cross bridge & other roadblocks	Travels slower than truck

When she was done, all three of them poured over the list together.

"I don't know, Dan. They look like the exact opposites of each other."

Jeremy agreed with Jackie. Dan nodded his head. "Yes, it certainly does. But…"

Jeremy slid the baby over to Jackie across the table. "What? What are you thinking, dad?"

Dan pointed to the list. "Some of these items carry more weight than others. For example, speed isn't as important as distance. If we can only make it halfway, then we may be better off staying where we are. At least here we have shelter, security, and all our supplies. If we can't make it all the way, I don't want to go at all." He moved his finger down to another item. "On the other hand, if a blizzard comes up and we freeze to death …"

Jackie threw up her hands. "It's six of one and half a dozen of the other! The problem is we don't know for sure what we face out there."

Dan shook his head. "That's not entirely true. We know from experience that security is going to be a big issue. There are people out there who will kill us just to take our gear."

Jeremy interrupted him. "But what about the weather, Dad? We have no way of knowing if we'll have snow or not. For all we know we could be driving into a tropical heat wave."

Dan and Jackie both nodded. "That's true, son. But we shouldn't make a decision based on variables we have no control over. With conditions as they are, we'll make it home faster with the snowmobiles. We can make the trip in two days, and it would take one heck of a heat wave to melt all the snow, especially this far north."

"Are the two machines dependable?"

Dan answered Jackie's question. "Yes, I've looked them over, and they're pretty new and seem in good shape."

Jeremy shook his head. "I don't know, dad."

Dan smiled. "No one knows but God, son. Especially when we're talking about the weather. But we have to go with what we know, not by what we fear might happen. If no one can argue with my logic, then we'll leave day after tomorrow as soon as this storm lets up."

There was nothing but silence around the table. Then Jeremy looked him in the eyes. "I think we should pray about it, dad."

Dan smiled. "Agreed. You go ahead, son."

All of them bowed their heads as Jeremy talked to God.

"Okay, God. Here we are, wondering what to do. We need to get home, and we need your help. Please give us enough snow to get us home safely. It's all up to you, God." And then he added. "And please forgive us for killing those two guys today. We didn't want to do it."

Jeremy said "Amen" and the others repeated it in agreement.

They opened their eyes, all smiling at one another, as if relieved that a decision had been made. The wind and snow blew outside, hammering itself mercilessly against the cabin walls, but the walls held. They spent the next hour creating a list of the food and supplies they could take with them, giving special weight to security and shelter.

When they finally went to bed, Dan lay awake for several hours just thinking, wondering about the decision they'd made, wondering if he was leading them all out to their deaths. He felt bad about the lives taken today, so he went over every detail of the skirmish over and over again. But, still… he could find no way around it, even with the calm and wisdom of retrospect. In the end, he fell asleep after 2AM. His chest rose and fell with steady breathing. Jackie's arm came around him as he slept and squeezed reassuringly. She nuzzled her face up to his neck, taking in the sureness of his smell and the solidness of his touch.

A few feet away, Jeremy lay awake, knowing instinctively that he'd crossed a line he couldn't take back ever again. His Social Studies teacher would call it the Rubicon, but… it didn't matter what she thought. She lived in Eau Claire, and was probably already dead.

The wind continued to howl outside, but, even in the warmth of the cabin, with the fire glowing in the hearth, Jeremy pulled the sleeping bag up over his neck, but … he still felt cold.

CHAPTER 25

Moonshadow Recon

"MOONSHADOW, this is Eagle Ranger. Say again your last, over."

The man keyed the SINCGARS radio again before speaking. "Eagle Ranger, I say again. I'm requesting a priority 1 recon patrol in your sector. I'm looking for two white males and one female, traveling together across the border into your sector. They should be heading towards my location."

"Roger that, Moonshadow. Please relay names and descriptions of each."

Moonshadow leaned back in his rocking chair, deep inside his underground bunker. Very few people in the Shadow Militia knew his real name, but that was by design. It had always been imperative that he remain anonymous, but the day was fast approaching when he'd shed his anonymity and go into full military battle mode. At that time, there would be no turning back. He keyed the mike again and gave Eagle Ranger the description of all three people, along with any other details he could think of.

The SINCGARS was a satellite-based radio using 25 kHz channels in the VHF FM band, from 30 to 87.875 MHz range, using single-frequency and frequency-hopping modes. The frequency-hopping mode hopped 111 times a second making it very secure. Despite that, Moonshadow and Eagle

Ranger were careful to follow protocol, using no names or exact locations. Everything they said would have been considered cryptic at best by any outside listener. Moonshadow was always amazed at the new technology. The comm gear they used now was nothing like the AN/PRC-77s they had used back in Nam.

And the Shadow Militia needed the security to protect them from the United States Government. The FBI and ATF had long made it a matter of routine to try and infiltrate and fragment all state militias, and that's why the Shadow Militia had been formed. They operated under the surface, in the shadow of the public militia. In fact, they were so secretive, that not even the Commanding Generals of the state militias knew of its existence. Their numbers were small, but they were all highly trained and well equipped, mostly special ops types, former Army Rangers, Marines, Green Berets, and a few Seals. They made Rambo look like a Cub Scout.

And Moonshadow was their unassuming leader.

"Roger that, Moonshadow. Is that all?"

Moonshadow hesitated, then keyed the mike one last time. "Affirmative, Eagle Ranger. Please advise when contact is made. Roger, over and out."

The old man placed the radio down on the steel barrel filled with red wheat. Off to the side was an entire pallet of 5.56mm NATO rounds in olive drab steel cans. Beside that was a pallet of Stinger missiles, one of fragmentation grenades, and still another of 7.62mm rounds. Just to be safe, Moonshadow never smoked down here.

Instead, he leaned back in the chair, placed his hands on the arms of the rocker and slowly moved back and forth, back and forth, back and forth. The movement and rhythm cleared his head and helped him think. But no amount of thinking and rocking could create the security he yearned for. He wanted the reassurance they were okay, but it just wouldn't come.

Departure day

The sun was shining on the day they left the cabin and headed east toward the Upper Peninsula. Jackie was seated inside the lead sled, facing the back, with Donna in her arms, wrapped inside blankets. She was set up to keep her daughter warm, out of the wind, and she could even breastfeed her while the snowmobiles were on the move.

Jackie found it a bit disconcerting they had to leave many of their supplies behind. There simply wasn't enough room in the sleds. But most disturbing to her was leaving the gravesite of her first husband. She glanced over at the wooden cross jutting out of the snow. This was the cabin she'd bought with Don to live in when everything else went bad. But the collapse had taken his life as well as many others, and things had changed.

She left a note on the table inside which said:

> To whom it may concern:
>
> This is my home. Please use it to keep warm and safe from danger. You may live here as long as you need shelter. Please take care of it as if it were your own. Leave it in good order for the next person in need.
>
> My husband, Don, is buried beneath the cross. Please respect his grave.
>
> May God bless and keep your family.
>
> Jackie Branch
> The Owner

Dan and Jeremy came over to her now and kneeled

217

down beside her and the baby.

"Are you ready sweetheart?"

Jackie looked into Dan's eyes and nodded, but said nothing. She didn't want to cry in front of him, afraid he would misinterpret her tears. She loved Dan and would follow him anywhere. She would even die for him, but … this cabin had given them safety and refuge and peace in the eye of the storm. Now they were leaving it behind never to return.

Dan held his right hand out. Jackie covered it with her own, quickly followed by Jeremy's.

"Dear God. We ask you for easy travel, for moderate weather, and for a safe passage all the way home. We praise you and lift you up. Amen"

Jeremy bent down and kissed the baby on the forehead. "Keep her warm, mom."

"I will, son. Drive safe."

Dan took one final walk around the cabin before placing the helmet on his head and mounting the snowmobile. He was anxious to get back, but this moment sobered him, and he couldn't help but remember last September, the day after the collapse, when he'd left his home in Menomonie.

So far, the nine-hour drive had taken him over six months. And he was only halfway home.

Dan fired up his machine, followed quickly by Jeremy's. They moved out over the snow toward the main road, leaving their place of refuge behind, not knowing what dangers lie ahead of them.

❧ ⸱ ⸱ ❧

Building an Army

"You don't need a police force. You need an army."

Sheriff Leif looked over at his friend, trying hard to hide his exasperation and impatience. Rodney had been pushing him into this for months now, but he was resisting every step of the way.

"I don't need an army, Rodney! I'm not a General, I'm a Sheriff."

218

Rodney smiled and pulled a pack of Camels out of his front right pocket.

"There's no smoking in the building, you know that, Rodney."

His Zippo popped open and torched the end of the cigarette. "It's okay, Joe. This is medicinal tobacco and I have a prescription from my doctor."

The Sheriff gritted his teeth together and tried hard not to grind his jaw back and forth.

"You are really starting to get on my nerves, old man."

Rodney blew smoke out the left side of his mouth so as not to envelop his friend in the cloud.

"I understand. I get that a lot these days. It's amazing. I don't even like myself anymore. But that doesn't diminish the validity of what I just said." He took another drag off the Camel and let the smoke sit in his lungs for a few seconds. "You need to train your posse in basic battlefield tactics. They need to know about flanking maneuvers, how to set up an ambush, basic recon, hand signals, battlefield first aid." Smoke came out of his mouth as he talked.

"Where are you getting all those cigarettes? Everyone else has been out for months now."

Rodney smiled. "Ebay, but don't change the subject. All I'm asking is that you let me train them in the basics. It's not like I'm going to form them up and have them parading around town like soldiers."

Joe looked away and focused on the picture on his desk of his wife and kid. His son was holding up a ten-inch Blue Gill and his wife was smiling at him. Vandalism had increased over the past month, probably stemming from the hundred or so refugees camped out in the state game area five miles down the road. Some of the residents had openly suggested they go and burn them out and force them to move on. Joe had come down hard against it, threatening to throw anyone in jail who took the law into their own hands. To top it all off, rumors had been circulating about bands of thieves roaming the countryside, in the counties to the south of them.

"Let's come back to that in a minute, Rodney."

The old man crushed out his cigarette on the heel of his boot and placed the butt in his left, front shirt pocket.

"Sure. You're the Sheriff." And he smiled when he said it, like it was the barb on the end of a fish hook.

Joe squirmed in his chair before speaking. "So, Rodney, what are you hearing on the short wave these days?"

Rodney gave him a cold, blank stare.

Joe pursued it further.

"Come on, Rodney, you're a patriot!"

His hard stare got colder.

Joe exhaled as if in defeat.

"Okay, Rodney, here's what I'll let you do."

Rodney smiled slightly.

"Go ahead and start training the military vets. But this is just a pilot program to see how it's received by them and by the community."

Joe leaned forward in his chair.

"Agreed?"

Rodney's face broke into a full smile now.

"Sure thing, Joe. After all, you're the Sheriff. if that's what you want, then I'll start right away."

He got up to leave, but Joe stopped him.

"Hold on there, not so fast. Tell me what you're hearing on the short wave. Are all those rumors true?"

Rodney hesitated before sitting down and lighting up another cigarette. He ceremoniously blew out smoke, knowing the Sheriff was waiting impatiently for him to speak. "Well, some of the rumors are true, and some are false. Which ones are you worried about most?"

Joe tried to steady his breathing before he spoke. "The rumors about two hundred murdering rapists heading our way. Is it true or not?"

Rodney paused for dramatic effect, and took another puff off the Camel before answering.

"It's true. But I would put their numbers more at 300, not 200. If they come here we can take them, provided we play it smart."

A faraway look settled in the Sheriff's eyes. He glanced back down at his wife and son in the picture. It had been taken at Lake Piqua right before the collapse on their last family vacation. It was quite possibly the last vacation they would ever take. Now, every waking moment was spent just trying to eat and survive.

"If you were in charge, how would you handle it?"

Inside the privacy of his mind, Rodney's aging body did a cartwheel and topped it off with a handstand. But on the outside, he remained stoic.

"Well, I suppose ... if it were me, I would ..."

And then he told him everything, holding nothing back. Joe's eyes opened wide and his pulse quickened.

CHAPTER 26

A Perilous Journey

THERE it was, straight ahead and to the right.
Lake Michigan. It had taken them four hours to reach the
Michigan border, but now, Dan's heart leaped upon seeing it.

There was ice still on the lake out to about 100 yards off-
shore. but it was breaking up around the beach. He wanted to
head for the bridge on the frozen lake, but didn't dare. March
ice was seldom stable, even this far north.

He came to a stop on the beach, and Jeremy's snow machine came up beside him. Both engines died down, until all
they could hear was wind.

"Is this Michigan, Dad?"

"Sure is, son. Can't you tell?"

Jeremy took off his helmet and scratched his head. "Not
really. Looks a lot like Wisconsin to me. I've never been to
Michigan before."

Just then the baby started to cry.

"Dan, I need to change her diaper. Can the two of you
form a windbreak around me so she doesn't get so cold?"

Dan nodded, then reached into the back of the sled and
pulled out a small, blue tarp.

"Come on, Jeremy. Let's wrap this around the sled so
they stay warm."

A few minutes later, the baby was changed and Jackie began nursing her. Dan and Jeremy drove the snowmobiles up into a small copse behind a dune where the wind was blocked and built a campfire.

"We won't be able to do this very much once we get to more populated areas, but this stretch south of Ford River on M-35 is pretty secure. Hardly any people at all around here. But the closer we get to Escanaba, the more dangerous it might get."

Dan spread out the paper map of Michigan on the back of Jeremy's sled, but the wind kept blowing it closed.

"Sure wish we had a GPS. But I guess those days are long gone."

Jeremy walked up behind him. "Why don't we just use the GPS on my cell phone?"

Dan and Jackie looked at each other, and then over at Jeremy. "You mean it still works?"

"I don't know. I haven't tried it. Trying to save the battery."

He reached into his front pocket and pulled it out. A few seconds later he smiled. "We can only get three satellites, but it's working."

Dan folded up the map and stuck it back in the sled. "Let me take a look."

Dan took the Blackberry from his son and smiled. "Will you look at this, Jackie. I can't believe it still works. Apparently the collapse didn't affect the satellites. We should be able to navigate around Escanaba without running into too much trouble."

The three of them huddled around Jackie's sled as they made plans. "See, we can go just past Ford River, then veer north until we get above Escanaba, then turn back east. That way we don't have to follow the lakeshore where all the towns are."

Jeremy clapped his father on the back. "Sounds like a plan, Dad."

Dan looked his son in the eyes. "Makes me wish I hadn't thrown my cell phone away so quickly. Thank you, son."

Jeremy caught himself blushing and turned away smiling. "No problem, Dad."

"Let's keep moving, honey. The baby's pretty restless and I want to get this done as quickly as possible."

Dan nodded and passed out some water, bread and dried meat. They all ate hurriedly and then Dan put out the fire. Five minutes later they were running northeast straight down M-35. There were very few houses near the beach, but when they came to one, they quickly skirted around it, giving it a wide berth for added safety.

A few miles from Ford River, Dan turned north away from the beach. Once inland, they saw more trees and swamps and Dan used them for cover as much as he could. They were making good time when all of a sudden Dan's snowmobile hit a large rock and bounced high into the air. Dan was thrown clear, but the snowmobile came down with a crash, overturning the sled with Jackie and the baby inside.

Jeremy swerved to the right, missing the rock and the crash. He came to a stop just a few feet away from the over-turned sled.

Dan landed in a snowbank unharmed, but Jackie's body was half out of the sled, pinched between the frozen ground with the sled lying on top of her.

By time he reached Jackie, Jeremy was already there lifting her head up off the snow.

"Mom! Mom!"

Jackie didn't move. Her eyes were closed and her face and forehead were bleeding.

"Don't move her, son until we know her spine is okay."

Dan looked around on the ground. "Where's the baby?"

Jeremy ran around the sled frantically, looking for Donna, but couldn't find her. Suddenly, they heard crying and traced it to a snowbank about twenty feet away. The baby was still wrapped in its blankets with her face down into the cold snow. She screamed as loud as she could until Jeremy scooped her up and cuddled her close. He talked to her all the way back to the sled where his father kneeled beside Jackie.

"Please God, let her be okay! Please God!"

Dan checked Jackie's legs and quickly saw the blood seeping through her snow pants. He carefully tipped the sled back onto the runners, then he pulled out his knife and cut away the cloth from her ankle. He shuddered upon seeing the white bone sticking out through her skin. A compound fracture.

The baby started crying again, but Jeremy couldn't silence her. "What do we do, Dad?"

Dan shook his head from side to side. "I can't believe I didn't see that rock. We should have stayed on the road."

He moved away from her leg on up to her head. He checked her pulse by feeling the carotid artery. It seemed weak and slow to him, but he didn't know for sure as his medical training was limited at best. He lifted up on her left eyelid and watched the pupil. It didn't seem to be responding to the light.

"I think she has a concussion. Nothing we can do about that. We'll know more when she wakes up. Right now I have to make a splint for that leg. Thank God she didn't cut an artery."

"Dad, I can't make the baby stop crying. I don't know what to do. Is she going to die, Dad? What's going on! What should I do?"

Dan looked up with fear and fire in his eyes. "Just shut up for a second and let me think!"

Dan's fingers pressed against his helmet. He quickly ripped it off and threw it to the ground. The icy, cold wind blew his greasy, blonde hair, making it slap against his bearded face.

"First, I'll keep your Mom warm with blankets, then build a fire. After that I'll cut the wood I need for a splint.

Hopefully by then she'll be awake and can tell us more."

Jeremy looked desperate. "But what about the baby? What should I do?"

Dan spoke as he moved to get the blankets. "Unwrap her and check out every inch of her body for wounds. If you find nothing wrong, then wrap her back up and keep her warm. Try to distract her by playing with her and feeding her some of that applesauce in the MRE packets."

Dan glanced over at his snowmobile. It had crashed into a tree when it landed and looked ruined. The afternoon sun would soon be going down, and with it, temperatures would fall. They both went to work, quickly, efficiently and desperately.

"Dad, she's waking up!"

Dan hurried over to Jackie just in time to keep her from choking on her own vomit. He carefully moved her head to one side and rolled her over slightly. Her splint was in place to lessen the chance of further injury to the leg, and the shelter was up as well, protecting her and the baby from the wind.

"Jackie! Sweetheart! Can you hear me?"

Her lips moved and Dan leaned down to hear her whispered reply.

"Stop yelling. My head hurts."

Dan smiled and kissed her on the cheek. "Don't worry, honey. You're going to be okay. You just have a concussion." And then, almost as an afterthought he added. "And don't move your legs. One of them has a compound fracture and you don't want to make it worse."

She smiled weakly. "Oh, is that all."

Then the baby started crying again, and Jackie tried to get up. "No, honey. Stay down. The baby's okay."

"I want to see her. Bring her here or I'm getting up."

Jeremy, just a few feet away by the fire, heard her words and came over with baby Donna. They propped up Jackie's head and then placed the baby in her waiting arms. "I have to nurse her."

Once she started to suckle, the baby quieted and Jackie smiled. "My head hurts, Dan."

"I know honey. I have the Tylenol ready." She took the pills with water.

"The light hurts my eyes."

Dan nodded. "Yes, I know. But just keep your eyes closed and rest until we get ready to move again. Are you warm enough?"

She nodded her head. "Ouch!"

"Don't move your head, honey. Just whisper. Just use words."

"I feel like I'm going to die."

Dan's heart-rate skyrocketed. "No, you're going to be okay. As soon as you're done nursing, we're going to load you up and get you some help."

But Jackie didn't answer. She was already drifting off to sleep.

CHAPTER 27

Moving out

THE snowmobile moved slowly, pulling the sled behind it. Every time it bounced, even slightly in the snow, Jackie winced in pain. Jeremy was driving while Dan walked beside the sled, cradling the baby in his arms. It was slow going, and the sun was setting. The wind was picking up now as it usually did at sunset, and the temperature began to plummet.

"Stop, Jeremy!"

Jeremy came to a halt in the snow, and his father walked up to him.

"Let's take a look at the GPS again."

Jeremy pulled it out of his front pocket and looked at it. "It says no signal, Dad."

A frown moved across Dan's face, but he said nothing.

"So what do we do now, Dad?"

Dan was getting sick of people asking him that question. He was tired of having to pretend like he knew what was going on. "No problem, son. We just keep heading east until we reach Lake Michigan. Then we turn left and follow it up the coast until we reach Escanaba. They have a hospital there."

Jeremy nodded. "Okay." Then he quickly added. "So which way's east?"

Normally, Dan would take this opportunity to smile and teach his son, but not today. "Just keep the sunset on your back and we'll be fine."

Jeremy's brow tightened up inside his helmet. He was thinking *What happens when we can't see the sun anymore?* But he didn't voice his thoughts. He was too afraid his father had no good answer. So he started the snow machine up and moved forward again, being careful to keep the sun on his back and trying to take the smoothest terrain.

Dan dropped back again, walking along the sled, trying to stay strong for the others, clinging desperately to the baby and what little faith remained inside him. He looked down at his wife's ashen face, then down at the baby. Dan was surprised to see her eyes open. Donna looked up at him and laughed. Dan smiled too. His heart took a step up, and he began to sing softly to his child.

> *"Oh there's a bright golden haze on the meadow. There's a bright golden haze on the meadow. The corn is as high as an elephant's eye. And it won't be long till it reaches the sky."*

Jeremy heard the singing and glanced back over his shoulder briefly. He whispered a prayer to God. *Please help us, Lord.* Then he started singing too, doing the best he could to keep from jostling his mother, all the while thinking, *If my Dad can do it, then so can I.*

తఁ *ఁ* తఁ

Rodney sat beside his short wave radio listening. The dog was at his feet, and the fire crackled beside him. He was warm. He was safe. He was frustrated.

He so much wanted to be up in the U.P. out in that late-winter storm, searching for the kid and his family, but it wasn't possible or wise. So he continued to sit in his rocking chair, forcing himself to monitor broadcasts, listening for any clues that might tell him three people had been found and rescued.

But no word came, and the silence was deafening.

❧ ⋅ ⋅ ❧

Dan huddled over his wife, trying to keep her warm. The baby was between them, and she was crying now. Jackie had lost consciousness again a few hours ago, and Dan had been unable to wake her. Jeremy sat over by the fire, but it was hard to get the wet wood to burn hot enough to make a difference.

As the wind howled all around them, Jeremy thought to himself *And I was worried about a spring thaw?* He took off his gloves and held them closer to the flames. After a few more minutes of shivering by the fire, he walked over to his Dad.

"Dad, is she going to be okay?"

Dan looked up and raised the visor on his helmet so he could be heard. He shook his head in frustration.

"I don't know, son. At first I thought she was going to be okay, but now I can't even get her to wake up."

Jeremy looked down at the baby. "What about baby Donna?"

"So long as she stays warm she'll be okay. She's eating enough. I've been chewing up the crackers and putting them in her mouth and she eats them okay. We have the canned milk, but I can't figure out how to make the nursing process work without Jackie's help, and we don't have a baby bottle."

Dan reached down and checked Jackie's pulse again. It was still weak.

"Maybe one of us should go for help, Dad."

His father looked up at him and shook his head from side to side. "It's too risky, son. We have no guarantee we'd find anyone in time, and no idea what kind of person we'd find.

We could end up making things worse."

His son looked out into the wind. "How could things possibly get any worse?"

Dan's brow furled as he winced at the question. "It can always get worse, son. Always."

Jeremy shrugged. "So what's the plan, Dad?"

Dan thought about it for a second. His reply was terse and unsure.

"I guess we just try to stay warm until the snowstorm lets up ... and we pray."

That answer frustrated Jeremy. He wanted to do something. He looked down at Jackie. The baby was still crying and it broke his heart to hear her cries. Everything inside him wanted to do something - anything.

"Okay, Dad. I'll pray."

"Eagle Ranger, this is Moonshadow, over."

There was nothing but silence coming from the radio. Eagle Ranger, this is Moonshadow. Please acknowledge, over."

Rodney put the radio down with a heavy sigh on the barrel beside him. It could be the weather. He knew it was pretty bad up there right now. It wasn't like Eagle Ranger to not respond. Maybe he was out looking for them right now. *No,* he thought, *Eagle Ranger would have his radio with him at all times.*

He turned back to his notebook and continued to jot down notes. He was in the process of writing up a draft training plan for Sheriff Leif. He didn't want to, but Joe had insisted he put it all down on paper before he started training his men.

Rodney was disgusted by paperwork. He liked the Sheriff, but was convinced the man was living a year in the past. Now was the time to cut through all the red tape. Now was the time to rise up and press on full speed ahead instead of forming committees and having brainstorming sessions and writing mission statements.

Nonetheless, he wrote down a few more words, then tried to organize them into something cohesive. Then he smiled to himself and thought to himself, *How's this for a Mission Statement. We train hard. We fight hard. We kill anyone who tries to hurt us.*

He shrugged and said out loud. "I don't think that one will fly, at least not yet. But Rodney knew from experience and from his study of history that his time would come. He was not a peacetime leader. He was more of a take-names-and-kick-ass kind of guy. He was reminded of Winston Churchill's famous quote about war and peace.

> *Those who can win a war well can rarely make a good peace and those who could make a good peace would never have won the war.*

Sheriff Leif was a good man, but he was still stuck in the peace of yesterday. Rodney couldn't help but wonder, *Will he be able to make the transition into war, because war was undoubtedly coming; it was coming like a freight train, straight at them, and it would not stop to wait for good men to get the stomach for killing.*

On the contrary, Rodney had the stomach for killing. He'd done it before and would do it again. He wouldn't enjoy it, but, nonetheless, he would do it without flinching and without hesitation.

He reached over and picked up the radio again.

"Eagle Ranger, this is Moonshadow, over."

Silence. "Eagle Ranger, this is Moonshadow, over." More silence.

Rodney spoke out loud to no one. "Where are you, Dan. Why aren't you here? I need you, son."

CHAPTER 28

The Impetuosity of the Young

DAN awoke to the sound of his snowmobile driving away. He quickly threw off the blue tarp, which was covered with a full foot of snow. It showered down on him, blinding his eyes for a moment, but by the time he was up and moving, the snowmobile was already out of sight.

He looked around quickly, taking everything in. The sun was up and shining, the fire was a weak smolder, the wind and snow had stopped, and his son, Jeremy, was no where to be seen.

He looked down again at his wife and child, sleeping soundly. They both looked so vulnerable and frail. And, as the drone of the snowmobile's engine faded into the east, Dan whispered a prayer before setting out to rebuild the fire.

Jeremy drove as fast as he could through the snow. The storm had lifted, so he was able to make good time. He remembered what his dad had said about direction, and headed straight into the sunrise. As he drove through the knee-deep fresh, powdery snow, he contemplated the ramifications of what he was doing. He knew his father would be upset with him, but he saw no other way to save Jackie's life. They needed help, and his father wouldn't do it, so that left only him. Besides, he'd learned from experience that it was sometimes better to ask for forgiveness than for permission.

After fifteen minutes he drove down into a cedar swamp, snaking through it, always looking for the high ground. He'd never been in a cedar swamp before. By time he was deep inside it, he realized how lost he was. He pulled up onto a mound and stopped his machine before pulling his cell phone out of his pocket. He had a signal now, and checked his location. He smiled. Not too much further and he'd be there.

The baby was crying again, and Dan held her, rocking her gently, talking to her in a soothing voice, but nothing he could say or do seemed to make her feel better. He looked down at his wife, lying in the sled. She was still alive, but she should be awake by now, and that bothered him.

He walked over to the fire and kept singing to baby Donna.

> *"He was singing, "bye-bye, miss American pie. Drove my chevy to the levee, But the levee was dry."*

Dan stopped in mid-verse. When was it he'd sang that song last? Then it came to him. It was the night he'd been beaten nearly to death in Eagle River. Perhaps he should choose another song.

> *Amazing grace! How sweet the sound That saved a wretch like me. I once was lost, but now am found, Was blind but now I see.*

Baby Donna stopped crying and looked up at him. She reached her little hand up out of the blanket and grabbed onto his shaggy, dirty, blonde beard. Dan smiled and then took her tiny fingers in his own. He'd never held a black baby before Donna. Perhaps it was odd he'd expected them to be different from white babies, but they weren't. The only difference appeared to be the color of her skin. He found himself wondering why blacks and whites didn't get along better. Personally, he didn't know any blacks in Menomonie. There just weren't that many. From his experience in the Marine Corps, he knew that most of them lived in the big cities. He recalled that in boot camp, the color of a man's skin didn't really account for much. Black and white pulled together or everyone failed. He thought about it for a moment and realized that it was probably that way all over the country now, whether in the city or country, whether black or white. People who pulled together would survive, and those who tried to go it alone would likely die.

Then his thoughts shifted to his son, traveling alone in the frozen north woods of the upper peninsula, and he shivered. Deep down, in his heart, he knew that Jeremy was right to go for help. There was no other way, but ... who could they trust? How would Jeremy know the good from the bad? He closed his eyes and whispered another prayer. When he opened them, baby Donna was smiling at him.

Dan smiled and began to sing again, this time softly and ever so tenderly.

> *When we've been there ten thousand years,*
> *Bright shining as the sun,*
> *We've no less days to sing God's praise,*
> *Than when we first begun.*

The little baby slowly closed her eyes and drifted off to sleep.

∾ ∾ ∾

"Eagle Ranger, this is Eagle Recon 3, over."
There was silence for a moment, and then a voice came

over the radio. "Eagle Recon 3, this is Eagle Ranger, go ahead, with your sit-rep, over."

Donny Brewster hesitated before keying the mike and speaking. "Dis is Eagle Recon 3, I finished da search a sector seven, but need ta head ta town fer food and get rested up a bit, eh. I go ta Ford River to da cafe and get warm, then head ta Escanaba by da river just ta see what I can see, eh?"

"Roger that, Eagle Recon 3." There was silence for a few seconds, then another transmission. "Also, be advised to cut the accent, Eagle recon 3. It gives away your location. Besides, you're from Detroit and we all know it. You're just another troll like me."

Donny heard someone laughing just as the transmission cut out. He spit at the ground in exasperation. He hated that disparaging troll label. Up here in the U.P. there were only two kinds of people: yoopers and trolls. Most of the others up here were either of Finnish, Canadian or Native American descent. And even though the locals had accepted him, he knew that in their minds, he would always be a troll, someone from under the bridge, someone who'd come up to escape the rat race and get a little peace in God's country.

He'd joined the Shadow Militia by invitation, because that's the only way it happened. Truth is he'd gotten out of the Marine Corps six years ago and hadn't been able to get a job. But then again, what kind of job could he get as a retired Marine Corps sniper? There just wasn't a whole lot of legitimate work out there for a man is his line of work. *"Hi, my name is Donny Brewster. I'm looking for a job. Is there anyone you'd like killed today? I specialize in 1,000-yard headshots."*

The more he thought about it, the more he realized that the reason he'd been accepted into the Yooper community was his affinity for firearms. Some people up here were great drinkers, others good at cutting trees or moving ore. Donny Brewster was just a guy from Detroit with good eyes and a steady aim.

He put the radio back in his pack and slung his M1 Garand over his shoulder and began the long trek back into town. He loved the Garand. He'd gotten it through the Civilian Marksmanship Program, and enjoyed shooting it. Sure, there were lots of other rifles that surpassed it in various ways, but Donny was nostalgic. His father had carried the M1 in Korea, and his grandfather in World War II. Somehow, when he carried it, he felt closer to them, even though they'd been dead for many years now.

The M1 was designed by John Garand and fired an eight-round clip of 30-06 cartridges. The rifle had plenty of knock-down power, and Donny was good with it out to 600 yards, even with the stock open sights. The rifle was a good shooter, and his was decked out with a few extra goodies, making him better able to reach out and touch someone using long distance. General George S. Patton had called the M1 "the greatest implement ever devised for battle".

Donny dug his ski poles into the snow and pushed off down the little hill. He was almost to the river when he heard the whine of a snowmobile engine.

At the top of the river embankment, Jeremy hesitated. He wondered if the ice could hold him, but then he saw a group of people out on the ice. It looked like they were fishing, so he nosed the machine down the slope and out onto the frozen river. He was relieved to reach the first two men who were watching his approach. When he pulled up, he killed the engine, hopped off the snowmobile and ran toward them, ripping off his helmet as he went.

""Hey! I need help! My mom is hurt and she needs a hospital!"

The two men held fishing poles in their hands and continued to fish as he talked. One man jerked his pole up and pulled in a Blue Gill about 8 inches long. His friend came over to look.

"What bait ya got, eh? I ain't got no bites yet."

"I use da mousies eh. Dey pretty good ya know."

Jeremy stood in front of them, wondering why they wouldn't respond to him.

"Hey guys I need your help. My mom is hurt really bad. She's got a compound fracture and a concussion. We've got a little baby, and my Dad is back there with them until I can get help.

Both men looked over at him and smiled.

Donny was near the river's edge now in a clump of trees. He settled down in the snow and took his spotting scope out of his back pack. He trained it on the group of men now surrounding the snowmobile and its rider. They appeared to be circling him like a pack of wolves. He noticed five of them as rough, local characters of disrepute he wouldn't trust alone with a goat, let alone a teen-aged boy.

And then he wondered, *Is this the father's son I'm looking for?* He pulled the radio out of his pack and called Eagle Ranger.

"But my Mom is dying, and all you care about is stealing my snowmobile? I can't believe this!"

The other men looked around each other and laughed out loud. There were eight of them now with more coming over.

"It ain't just the machine, boy, though that would be enough. You also got a good shotgun there."

Jeremy looked the man in the eyes, noting his lack of yooper accent. He must be from the lower peninsula or Wisconsin. It didn't matter though. Jeremy recognized the look in his eyes and the tone of his voice. The man he'd killed had the same look and sound. He wanted to cry, but he held it in. It would only encourage them, like blood in a shark tank. And then he thought to himself, *There has to be someone good here. Not everyone can be this bad. There must be someone good enough to help me.*

The man who spoke last took a step forward and held out his hand. "Give me the gun, kid, and we'll let you walk away, minus the snow machine, of course."

A determined look came over Jeremy's face, and he clenched his jaw and hardened his gaze. Oddly enough, he was more angry than afraid. Slowly, he unslung the Winchester shotgun from his back and pointed it at the man in front of him.

"I've got five rounds of double-aught buckshot that says the gun and the machine are mine."

Donny put his radio back in his pack and laughed out loud while he watched through the spotting scope as the boy drew the shotgun down on eight men. "I like this boy. He's got spunk!"

His M1 was already out on the snow in front of him as he lay in the prone position readying himself for the shot. He tucked the stock into his shoulder firmly and put down the spotting scope. Then he nestled his cheek on down into his favorite spot and started to breathe slowly. He guessed the distance at two hundred yards with a four-mile-per-hour west wind. An easy chip shot to the green. Slowly, he breathed, just barely. Gradually, he took up slack on the trigger. For now, he just watched and waited to see what would happen.

The man laughed out loud. "Nice bluff, kid. But you just told us you only got 5 rounds. And there's eight of us. Now, I'm no accountant, but …"

The words never left the man's mouth, because suddenly … his mouth was gone.

Jeremy hadn't consciously fired his gun, but somehow it had come up to his shoulder and fired directly into the man's face. And just as mysteriously, Jeremy pivoted to take a bead on the next man who was moving toward him.

Just as he was about to pull the trigger, the man's head exploded in a misty cloud of crimson. Two of the eight men now lay fifteen feet away on the snow, painting the ice red. The boy quickly switched targets, but the man he was aiming at quickly turned and ran. Jeremy let him go and brought another man's head into his sights. But this man turned and ran as well.

Then, almost as if they all shared the same brain, the other men turned and ran off the ice, leaving their fishing gear and their foolish pride behind.

Suddenly, Jeremy was standing on the ice alone. There were other onlookers, but they stayed back. His hands started to shake, and he felt his throat constrict as the bile rose up into his mouth. The boy bent over and heaved his stomach out onto the ice. As he kneeled there alone, he heard someone coming up behind him and turned. He tried to bring the gun up and aim, but the adrenaline dump had left his muscles weak and his nerves frayed.

"You okay, boy?"

Jeremy started to cry now and let his butt drop down onto the snow. The man moved his skis across the ice and was soon kneeling beside him. "What's your name, boy?"

Jeremy caught his breath in mid sob. "I'm … I'm … My name is Jeremy Branch."

Donny Brewster smiled. "That was good shootin', son." He put his arm around the boy. "and those guys needed killin'."

Suddenly, Jeremy was reminded of his father. "My dad and mom and my baby sister need help."

Donny nodded but didn't say anything. He took his pack

off his back and pulled out the radio.

"Eagle Ranger, this is Eagle Recon 3, over."

"This is Eagle Ranger, go ahead, over."

Donny smiled at the boy while he talked.

"I have Jeremy Branch and need extraction, over."

"Roger that, Eagle Recon 3. Any news on the other priority ones?"

Donny looked down at Jeremy.

"Where's your dad, son? Can you take me to them?"

Jeremy nodded as he pulled his cellphone out of his pocket and handed it to his rescuer.

"They're at waypoint A."

Donny laughed out loud. "You are good, son. Who trained you?"

Jeremy tried to smile. "I'm my father's son."

Donny nodded. "I bet you are."

He keyed the mike again.

"Eagle Ranger, this is Eagle Recon 3. That's affirmative. Stand by for grid coordinates, over."

Donny read off the coordinates from the GPS before signing off. Then he put the radio back in his pack and slung it over his shoulders again.

"Let's go get your family, kid."

Jeremy looked up with awe in his eyes.

"Who are you?"

Donny laughed out loud. "A year ago I was Donny Brewster from Detroit. But today, I'm Eagle Recon 3."

Then he helped Jeremy up to his feet and over to the Snowmobile. "Let's go, kid. We got clicks to turn."

CHAPTER 29

The Shadow Militia

FOR the next two weeks Jackie and baby Donna resided at St Francis Hospital in Escanaba. Jeremy and Dan stayed at the home of Colonel Roger "Ranger" McPherson who lived just outside town.

The rescue had come just in time to save Jackie's life. She'd lost a lot of blood and suffered from exposure. The doctor said the concussion would heal in time. With the help of an operating room and modern instruments, her leg was quickly set and the wound sewed shut.

Dan was amazed to see that Escanaba was an island of civilization surrounded by anarchy and violence. One night at dinner, Dan asked Colonel McPherson how they'd managed to maintain law and order.

"It's really quite simple. We saw it coming, and we made a plan. We set out the rules and we hold firm to them."

Dan lifted a fork full of canned corn to his mouth and questioned him further. "So what are the rules?"

The Colonel's eyes grew stern. "You steal - you die. You murder - you die. You rape - you die."

Dan stopped chewing his corn. "How do you enforce that? I mean, by what authority?"

Jeremy was interested and he stopped eating as well.

"We enforce it with steel resolve and the help of God. We

try to be fair, but the days of impunity are over. We worked it out with the Delta County Sheriff soon after the fall."

Dan nodded. "The fall? That's what they're calling it now?"

Colonel McPherson set his fork onto the table. "Yes, the fall, the collapse. They both mean the same thing. Society has broken down and chaos and evil are loosed upon the earth."

Dan took another bite of corn, and Jeremy chimed in. "Is that why people can walk on the streets without dying here?"

The Colonel laughed out loud. "You have a blunt way about you, kid. I see why Donny took a shine to you."

He moved his hands up onto the clean, white tablecloth and interlaced his fingers beside the white china plate of food. "Edmund Burke said, "All evil needs to triumph is for good men to do nothing." He paused. "We organized the good men, and we did something. We defeated the evil. And we continue to do it everyday."

Jeremy looked over at his father. "Dad, can we stay here?"

Dan smiled and shook his head. "Sorry, son. We have to get back to Uncle Rodney. He's an old man and he needs us."

Colonel McPherson looked over at him and started laughing so hard the table shook. Dan and Jeremy stared at him with no idea of what to say. Finally, Dan spoke. "Why is that funny?"

"I'm sorry." It was all the Colonel could do to stifle his laughter. "I'm sorry, Dan, but your Uncle Rodney is the last person on this planet who needs your help." Then his face grew serious again. "Don't you have any idea who your Uncle Rodney is?"

Dan looked offended. "Of course I do! He raised me when my father died. I know everything there is to know about him."

The Colonel shook his head from side to side.

"Negative, son. Not everything." He thought for a mo-ment, placing his clasped hands beneath his chin and resting them there while he decided what to say. At last, he pulled his hands down and smiled.

"I may as well tell you both now. You'll find out soon enough as it is."

He pulled the white, linen napkin from his lap and wiped his mouth before speaking. "People call me Colonel because I'm the commanding officer of the Upper Peninsula Shadow Militia."

It sounded ominous and impressive, but neither Dan nor Jeremy had any idea what he was talking about. The Colonel could tell they were confused, so he pressed on.

"The Shadow Militia was formed decades ago in the event society collapsed, or, God forbid, our government needed major realignment." He let that sink in before continuing on. "We are a small, but well funded and equipped group of highly trained, elite individuals, dedicated to the continuity of a constitutional society."

Jeremy raised his hand, and the Colonel laughed again. "You don't have to raise your hand, Jeremy. What do you want?"

"Colonel, I'm only fifteen, and I have no idea what that means."

The Colonel looked over at Dan and nodded. Dan smiled and looked over at his son. "It means, Jeremy, that the Shadow Militia is the good guys. And they can really kick ass!"

The Colonel clapped his hands together once, and a servant came into the room. "Well said, Dan." He looked over at the servant. "Felicia, we're ready for our cherry pie now."

Dan turned away from the servant and back to their host. "But … what does the Shadow Militia have to do with my Uncle Rodney?"

Jeremy laughed now. "Don't you get it, Dad? Your uncle is in the Shadow Militia." He looked across the table at the Colonel as if asking for confirmation.

"Well done, Jeremy. But it's even bigger than that."

He turned and looked Dan square in the eyes. "Your uncle isn't *in* the Shadow Militia. He *is* the Shadow Militia."

Dan's face clouded over. A million thoughts ran through his head, connecting dots, memories, conflicts that now seemed to make sense to him after years of hiding in the dark.

"Why do you think we went looking for you? The General ordered it. Priority one."

Felicia came in with the pie and placed it at each setting. Dan looked down at it with disbelief. So many people out there starving, dying, suffering, and he was here surrounded by clean linen, eating roast beef, corn and cherry pie. He took a bite and it exploded with flavor inside his mouth. Dan closed his eyes and almost cried. The Colonel smiled at his response.

"General Branch has ordered you transported out of here back to his location at 1300 hours tomorrow. Your wife and baby are fit to fly, and I'll see that everything is in order. I'm taking you home myself."

Jeremy's jaw dropped open and he looked over at his father in shock. Finally, he spoke. "General Branch?"

Dan smiled to himself all the while enjoying the cherry pie. He loved his Uncle Rodney. Then he looked over at the Colonel.

"Colonel McPherson, there is one thing we have to do before leaving."

The Colonel nodded. "Anything. Just ask and you'll have it. You're priority one."

Dan smiled. "Can you have an ordained minister of some type meet us at the hospital tomorrow morning?" He placed his left hand on his son's shoulder. "We have some unfinished business to attend to."

Jeremy breathed a sigh of relief. "Thank God! It's about time!"

The wedding ceremony took place beside the hospital lawn on the freshly shoveled sidewalk. Jeremy was the best man and Colonel McPherson and Donny Brewster signed as witnesses. Baby Donna was the Maid of Honor. The ceremony was presided over by Father Francis Connors. The sun shown during the whole wedding, and then quickly slipped behind a cloud when Father Connors announced, "I now pronounce you husband and wife. You may kiss the bride."

And he did.

Rodney Branch stood on the courthouse lawn beside Sheriff Leif. The weather had turned mild the night before and the snow was thawing quickly. Rain was coming, and soon the roads would be clear again.

"Why did you want to meet me out here, Rodney?"

Rodney pulled out a pack of Camel nonfiltered and placed one white tube between his chapped lips.

"There's some things I have to tell you before they get here. I've been keeping some things from you, and I don't want you to be blind-sided."

Joe Leif grimaced. "What have you done now, old man? Whatever it is, I bet you a million bucks it's going to get me in trouble isn't it?"

Rodney shook his head and smiled as he pulled out his Zippo and lit up. "No, it won't get you in trouble. To the contrary. It's good news. They found my nephew, Dan."

The Sheriff's face changed from a grimace to a beam in a second's time. He reached over and hugged his friend in a rare embrace. "Oh, thank God, Rodney! Thank God! I can't wait to see him again. It's been years. Is he here now? Can I see him?"

Rodney's face clouded over just a bit. "Well, yes, he'll be here any minute now. But that's what I wanted to talk to you about."

Joe cocked his head to one side and looked up into the northern sky. "Can you hear that?"

Rodney looked down and sighed. "Yup. Sure can. Sounds like a helicopter. Just a wild guess, but I'd say it's an Apache AH64 attack helicopter by the sounds of it."

Joe looked back down and over at his friend. "Rodney? There's more than one. What's going on?"

The sounds came closer now, getting louder by the second. "Oops, here comes a different one. That's two Apaches and what's that other sound? Hmm, sounds like a Bell UH-1 Iroquois. You know … a Huey."

As Sheriff Leif looked on in surprise three helicopters circled above the courthouse lawn. The two gunships continued to circle, providing security, as the Huey touched down gently on the snow-covered lawn. Joe covered his face as the wind whipped snow up all around him.

As the engine was cut and began to wind down, a tall man in olive drab fatigues stepped off and strode quickly over to them with his head down low. Upon reaching them, he stood stiffly at attention.

"Colonel McPherson reporting as ordered, sir!"

Joe looked at the soldier, not quite knowing what to do or what to make of it. He glanced over at Rodney and saw him smile. Rodney snapped to attention and smartly returned the Colonel's salute.

"At ease, Colonel. Thanks for coming."

Then he turned to Joe and made introductions.

"Colonel McPherson, this is the Sheriff of Iroquois County, Joe Leif. Sheriff, this is Colonel Roger McPherson of the Shadow Militia. He's the commanding officer for the Upper Peninsula."

The Colonel reached out his hand, and Joe reacted by extending his own weakly. The Colonel pumped it heartily up and down. "Pleasure to meet you, Sheriff." Then he turned back to Rodney. "General, we have your priority one personnel on board as ordered, sir."

Sheriff Leif turned away from the Colonel as his mouth dropped open in confusion. "Rodney, why is this man calling you a General? And what is the Shadow Militia?"

The Huey's rotors had almost stopped turning now, and Dan Branch hopped down, followed by Jeremy who was holding baby Donna, and his new wife, Jackie, who hobbled on crutches. Dan raced over to them and threw his arms around his uncle. "Uncle Rodney! Thanks so much for saving us! It's so good to be back home!"

Joe moved his hand up to his chin and stroked it gently, all the while wondering, *Okay, Rodney, what have you done now?*

"Dan, you remember Sheriff Leif?"

Dan smiled and shook his hand. "Of course, hi Sheriff. Good to see you again. You've put on a little weight."

Rodney laughed out loud, and Joe frowned at him.

By now the others had reached the sidewalk. "Uncle Rodney, allow me to introduce my wife, Jackie, my son, Jeremy, and my daughter, Donna."

Rodney put out his cigarette, field stripped it and stuffed the butt inside his front, shirt pocket. He bowed slightly.

"Pleasure to meet you, ma'am. I suspect there's a long story to all this. I trust you're helping my vagabond nephew grow up a bit?"

Jackie smiled. "Yes, General. I'm doing the best I can, but you have to understand that he's quite a handful."

Rodney laughed. "Of course he's a handful! He's a Branch! We were born to be wild!"

Joe looked on in amazement. "Rodney, why are they calling you General? Where did you get three helicopters?"

But before he could answer, the Colonel interrupted.

"General, we did the flyover south of here you ordered."

Rodney's face grew more serious. "And?"

The Colonel looked him straight in the eyes.

It's not good, sir. It's as you suspected. A large force heading northwest in your direction."

Rodney's eyes took on a faraway gaze and he reached up to stroke his cheek. "How many?"

"About one thousand strong, sir, gaining strength as they go."

"Armaments?"

"A few armored personnel carriers, a dozen Humvees, but mostly civilian transportation. Mostly light arms with some fifty cals. We were fired upon."

Rodney nodded. "Estimated Time of Arrival?"

The Colonel's face took on a grave look when he answered. "Not long, sir. Maybe a week. maybe a bit longer."

Rodney nodded. Then he turned to Joe. "Sheriff, we have strategy to discuss. May we use your conference room?"

Joe looked at him, all of a sudden feeling a hundred years older. He hung his head down and stared at the sidewalk.

"Okay, let me get this straight. He's a Colonel?"

Rodney nodded...

"You're a General?"

Rodney's head moved up and down again.

"There are one thousand bad guys heading this way?"

"Yup."

Joe nodded. "Okay, so far so good. Now here's the most important question." He pointed to the Apaches circling over the town. "Those helicopter gunships? They belong to you?"

Rodney smiled. "Well, not exactly. I don't own them. I just command them."

The Sheriff smiled. "Okay, Yeah. Sure. You can use my conference room."

As they all walked down the sidewalk to the courthouse, Joe couldn't help but ask. "So, tell me. Where does a guy get military attack helicopters?"

Rodney laughed. "You know. Same place I got my Abrams Tank. On Ebay!"

Jackie looked over at Dan as she struggled to keep up on crutches. "Your uncle has a tank?" Dan shrugged. "I don't know." And then his mind switched over to the horde of one thousand men heading this way, raping, destroying and killing everything in their path. He'd seen them himself on the flyover. As he'd looked on from the relative safety of the helicopter, he'd watched as a man raped a little girl in broad daylight. Bodies had been strewn everywhere, and, while he flew over, men, women, and children had been lined up and shot in the streets.

It was the Golden Horde that his Uncle Rodney had taught him about. And it was coming here. Coming here to kill his family.

Coming soon!

The saga continues in

—The Shadow Militia—

Other Books by Skip Coryell

We Hold These Truths
Bond of Unseen Blood
Church and State
Blood in the Streets
Laughter and Tears
RKBA: Defending the Right to Keep and Bear Arms
Stalking Natalie

Skip Coryell now lives with his wife and children in Michigan. He works full time as a professional writer, and *"The God Virus"* is his eighth published book. He is an avid hunter and sportsman, a Marine Corps veteran, and a graduate of Cornerstone University.

For more details on Skip Coryell, or to contact him personally, go to his website at www.skipcoryell.com